HIT AND RUN

CALLAHAN SECURITY BOOK 3

LORI MATTHEWS

ABOUT HIT AND RUN

Gage Callahan knew his latest assignment with Callahan Security was going to be a disaster. He traipsed around Europe to locate the computer programmer he was hired to protect only to discover she's actually a hacker hiding in Alaska. Tensions mount when she narrowly escapes becoming roadkill as a vicious organization comes after her. It will take all his ingenuity to rush her to safety, especially when Gage's primary objective…get her and the prototype to New York…becomes secondary to protecting his heart from a fatal attraction to the spunky woman.

Dani Pierce is used to working on the dark web but now she is truly scared because deadly trouble has arrived at her front door. The self-reliant hacker knows she'll need help to survive her contract to build facial recognition software. The aggravating yet handsome man hired to protect her makes it clear he detests her, but that doesn't stop her from developing feelings for him.

It soon becomes apparent to Gage that Dani's in deeper than she'll admit but her answers don't explain why the deadly gang after her is always one step ahead. It will take his military skills and her hacking know-how to save not only their butts, but the budding love they've discovered in the midst of danger.

Hit And Run

Copyright © 2020 Lori Matthews

For Shelley and Merrill

Forever, sisters. I wouldn't be me if you weren't you.

ACKNOWLEDGMENTS

Thanks once again to all the inhabitants of my city – the one it takes to bring this book into the world. My deepest gratitude my editors, Corinne DeMaagd and Heidi Senesac for making me appear much more coherent than I actually am; my cover artist, Llewellen Designs for making my story come alive; my medical peeps who never failed to answer my questions, day or night, Dr. Shivani Srivastava and Dr. Shalabh Singhal. My virtual assistant who is a social media guru and all round dynamo, Susan Poirier. My personal cheer squad which I could not survive without: Janna MacGregor, Suzanne Burke, Angi Morgan, Kimberley Ash, Stacey Wilk. Thank you all for talking me off the ledge more than once. My mother and my sisters who told me to dream big. My husband and my children who make my life complete. You all are my world. A special heartfelt thanks goes out to you, the reader. The fact you are reading this means my dreams have come true.

CHAPTER ONE

The roaring of an engine and the crunch of metal hitting bone caused Dani Pierce to look up. Her stomach lurched as she watched the blond woman who had been crossing the street directly in front of her catapult twenty feet in the air.

The woman twisted, her eyes huge, round and glassy like marbles. Her mouth formed a perfect *O*. Her arms flailed as she flew, her salmon-colored jacket bright against the light blue sky. She landed with a sickening thud. Bone hitting pavement this time. Her head bounced like a deflated basketball and came to rest at an awkward angle.

For one brief instant, it seemed like the world had frozen, time had stopped moving. Dani could hear her own breathing and her heart hammering in her chest. Then it was as if the world had exhaled simultaneously, and all hell broke loose.

Tires screeched. Someone screamed while a cacophony of voices cried out, demanding help and yelling for the police. The smell of exhaust filled her nose.

The van that had caused the accident zigzagged around

the body then sped off down the street. Dani craned her neck to see around the crowd and caught a glimpse of the van as it turned the corner a few blocks down. Then it disappeared from view.

Sirens drew closer. An ambulance. Dani knew there was no rush. The woman was gone. She was dead when she was flying through the air; the woman just didn't know it yet.

Tearing her eyes away from the scene, Dani scurried through the growing crowd, shoulders hunched, chin tilted down toward her chest. *Police.* The last thing she needed was to get mixed up in some investigation.

There were plenty of witnesses. Many had had their cameras out, so the police were likely to have pictures of the whole thing. She bit her lip and slowed her steps. She was abandoning the woman. Her hand shook as she brushed back a stray strand of dark brown hair. Hair that had been the same shade as the dead woman just yesterday. She picked up speed again. Not to be cold about it, but her life was on the line, and that woman's was over.

CHAPTER TWO

Dani turned down the driveway and was heading past the little white house to her garage apartment when the front door banged open and Mrs. Williams came out on to the porch.

"Dani!" she barked. "Thought we lost you there for a minute."

Dani blinked. "What do you mean, lost me?" Mrs. Williams looked visibly upset. Her grey-brown hair was coming out of its messy bun, and her plaid shirt was only half tucked into her old, faded jeans.

"Delilah just called and said there was a hit and run in town. The woman was killed. She worried it might have been you." Mrs. Williams reached out and grabbed the porch railing for support. She was deathly pale, and her chest heaved with every breath.

"Me?" Dani's voice cracked as her hands tightened around the bag she'd been carrying, her knuckles turning white. So she wasn't the only one who thought the woman could have been her.

"Delilah said she had on the same color coat you have,

the coral one, and her hair was blond." Mrs. Williams sagged against the house while still holding the railing. "Glad to see you're okay. I haven't lost a tenant yet, and I'd like to keep it that way."

Dani opened her mouth but closed it again. Her lungs were frozen. She was having trouble sucking in any oxygen. The woman had looked like Dani, or rather how she used to look. Dani's hand flew up to her hair. She'd dyed her hair back to her natural dark brown last night.

She glanced down at the faded jeans and ragged blue T-shirt she was wearing. She hadn't bothered with the coral coat today because it was so warm. It wasn't a coincidence. That woman died because... Her insides tied into knots. Panic crawled up her throat. She slumped, leaning against the porch.

Oxygen returned to her lungs in a rush. "Ah, Mrs. Williams, I'm sorry you were scared." She meant it. Dani was scared shitless, but she didn't want the old woman to be upset. Mrs. Williams had been kind to her. One of the few in life who had. She reached up and gave the elderly lady's hand a squeeze, then quickly put her shaking hand into her jeans pocket.

Dani cleared her throat. "I saw the accident in town. It was...shocking. The van didn't even stop."

Mrs. Williams gave her a quick nod. "That's what Delilah said. It must've been tough to see. Come inside, and I'll make you a cup of tea. I think I have some of those chocolate chip cookies you like. Did you eat dinner?"

"Um, no, but I'm okay. I don't really have an appetite at the moment." She took a deep breath and swallowed hard.

Mrs. Williams seemed fully recovered now and was giving Dani the once over. "You sure? I can whip up some leftovers quick-time. I ate earlier."

Dani nodded. "Yeah, I'm sure. Thanks, though. I just

need a bit of time alone." As much as she wanted the comfort of Mrs. Williams' cozy white house with its big front porch and tiny front yard, she needed a moment to breathe. To think. Cookies would have to wait.

Mrs. Williams nodded again. "You take it easy. I'll bring over some of those cookies in a bit."

Dani nodded and then turned toward the garage apartment. She heard the front door of the main house close as she walked to her place. She needed to call Jameson Drake asap. As her employer, he needed to help her out of this mess. And she needed to get out of town as quickly as possible.

Whoever was after the software had found her for real this time, but Dani wasn't finished.

Whoever. She had a pretty good guess as to who that was, or at least which group. She frowned. The prototype she had sent Drake worked, but only so far. The software still had a major flaw. Eventually, it froze, the curser unblinking permanently. She needed time to fix it. Carly was counting on her.

But why kill her? It made no sense. Wouldn't they want her alive? At least until they had the software?

She bit her lip as she slipped her key in the lock and paused, doing a quick check for the one strand of long hair she always stuck in the doorway when she left. She looked again. The hair was gone. Her palms dampened. Could it have fallen out on its own? No. She scrubbed her hand on her jeans and stepped back from the opening. What if they were still inside? She started to turn away. They just ran over the woman in town, so they couldn't be here.

She quickly reached out, unlocked the door, and thrust it open.

Dani's heart galloped in her chest. The place was trashed. The furniture was turned over, and her meager belongings were scattered all over the room. She scanned the counter in the kitchen area where she had left her USB stick. It was gone. They must have thought they had the software, so they killed the woman in town. They thought they didn't need her —Dani—anymore.

It wouldn't be long before they realized they'd hit the wrong woman. Dani's stomach rolled. When she closed her eyes, she saw the woman sailing through the air again.

She opened her eyes, dropped the bag she'd been carrying and her backpack on the floor, and ran for the bathroom. Her whole body shook as she violently emptied the contents of her stomach repeatedly. When she finished, she leaned against the wall. Her legs gave out and she slid to the floor.

She needed to make a plan, and it had to happen now. Her hands shook. She flexed her fingers as she took deep, cleansing breaths. She'd been through so much. But this, this was beyond. It wasn't that people wanted to hurt her; she was used to that. It was that they were willing to hurt others to get to her. Again she thought of the woman in the salmon colored coat. This was a whole new ballgame.

A couple minutes later, she got up off the floor and brushed her teeth. At least they hadn't thrown her toothbrush on the floor.

She left the bathroom and ventured into the main living area. She righted the sofa and cleaned up the rest of the mess. It only took a few minutes, and she needed to do something to calm her nerves. Thank God they hadn't hurt Mrs. Williams.

Once the room was passable, she retrieved her laptop and the snacks she'd purchased. She closed the door and bolted it. She even turned the lock in the doorknob. It was flimsy, but she'd take any precaution available.

She brought the bag to the coffee table by the sofa, sat down, and after setting her laptop across from her, opened the lid.

She quickly fired off an email and then a text message to

Drake. He'd hired her to write the software. This was his mess. His responsibility. She needed his help to get out of it. Alive.

She bit her lip. Would he believe her? She'd cried wolf a few weeks before and demanded his help, only to walk back that need twenty-four hours later. How was she supposed to know the stalker she noticed was stalking her neighbor and not her? He was slunk down in his car on the street at all hours, staring in her general direction, and she saw him a few times in town. It was an honest mistake.

Drake's voice had been icy when she explained the situation. Then it turned loud. He'd already had a man in the air on his way to Europe when Dani had gotten back to him. Well it wasn't her fault he'd jumped the gun. Besides, she'd never told him she was in Europe. He'd made his own assumptions.

Drake immediately tried to cancel the project. He wanted the code as is, and he wanted her to stop. Said it was too dangerous.

So, she'd refused to tell him where she was. No way in hell was she giving up all her hard work. She intended to… no, needed to finish this project no matter what.

She knew Drake was going to curse up a storm when he got her emails and texts, no question. But the danger was real this time. The men had found her.

The phone shook in her trembling hands. Still nothing. Should she send Janet a text? The woman was Drake's assistant. She might be able to get word to him. Dani quickly sent off the message and then put down the phone. Janet would get back to her. She was the epitome of efficiency. Dani flexed her fingers and then looked up flights out of Juneau.

The benefit of being in a small Alaskan town was not many people came here and it was easy to hide. The downside was it was hard as hell to get out in a hurry. She glanced over at her phone, but still nothing from Drake. There were no seats on any plane leaving Juneau that evening because there were no planes leaving period. That couldn't be right.

"What the hell?" she murmured as she typed on her keyboard. A storm. A big fucking lightning storm was moving in. No more airplanes in or out. Dani looked out the window. What had been a cloudless sky twenty minutes ago was now full of angry-looking puffs of dull gray. It was summer, so it would still be light for hours, but the clouds made it appear much darker than usual.

She drummed her fingers on her keyboard. How else could she get out of town? Driving wasn't an option. If they found her, she' be dragged off into the woods and never heard from again. She shuddered at the thought. Maybe Mrs. Williams knew someone who could fly her out in a private airplane. Maybe she could still get out somehow. She stood up. She could use one of Mrs. Williams' cookies right now. Hell, she could probably eat a dozen.

She grabbed her keys and carefully locked the door after she left the apartment. She paused long enough to put a hair back in place, her early warning system. As she walked back down the driveway to Mrs. Williams' she studied the street. She had to be very careful. One wrong move, and she'd be the woman flying through the air.

CHAPTER THREE

"I promise I'm not here to hurt Daniella Pierce. I'm here to help," Gage Callahan said as he stared down the barrel of a shotgun. He had no doubt the woman aiming at his forehead was prepared to pull the trigger.

"Sure. That's why you were sneaking around the back of my house. I know all about you. She told me. You're a no-good piece of shit that no one will miss so don't move a muscle. I'm tempted to use this as it is. Would make it much easier for her, and that girl has been through the wars. You can just tell." Mrs. Williams shifted slightly, resting the double-barrel shotgun against her hip.

Gage ground his teeth. He hadn't expected an old lady with a shotgun when he was making a circuit of the house. Perhaps he should've. So far, this trip had more twists and turns than a funhouse maze.

Who the hell knew Alaska would be so warm? He made a move to tug at the collar of his shirt, but the old lady gave him a look, and he put his hand back in the air.

"Look, if we could just talk to Daniella, we could sort this whole thing out," Gage said as he tried to think of anything that would convince the old lady he was here to help not hurt.

She shook her head. "You leave Dani alone."

Dani. Good to know. Sweat was trickling down his back. He glanced around the kitchen. No air conditioning. Probably didn't need it usually. The woman made him come inside so she could call the police, but now she seemed to be toying with the idea of shooting him.

He glanced at the countertops to see if there was any other weapon handy but, apparently, Mrs. Williams was a very neat housekeeper. The place was spotless, and the counters were bare except for some rather delicious looking cookies in a Tupperware container. Gage's stomach growled.

He took a deep breath. His levels of crankiness and exhaustion were high at the moment, but he'd survived Afghanistan and Iraq without losing his shit under pressure. Some old lady with a shotgun was not how his time on the planet ended.

Gage tried again. "We can't stand here all day, so why don't you put the gun down so we can have a reasonable conversation."

"Why don't I call the cops, and they can sort you out?" She took a step sideways, bringing her closer to the handset on the counter. Just then the phone rang, and the woman jumped.

Gage's gut knotted. This woman was nervous, and her finger was on the trigger. She moved to answer the phone. Gage shot out a hand toward the woman. "No, please don't do that. It could endanger Daniella—Dani's life further." He didn't have time for her to be chatting away while holding him hostage.

"Why would answering the phone or calling the sheriff put Dani in danger? Hal's a good man, and he knows what he's doing." She moved next to the counter and glared at Gage as she reached for the phone.

"He's right, Mrs. Williams," Dani said.

Both their heads swung in her direction. She was standing in the dining area off to the right and behind Mrs. Williams' left shoulder.

She wasn't what Gage expected. She looked young, like in her late teens, but Gage knew that couldn't be true. She might be five-feet-four on a good day. Her hair was a dark brown bordering on black. Her eyes were so dark that with the distance separating them, it was hard for Gage to distinguish her pupils from the irises.

She wore baggy clothes, but they didn't disguise her curvy figure. She looked like a college kid, but those eyes were definitely older. They'd seen a thing or two. Something about her made Gage instantly want to protect her. There was a vulnerability there he hadn't seen the likes of in a long time. It appealed to him in ways it shouldn't.

He hadn't even heard her come in. Sloppy. He needed to do better than that. He cleared his throat. "Dani, my name is —that is, your boss sent me. I'm with Callahan Security."

Her eyes narrowed. "He didn't mention it."

Mrs. Williams' glanced back and forth between the two of them. "Do you want me to call the sheriff? Hal will take care of him."

"Uh, let's hold off on that a minute." Dani whipped out her phone and snapped a quick picture of Gage and then texted with a speed that was far beyond anything Gage could manage. She glanced up at him and started chewing the corner of her lip. She looked back at her screen, waiting for a response.

"Dani," Gage said, "we really don't have time to waste. Clock's ticking. We need to get out of here."

Mrs. Williams waved the shotgun again. "Don't you say anything else. You need to leave her be."

Dani shot Mrs. Williams a grateful look and then went back to staring at her phone. An eternity later, the phone pinged, and Dani nodded.

"You can put down the gun, Mrs. Williams. Janet, my boss's assistant, confirmed he sent this man to help me."

"You sure, child?" Mrs. Williams asked.

"Yes, it's fine."

Mrs. Williams lowered the gun but didn't put it down.

Gage dropped his hands. "We should talk somewhere privately, don't you think?"

Mrs. Williams started to bring the gun back up, but Dani took a step forward and waved her off.

"Mrs. Williams, I haven't been completely honest with you. It's not really a crazed boyfriend I've been avoiding. It's more...more of a work thing." Dani glanced at Mrs. Williams' face and then looked down and fidgeted with her phone. "I'm sorry I lied to you. I just really needed to be safe."

"Girl, no apology necessary. Makes no difference to me who you were hiding from. As long as you're safe, we're all good."

Dani smiled, and Gage could see the relief etched across her face. She obviously cared about the old lady. "This man, uh...Gage, is here to help me."

"Okay then." Mrs. Williams put the shotgun down in the corner of the kitchen. "How about those cookies?" Just then the phone rang again.

Gage glanced at it. "Ah, ladies, as much as I like the idea of a cookie, Dani, I think we need to chat and maybe get a move on."

She nodded at Gage. "Maybe in a bit, Mrs. Williams, okay?"

"Okay. You go get yourself sorted," she said as she reached to answer the phone. "That's probably another one of the girls calling to tell me about you being in a hit and run."

"Wait! Don't answer that." Gage spun around to face Dani. "What hit and run?"

"There was a woman who was hit by a van downtown. She was wearing a coat like mine and her hair was blond like mine was—well, until late last night." Dani shrugged. "I guess she kind of looked like me." There it was again, the tough exterior trying to hide the worry and fear. Gage blinked, and the look was gone from Dani's face.

"I see. People think it's you. I assume the woman was badly hurt?"

"She's dead," Dani said in a flat voice.

Mrs. Williams nodded. "One of my friends already called to tell me. Damn near gave me a heart attack 'til I saw Dani. I 'spect that's why the phone is ringing off the hook this afternoon."

Gage grimaced. "You tell Drake?"

"Yes. It seemed like too big of a coincidence."

"Okay. Mrs. Williams, please don't answer the phone. I need people to think the dead woman is Dani for as long as possible. There are some people out to hurt Dani, and if they think they already succeeded, we've gained some breathing room."

Mrs. Williams frowned. "Well, I guess I could avoid it, but soon enough, people will start dropping by. Juneau may have thirty thousand plus people but it's really a small town. We all know each other."

"We'll go as quickly as we can. Let's get your stuff, Dani," Gage said as he turned and headed for the front door. He peered out the window and checked the street. It looked clear. He gestured for Dani to follow him out and gave a quick nod of acknowledgement to Mrs. Williams. Then he and Dani were out the door.

Gage moved quickly off the porch and headed to the garage apartment. He stayed close to Dani, keeping his body between her and the street while he kept his head on a swivel constantly checking for any danger. "Do you know why they tried to kill you? It kind of doesn't make any sense."

Dani snorted. "It does if they think they already have the software."

CHAPTER FOUR

"What?" Gage swung around and looked directly at Dani, but she just continued past him to the apartment and then opened the door. "Do they have the software?" he asked as he walked in and took stock of the small apartment.

"No. They took a USB drive I had on the counter. It was encrypted. I suspect they think it has the software on it."

Dani walked directly across to the little dresser in the corner. She reached behind it and grabbed a duffle bag. She hadn't brought much when she moved here, and she hadn't bought much since she arrived. It was a small town, and she'd spent all her time programming. It wouldn't take her long to pack up her life.

"Wait. They were here? At this place?"

"Yeah. They must have broken in when I went out this afternoon. When I came back a while ago, the place was trashed and the USB drive was gone."

"Why would they think this USB drive was the software? What about your lab? Wouldn't it be there?"

"My what?" Dani asked as she moved around the room, packing her stuff.

"Your lab. You know, where you do all your coding. And what about your people? Drake didn't say anything about the rest of your team. Just that you were his coder."

"Coder. Lab. That's funny. Yeah. No. I'm the hacker Drake paid to build his software. There's only me, and this"—she spun around with her arms out—"is my lab."

"Son of a bitch." Gage ran his hands over his face. "I thought you were legit with a company or something, but you're not a professional. You're just some hacker kid Drake hired."

Dani narrowed her eyes. "I'm a *professional* hacker. I'm damn good at what I do. If you're looking for a bunch of dorks in a lab, you're barking up the wrong tree."

Gage sighed. "I should have known something was up when I was chasing your shadow all over Europe."

The heat crawled up her cheeks. "I am…" She swallowed. "That…wasn't my fault. I didn't tell Drake I was there. I just didn't correct him. I also said I needed to check something so not to send anyone until I was sure. It's not my fault he got all excited and sent you out.

"I told him it was a false alarm, but he was going on about how it was too dangerous anyway and he insisted I stop the project." She took a breath and silently added *I need to finish it for Carly*. "I…couldn't leave it undone. So I refused to tell him where I was. I set up the whole European false trail thing a while ago just in case anyone was looking for me."

Gage glared at her. "Someone was." He pointed to his own chest. "Me! And I wasted a hell of a lot of time doing it." He ran a hand through his hair. "I have no idea why Drake let you get away with not telling him where you were. Especially after you called for help. It's stupid."

"He had no choice. I refused to tell him, and he knew that if I found out he was looking, I would stop working on the software. It's safer for me to work on my own."

Gage turned away from Dani and started prowling around the small space, checking every window and then re-checking them. He kept clenching his hands into fists and then opening them again.

She watched as his gaze did a complete sweep of the apartment.

"And when did the hit and run happen?" he asked through tight lips.

"I dunno. Maybe an hour ago now." She stuffed clothing into her bag. When she advanced toward the ladder, she banged smack into Gage as he was leaving the kitchen area underneath her sleeping loft.

"Ooof," she mumbled as she bounced off his chest. He grabbed her arm to steady her, but she shook him off. The last thing she needed was to be close to him. He threw her off her game. He had since she first saw him.

He was so damn big and scary looking and sexy at the same time. It made her feel all jumbled up. She needed to keep her focus. It was the stress of the situation, she kept telling herself as she climbed up to her sleeping loft. *Yeah, that's what was making her jumpy and a mess. Clearly.*

She reached under her pillow and grabbed her favorite T-shirt. It said *Champlain* across the front in green letters. It was soft from the many washes it had endured over the last three years.

Dani held it tightly for a second as she remembered the day Carly had given it to her. It had been her birthday. Dani was auditing a video game programming class at Champlain College, and Carly had somehow managed to get her the T-shirt to celebrate, not only her birthday, but the fact that Dani was actually taking a class. Well, sort of. She smiled and then swallowed hard as the tears started to fill her throat. Now wasn't the time. Besides, Carly was going to be fine. Just fine.

Gage rolled his shoulders. "I guess the USB bought us some time, but soon enough they are going to find out it's not the software. What was on the USB?"

She hesitated but decided it couldn't hurt to tell the truth. Anyway, she could tell he wasn't going to stop asking until he got an answer. He seemed like an asshole that way. "It contained info on some people I worked with. Screen names of other hackers with notes about them. It's all written in code, so I'm not worried about them reading it."

"You coded the list and you encrypted it?" He raised an eyebrow. "Must be some list."

She nodded. "I'm all about keeping people's personal information secure." She tried not to laugh at the irony.

"Isn't stealing people's personal information what you do?"

She scowled at him. "It's called sarcasm. And not all hackers are created equal. Some of us do things for the right reasons."

"Uh huh," he grunted in response. "Sure, you do."

So maybe she hadn't started out that way, but that's where she was now, and she wasn't going to take any shit from him about it. "I don't give a rat's ass about your opinion, so why don't you just spend your energy on getting us the hell out of here?"

Gage froze. He turned and looked up at her. "Why don't I get us out of here?"

His voice had gone soft. His eyes were a deep blue-gray and were so intense, Dani wanted to lean back into the loft so he couldn't see her, but she forced herself to remain still.

"You listen to me, little Ms. Hacker. We would've been already safe in New York, not running from some unknown killers, if you would've told Drake the truth about where you were. Instead, I had to traipse all over Europe looking for clues. The situation here is much worse than I thought. You've already been found. So now you are going to finish getting ready as quickly as humanly possible so we can leave ASAP." He turned back around and walked over to stand by the front window.

Dani sighed and crawled down the ladder and went to her bathroom. "Fun times," she mumbled under her breath as she rolled her eyes. Well, it didn't have to be fun. He just had to keep her alive. That's all that mattered.

She shivered and then started to collect her things. She opened the closet behind the bathroom door. They hadn't touched the laundry she'd left in the stackables. They must have missed the closet entirely. They'd probably found the USB by that point.

Her stomach dropped. There was her coral coat. She'd hung it to dry in the small space next to the washer/dryer unit. She put her hands on the unit to steady herself. Taking deep breaths she tried to control the weakness in her knees. She ran through a couple of lines of code in her head, focusing on every detail. Finally, taking one last deep breath, she grabbed her laundry but left the coat. She wouldn't ever wear it again.

"How are we getting out of here?" Dani asked as she shoved the last items into her duffel bag. She walked over to the coffee table and started packing up her computer stuff.

Gage glanced over at her. "Flying."

She saw him take in the stickers on her laptop cover. He blinked and then his lips twitched. She wasn't about to explain why she had *Frozen* stickers on her laptop. It was none of his business. "Not unless you've got a private plane. All the regular flights are grounded."

"What? Why?"

"Big storm moving in. Something about all the heat and some sort of pressure thing. Anyway, there're storm warnings about torrential rain with thunder and lightning. A possibility of hail. It's about to get ugly."

Gage quickly jerked his phone out of his pocket and started typing what was probably quickly for him, which wasn't bad, but not really good either. He could type faster if he didn't pound so hard on the screen.

She turned and then paused for a second, took a last look around. This was it. She was leaving what had been her home for the last few months. Funny, she had stayed longer in a lot of other places, but here was one of the only times where she'd felt safe. In another life, it might have been her home. She shrugged that thought off and said, "Ready."

Gage didn't seem to have heard her. He was busy reading something on his screen. Then he made a call.

She watched him walk around the room as he spoke in a low voice into the phone. His dark brown hair was a bit long, and a lock fell over his forehead. His eyes were now a deep blue that complemented his navy sweater. Did they change according to his mood or the lighting? They were eyes that had seen a lot in life, she could tell. *It takes one to know one.*

His nose must have been broken once or twice because it was slightly crooked, but if she was honest, it was his hands that drew her attention. He had big, masculine hands. Dani always noticed hands. It was instinctive.

Growing up in foster care, she would look at the hands of any new boyfriend her foster mom brought into the house and try to calculate if they had hands that liked to hit.

Gage's hands were strong and tanned. They were banged up a bit and had plenty of scars, but they gave her the impression he could take care of things. There was no doubt in her mind they were hands that could hit, but for some reason she couldn't fathom yet, she was sure they weren't going to hit her.

"Fuck!" Gage had ended the call and was back to pacing between the windows. "Flying is out. Even private planes are grounded, and no one wants to take the chance, no matter how much I offer them."

"Thunderstorms here are no joke. Since we've had record-breaking heat this summer, we've had a lot of storms. Ten thousand lightning strikes in the last two weeks alone over the whole state. Lots of forest fires, too." Dani dropped her duffel, eased the backpack off her shoulders, then plopped down on the sofa.

"So they keep telling me. I've asked about boats, but no one wants to chance getting caught in the storm." Gage leaned his back against the pole that held up the sleeping loft.

Dani breathed a sigh of relief. As much as she wanted out of Juneau, taking a boat, any kind of boat, was her nightmare scenario. She wiped her palms down her jeans.

She glanced around her safe haven again. It was one room, the back wall with a kitchen that had a sleeping loft over it. It had a tiny bathroom as an addition off the back corner. It was good they couldn't stay. It would be a tight fit for the two of them. Gage was so large. He took up a lot of room. Suddenly, the idea of being stuck with him in the tiny space seemed unbearable.

"What about driving?" she asked

Gage shook his head. "We wouldn't get very far before the storm hits, and I don't want to be stuck on the side of a highway in Alaska. There's no upside to that, and we can't wait it out here either. Whoever tried to kill you earlier will find out soon enough they didn't get the software. They're oh-for-two if they don't know already. Then they will come looking for you here."

"So, what are we going to do?" The panic bubble that had subsided earlier was back, clawing its way up Dani's chest.

Gage cocked his head, and his eyes narrowed. "Did you hear that?"

Dani shot off the sofa. "What? Are they here?" Her heart hammered in her chest.

"What? No. Relax." Gage was using his phone again.

Dani fell back onto the sofa and wiped her palms on her jeans. *Get it together.* Normally, Dani could take the punches because she'd had a tough upbringing. But being stalked because of her project was a whole new experience, one she hated.

She was helpless, or that's what it felt like, and that was not something Dani had ever let herself feel in the past. Not being in control of the situation was hard enough, but being out of options was a brutal reality she was refusing to acknowledge.

"Okay, grab your stuff. We're out of here," Gage said as he moved toward the door.

Dani stood and grabbed her backpack. She slung it over her shoulders and then grabbed her duffel bag. "Where are we going?" she asked, but Gage was already out the door. "Wait!" she called as she ran after him. She went out the door and closed it after her. Gage was moving quickly down the driveway toward the street. He checked both ways, which must have been clear because he glanced back at Dani and motioned for her to catch up.

"I have to say good-bye to Mrs. Williams," she said as she caught up to him.

Gage's jaw tightened, and his eyes narrowed slightly. "You have precisely two minutes." He held up two fingers as if to emphasize his point.

Every cell in Dani's body urged her to tell this pain-in-the-ass man to fuck off, but she clamped down on her tongue and walked around Gage to go up onto the front porch. She needed him to protect her so she could finish the software and help Carly. Carly. If it wasn't for her, Dani would have been… Well, she didn't know where she would have been, but it wouldn't be here. Most likely dead on a street somewhere. And Carly needed her.

When she knocked on the front door, Mrs. Williams opened immediately. "Come in and have some cookies," Mrs. Williams said as she stepped back into the living room.

"Uh, I can't. I, um, just wanted to say thank you and good-bye." She held up the key to the garage apartment.

"You're leaving? Where are you going to go, and how are you going to get there with the storm coming?" Mrs. Williams stepped back into the doorway.

"Yes, time for me to go," Dani said, ignoring the rest of the questions she didn't have answers to. "Thanks for renting me your place."

Mrs. Williams wrapped her in a tight hug. Dani went stiff and swallowed hard. She hated being hugged. She didn't like being touched in any way. But this woman had been kind to her, so she made the effort to relax and gave her ex-landlord's back a couple of awkward pats.

Mrs. Williams let go and stepped back. "Girl, you ever need a place, you come back. You always have a home here."

Dani swallowed hard again, but this time she was trying to dissolve the lump that was in her throat. She just nodded.

Gage spoke in a quiet voice, "Mrs. Williams, chances are excellent some men are going to come looking for Dani. Tell them the truth. She did live here, but she left. Do not lie to them. Do not try and cover for Dani in any way."

"But I—"

Gage shook his head. "If you lie to them, they will hurt

you. They've already killed one woman today, and they won't hesitate to kill another. Do you understand?"

"Please," Dani said, her eyes pleading words she couldn't speak. *I don't want anything to happen to you.*

Mrs. Williams nodded. "Don't you worry, Dani, I know how to take care of myself." She smiled then and gave Dani's arm a squeeze.

"Let's go." Gage turned and left the porch. Dani nodded one last time to Mrs. Williams and followed Gage down the steps.

CHAPTER FIVE

Gage threw Dani's stuff in the back of the rental Jeep except for her backpack, which she insisted on keeping with her, and then climbed into the driver's seat.

"I thought you said we weren't driving" Dani fastened her seatbelt.

"We're not." Gage maneuvered the Jeep away from the curb and headed down the street. He turned right at the end of the block.

"Where are we going then?"

Gage ignored her and glanced down at the map on his phone. He made another turn toward the downtown area. All this time he thought he was tracking down some geeky coder, and instead it was some black hat hacker he'd been hired to protect. He clamped his jaws together and curled his hands tightly around the steering wheel. His desire to break something was extreme. *Fucking hackers.* They'd cost him his career and his best friend's life.

"What's going on?" she demanded.

The edge in Dani's voice was unmistakable. He quickly glanced in her direction. Her foot was tapping a steady rhythm on the floor mat and her hands were curled into fists. Great, she was getting really pissed. He didn't have time for this shit. He wasn't handholding some hacker, no matter how cute she was.

"Hey, asshole! I'm talking to you."

Just as Gage's head whipped around in her direction, there was a loud popping sound. "Damn!" he roared as he fought to keep the Jeep on the road.

"What was that? Are they shooting at us?" Dani hunched down in her seat.

"No one is shooting at us. Jesus!" He shook his head. "I hit a pothole, and now we have a flat."

He pulled over to the side of the road and brought the SUV to a stop. They were in an industrial looking area, not far from the docks. The warehouses were covered in rust and one set of doors hung of their hinges. There was no one around and nothing was moving.. Gage didn't want to spend any more time than necessary here.

"You okay?" he asked.

"Well, at least you're finally listening to me. You need to tell me what the fuck is going on. I'm not just going to sit here and let you make all the decisions about my life, so fill me in or I'll get out now."

Her hand was on the door handle. One look at her face said she wasn't joking. He didn't need this shit right now. Not at all. When he bit his tongue to stop himself from telling her to get out, he tasted blood.

He looked at his watch. "We don't have time for a discussion now. I'm not sure what's going to happen just yet. I have a call in to Drake for some help. I'm hoping he or Janet, his assist—"

"I know who Janet is," she said while rolling her eyes.

Gage clenched his teeth. She had no idea how close he was to leaving her in the Jeep and just walking away. If his brothers weren't depending on him to complete this job, he'd be gone.

"As I was saying, I'm hoping they can pull some strings. If they don't come through, we'll probably have to drive to the next town and wait out the storm. So cross your fingers and stay in the Jeep. I have to see if we have a spare tire." Gage opened the door and climbed out.

He heard her ask, "Cross them for what? What's Drake—"

He slammed the door. If she hadn't distracted him, he wouldn't have hit the damn pothole. Pothole, hell, it was a damn crater. He went around to the back of the Jeep and pulled the cover off the spare.

At least they had one. Most rentals didn't. Then again, he was in Alaska. The roads were tough here. He imagined people got a lot of flats.

He opened the back and heaved up the cargo floor to get out the tools to change the tire. It was damn heavy with all the stuff on it, but he wasn't wasting time taking everything out.

She started yelling at him over the back seat. "Don't fucking ignore me. What is Drake—"

He slammed the back closed. She was cute when she was angry, her dark eyes snapping at him. Well, she'd have to wait. He wasn't saying anything until he knew for sure. If she got her hopes up, and it didn't work out, he had a feeling he'd never hear the end of it. If her outburst was anything to go by, she wasn't the forgiving type.

He fervently wished his brother Logan was here. He was great at dealing with people. Gage could do it, but he had his limits. He smiled. But then his limits were far greater than his brother Mitch. Mitch was way too take-no-bullshit for his own good.

Gage went around to the rear passenger side tire and bent

down. He worked as quickly as he could, but they were losing time.

Finally, he was finished. He put everything back in the Jeep and closed the back door. He walked around to the driver's side, took a breath, and squared his shoulders before opening the door, preparing for the onslaught.

Silence greeted him as he slid into the driver's seat and took a quick peek at Dani. She sat stone-faced, staring straight ahead. He started the Jeep, and after putting on his signal, pulled out and continued toward their destination.

Dani turned on the radio and switched it to a local channel. Surprised, Gage's eyebrows went up. *Music?*

"The weather report comes on every hour at ten after the hour," she said.

He swore silently. She'd noticed his surprise, and he'd had no idea she was paying attention. Not good. He was all over the place and unfocused. Too much time traveling and not getting anywhere over the last while. *Sure, that was the reason.* It couldn't be the hundred-and-twenty-pound curvy distraction seated next to him.

But she was a hacker. *Better remember that.* He took a deep breath. Mistake. *Damn.* She even smelled good. Some sort of wildflower scent and mint.

He cursed again, aloud this time. Dani looked over at him. She was stiff against the seat, and her hand still lingered on the door handle. There was no doubt in his mind she would jump if he did the slightest thing that she found threatening.

Note to self—move slowly like she was a wounded animal. The last thing he needed was for this girl to start working against him. He had problems enough with the bad guys, whoever they were.

Work the problem. That's what the navy had taught him. Just focus and work the problem. He took another deep breath. Even though the AC was on high to keep them cool, he opened the window just a bit to chase away Dani's scent.

It still grated on his nerves they had no clue who was behind all this. He thought by now, for sure, he and his brothers would have figured it out. *Work the problem.*

Doubting himself and his brothers didn't help. He peeled his fingers off the steering wheel one at a time and tried to relax them. He needed to focus on the job at hand. He could fix problems. "Did you see any of the men in the vehicle that hit the woman? Or do you have any idea who is after the software?"

"Nope to both. I assume it's someone Drake pissed off."

The announcer's voice cut in at the end of the song. "Well, folks, it looks like the storm isn't too far away now. There are reports of the rain starting just outside of town. So batten down the hatches. The temperature has already dropped about fifteen degrees since this morning."

Gage looked out the windshield. The sky was filled with dark purple clouds, and the wind was picking up. He glanced at his phone again. They had maybe fifteen minutes to get to their destination or they were screwed.

He made another turn and saw out of the corner of his eye that Dani's hands were clenched into fists again. At least she'd stopped asking questions and taken her hand off the handle, but she was still stiff in the seat. Life was no picnic for her at the moment.

Stop. Don't even think it. He didn't need to solve this woman's problems despite his instincts. He needed to take care of his brothers and the family business. Solve his own problems.

He glanced over at Dani and shook his head. He was not taking on another extracurricular project, no matter how cute she was. She was trouble, and he didn't need any more trouble in his life. It was his job to protect her and get her to

New York. Whatever her issues were, she'd have to figure them out herself.

Gage checked his GPS once more. They were almost there. A text popped up on his screen. "Yes! Janet came through."

His gut loosened a bit. They had a way out of town. He made the last turn into a parking lot on the pier. He parked the Jeep in the first empty slot he found. They had about ten minutes to make it.

"Grab your stuff," he said as he opened the door and hopped out of the SUV. He put the keys under the mat. He'd call the rental company when they were safely back in New York. Once their pursuers discovered that Gage was helping Dani, they would track his movements, and he didn't want them to know they'd left town or how they'd done it.

When Gage opened the back of the Jeep and took out his large duffle bag and his backpack, he realized Dani was still sitting in the passenger seat. "What are you waiting for? We're out of time. Grab your stuff. Let's move."

Dani turned around and looked at Gage over the back-seat of the Jeep. "Not 'til you tell me what's going on. How are we getting out of town?"

Her voice had cracked, and she looked pale. What was up with her? He tensed. Something was off. "We're leaving on that. He pointed directly in front of her. Just then the huge cruise ship gave a long pull on the horn. When it stopped, Gage said, "And we have to move, or we'll miss it." He heard Dani's voice but couldn't make out her words. "What?"

"I'm not going!" she yelled.

"Right. Don't forget your backpack," he said, and then he closed the tailgate. He picked up all the bags and started walking toward the ship. He glanced over his shoulder and saw that she hadn't been kidding. She was still sitting in the car.

"Fuck!" He dropped the stuff in the middle of the pier and walked back to the Jeep, his jaw clamped so tightly his teeth ached. *Work the problem.* He opened her door and said, "Want to tell me what the fuck is wrong?"

Dani looked up at him defiantly. "I don't like boats."

"I don't like broccoli, but that's life. Get out of the car and let's go. We've got two minutes to board."

"I. Don't. Like. Boats." She glared at him this time.

"I. Don't. Care." He spoke exactly as she had. He reached around her and undid her seatbelt. "Get your ass out of the car and over to the ship. This is the only thing that's leaving this city today. We need to be on it because the men chasing you will not be on it. They will have no way of reaching us. They will not be able to find us. We, as in *you*, will be safe. Now get your ass moving." He stepped back and waited for her to get out the car.

She sat where she was, unmoving. Gage felt his temper snap like it was a rubber band that had been stretched too far. He leaned closer.

"I spent the last couple of weeks running all over the world, tracking you down, following all the false trails you left, because I was hired to keep you safe. It was a colossal waste of my time," he ranted.

"Now, I'm exhausted and very pissed off. I haven't seen my bed in far too long. So you need to tell me anything that is relevant *now* and stop being any kind of secretive. I have zero patience for your bullshit. And remember, your life depends on me.

Dani remained silent.

"So, get. Your. Ass. Moving," he roared.

Her eyes snapped, shooting sparks in his direction. He'd be six feet under if she could kill with a look. He hated being mean, but he just didn't have a choice. She slowly moved out of the car, but once she shut the door, she stopped.

"What now?" Gage was fuming. It took all of his willpower not to throw her over his shoulder and make for the gangplank.

"Boats…I don't do well on boats."

He stared at her. Was she kidding? What the hell was her problem? He studied her face. Her eyes were changing. She wasn't angry any longer. When she glanced at the ship, her face got paler. Her breath was coming in short gasps. Fear. She was afraid. She'd hid it before, but it was now written plainly on her features. Her eyes were darting all around, and she kept rubbing her palms on her thighs.

"First, it's a ship not a boat. Do you get seasick? Is that the problem?"

Her nod was slow in coming. She was biting her lip now.

He sighed and counted to ten. It wasn't just seasickness. Her fear was too great for that, but he just didn't have time to coddle her. Whatever was going on was going to get them both killed if he couldn't find a way to get her on that ship.

"Look, you'll be fine. Cruise ships are a very safe way to travel, and they have massive stabilizers so you won't even feel the waves. It's a hell of a lot better to be puking your guts up than being dead, so pick up your stuff and move."

He turned around and walked back to the pier, grabbed his bags, and kept going. If she didn't want to come with him, then fuck her. He was done.

Right. He hoped his bluff worked. There was no way in hell he could leave her behind. He wouldn't do that to his brothers. He wouldn't be the one to wreck the business their father had built.

CHAPTER SIX

She watched Gage's back as he walked across the pier toward the walkway up to the ship. Fuck him! She hated him. It was easy for him to say "come or die," but for her it was the same thing. She glanced over at the side of the pier. The water was black, and she was sure it was very cold. It didn't matter that it was summer. The ocean was always cold to her. Cold and deadly. Images of her foster mother flashed behind her eyelids. The woman would laugh and laugh and then force Dani into the water again. Dani's entire body shook with the memory.

Her eyes snapped open. She wasn't a small child anymore. If she didn't want to get on the damn ship, she wasn't doing it. She looked around. But where would she go? She couldn't go back to her comfy little apartment.

Mrs. Williams. Her breath caught in her throat. *Please don't let the bad guys hurt her.* Dani had never been anything but distant toward people. But, somehow, she was getting softer. First Carly and then Mrs. Williams. Being soft with them made her vulnerable. The last thing on earth she wanted to be. She wouldn't put Mrs. Williams in anymore danger than she was already in.

She stood next to the Jeep. She could take it and drive out of town, but Callahan had been right. Driving would mean running into the storm. No way she wanted to do that. Suddenly, the final horn sounded on the boat, making her jump. There was moisture on her face. The rain had hit. Chances were excellent it would turn into hail at some point. Maybe even snow. There was just no predicting the weather these days.

She looked around for Gage. He was almost at the walkway now. He really was going to leave her here on her own. Bastard! She was smart and street savvy, but these guys frightened her. More than the ship. Being dead *would* suck.

She took a deep breath and grabbed her backpack. She started after Gage at a jog. Served him right if she puked on him. She'd make sure she aimed in his direction when it happened. No way would she be the only one to suffer. She could feel the smile grow on her face. It was always good to have a plan.

"We're on deck twelve," was all he said as he started up the walkway ahead of her.

She didn't bother replying. She had nothing to say. Plus, she was desperately trying not to think about the fact she was getting on a boat that was on water. She could feel the sway of the stairs under her feet. She must have made a noise because Gage glanced at her over his shoulder.

"You gonna make it up, or should I throw you over my shoulder?"

She gave him her best "curl up and die" stare but he just turned around and kept strutting up the steps. *Asshole!*

When he reached the end of the walkway, he stopped and handed his passport to the crew member. He turned to her. "Get out your passport."

She dug through her bag and handed it over.

"Welcome aboard," the guy in the uniform said with a huge smile. "You made it just in time. My name is Jeremy. I'm one of the crew. Now, I need you to look straight into the camera so we can get a picture and get your ID all set up." She nodded and moved slightly so she was lined up with the camera. A few keystrokes later by Jeremy, and she was finished. He showed her the picture. Great. She looked like death warmed over. *Whatevs.*

"We don't often get people joining us this far along in the cruise," Jeremy said as he lined Gage up for his ID photo.

"Last minute change of plans," Gage said.

Jeremy opened his mouth but took one look at Gage's face and promptly closed it again, putting his smile back in place. He spent another minute typing and then handed her and Gage each a band. "This is your medallion. In coordination with the app you can download, it can be used to book dinner reservations, order drinks, book times on certain sports or entertainment features onboard, and it's also your room key. Most people wear it around their neck or on their wrist. It can also be used to find each other on the ship just in case you get lost." The smile was so wide now Dani was sure Jeremy's cheeks had to be hurting.

Gage grunted out a, "Thank you."

"Have a great time," Jeremy said, but Dani just nodded and followed Gage inside. This whole thing was bothering her.

"So, if we're using our real names, won't the bad guys find us?" she asked as she jogged up the stairs behind Gage. Silence. Did he not hear her, or was he ignoring her?

"Hey, asshole," she said in a loud voice just as she hit the top step. She turned to follow Gage, who had swung right and immediately barreled into a group of elderly ladies. They looked like they'd all eaten too many prunes. Their faces were all pinched. *Great. Guess they heard me.* Not that she cared. "I'm talking to you." She caught up to Gage and hit him on the back.

He stopped and turned around. "I know, and so does half the ship. Think you can keep it down a little? I'm not into the whole ship knowing our business."

"Well, if you'd answer when I talk to you, we wouldn't have a problem." She glared at him, hands planted on her hips.

"And if you used that supposedly large brain of yours for just one second, you'd realize this is not the place to have this conversation. Now, let's get to the room, and you can tell me all about what an asshole I am, okay?"

She instantly regretted she hadn't hit him harder a second ago. Her fingers curled into a fist. It was so hard not to let loose and smoke him in that "oh-so-perfect jaw." Or maybe break his nose again.

He walked away from her. She took a deep, calming breath and followed. She prided herself on being able to maintain control. If she kept herself neutral and controlled, she won. In the past, if she lost control, then her foster mother won, and Dani was punished. She started running lines of code in her head. It was what she did to calm herself down.

They came to what could only be described as a park in the middle of the ship. Dani stopped dead. "What the hell?"

Gage glanced over his shoulder. "Keep up. You can admire the sights later."

Dani started moving again but couldn't stop herself from trying to look everywhere at once. There was a pond and a tree. There were people everywhere, and shops. High-end shops, restaurants, and there was even a cocktail bar moving between floors like an elevator with people sitting and drinking. It really was a floating city.

When Gage stopped suddenly, she almost bumped into him. There were quite a few people standing around, waiting. It was a mix of young kids and elderly people. Dani must have looked confused because an elderly gent beside her pointed and said in a proper British accent, "We're waiting for the lift."

Dani smiled slightly and nodded. Then she turned to Gage. "I always wondered who took cruises. Who wants to be stuck on a boat for a week at a time?"

"Everyone, apparently," Gage murmured.

The doors of several elevators opened at once, and Dani surged ahead with the crowd. The ride up was long. The damn thing stopped at every floor. Finally they got off, and Dani followed Gage again. She had no choice since he hadn't told her the room numbers. When he stopped suddenly, she barreled into him.

"This is us." He opened the door and moved into the cabin, holding the door open for her.

"There's only one?" Dani asked.

Gage turned around and stared at her. "We were lucky to get this. Now get in here so I can close the door."

She gingerly moved inside. The bathroom was immediately on the left and then one large king-size bed was in the middle of the room. There were chairs and a coffee table beyond the bed and then floor to ceiling glass doors that led to a balcony with a couple of chairs. Through the rain and the gloom, she could see the water.

She dropped her stuff and leaned heavily against the wall. She'd thought her apartment was small but spending time with Gage in this tiny room while staring at the water was going to be hell on earth. Her stomach churned as fear started coursing through her. She was going to puke. No question.

Gage promptly walked over and closed the curtains to

the balcony. He turned to face her. "Your point about our real names is valid. So, since you're such an amazing hacker, it's up to you to fix it."

CHAPTER SEVEN

error. She was truly terrified of the water. He'd closed the curtains to block her view, hoping that would calm her down, but she still had a death grip on her duffle bag.

No one should ever have to feel fear like that. Guilt washed over him. It was his fault she was terrified. He practically forced her onto the ship. *There was no other way out of town.* Still. He owed her. As much as he hated hackers, he didn't want her to suffer like she was suffering now.

"So, are you going to get to work or what? The longer you take, the greater the chance they'll find us." He was hoping the distraction would calm her down. He was all out of ideas. It was the best he had.

"Wait. What? That's your plan? Have me fix the problem you just created?" She stared at him.

Her eyebrows were sky-high. Disbelief was better than terror. He'd take it. Her fear had shaken him. God only knew what she'd been through. How she was going to make it on a ship over the next few days, he had no idea, but it was better than being dead. But that thought didn't lesson his guilt.

He'd work the problem, just like always, and find a way

to make her okay with it. He never wanted to see primal fear like that on her face again.

"You're the expert. You got us into this mess by hiding out instead of coming to New York, so now you can help fix the problem." He walked over and threw himself into a chair. Then he brought out his phone and proceeded to check his email. "I'm going to do some work. You might want to get started."

He heard her gasp and then curse. He was guessing the word she used was aimed at him, but he didn't look up. It would only make them argue longer, and although he was sure fighting would take her mind off things, they really did need to solve the name issue quickly.

She started to sit down and then staggered and yelped. The ship had started to move. Her face lost all remaining color. He started out of his chair to help her, but she waved him off. He was surprised she felt it that strongly. Guilt sucker punched him again. She was suffering, and it was his doing.

She looked at him and then bit her lip. She slowly pushed the chair opposite him out of the way and then lowered herself onto the floor.

Gage sighed. She was going to have to get used to the movement or this trip was going to be a nightmare for both of them.

Relief flooded him when she got out her laptop and then set it up. "Is there internet?" Her voice sounded hoarse. She swallowed. "I know there is now because we're close to shore, but how good will it be later? You should buy whatever package they're selling. Get the top one."

He raised an eyebrow at her demand, but she didn't notice. She was already engrossed in what she was doing. He went online and did as she asked. "You're all set."

She grunted in response but didn't stop. Her fingers flew

"Um, I'm good. I think I'll just..." She opened her laptop again. "I have to work on the software. There're a few wrinkles to iron out. Besides, I'm not really hungry after all." She put a hand on her stomach.

He could hear it rumbling from where he was sitting. Her fear was too much. Here was the weakness. Dani was willing to take on the world, but she couldn't deal with seeing water. No need for her to suffer. He'd bring her food. She needed to eat.

"If you're okay to be here by yourself, I'm going to go check out a few things. That work for you?"

Dani looked up at him. "Sure. Whatevs." She waved her hand, and her eyes went back to the screen.

He studied her. Her nose was pert and sassy. It suited her face. Although her lips were full, the bottom one was dry and peeling, probably from her biting it all the time. Anxiety came off her in waves, and it triggered him. The urge to protect her was strong. It didn't matter if she wanted him to or not.

Damn, she was a ballsy spitfire. He hated to see her fears win. He'd been full of piss and vinegar. Once. He'd thought he could take on the world and win, too. It was obvious that life had slapped her down a few times already. Hard. He'd help her. Even if he hated the fact that she was a hacker. Everyone deserved a bit of help now and again. Plus, maybe if he was nice, she'd stop pissing him off so badly.

He put his hands in his jeans pockets so he wouldn't brush her hair back from her face. He knew it would be soft. Sitting here staring at her really wasn't a good idea. *Control*, remember? Gage shot out of the chair and grabbed the medallion off the dresser where he'd thrown it when they arrived. He went to the door, and with his hand on the door-knob, he turned. "What's my name?"

"What?" Dani yelped like he'd scared her.

"What's the name you gave me?" he said.

"Oh right, Robert Barker."

Bob Barker. Seriously. He sighed.

"What's yours?"

"Marie White."

He opened the door and closed it after him. Marie was Vanna White's middle name. He knew because his mom had all of Vanna White's crochet books and was a big fan. So Dani was a game show junkie. Why wasn't he surprised?

SHE WAITED FOR THREE MINUTES AFTER THE DOOR closed just to be sure and then brought up the app on her computer. She hit the video call button. Her stomach growled again. She was starving. Lunch had been long ago, and she'd left most of it in the toilet back at her old place. Still, the idea of going out of the room seemed too scary to contemplate. Plus, she hadn't spoken to Carly today.

The call timed out. She frowned. It was late where Carly was but, still, she was usually up. She bit her lip. What if something was wrong? Should she call the hospital switchboard and ask for the nursing station on Carly's floor?

The computer buzzed with an incoming video call. Dani hit the button, and Carly's face lit up the screen. "Carly!" Relief flooded through Dani at seeing her little sister's shining face. "How are you? Did I wake you?"

"No, I was just dozing," Carly said and then promptly yawned.

"Do you want to go back to sleep? I can call you tomorrow." Dani clenched her fingers into fists. Carly didn't look so good. Her color was grayish, and her usually bright blue eyes were dimmed.

"I'm okay. They'll come in and check on me shortly

anyway, so I'll stay up and chat with you until then. How's everything going?"

Even her voice sounded weak to Dani's ears. "I'm fine. The usual."

"Where are you? Not at your apartment. I don't recognize the chair behind you."

At least her brain was still sharp. Dani swallowed. Hard. This little girl was her life. Her little sister, even if not by blood. All the family Dani had and all she would ever need. "I'm on a cruise." Dani tried to sound excited, but her voice broke.

"What? You hate water. Why would you do that to yourself? What's wrong?"

Concern was etched in her tired young face, and it was breaking Dani's heart. "Don't worry. Nothing's wrong. Remember I said I might have to move around a bit while working on this project? It was time to hit the road, but unfortunately a storm came up, and this was the only way out of town."

"Why didn't you just wait 'til the storm passed?" Carly asked and then immediately yawned again.

Dani dug her nails into her palms. Carly wasn't doing well. "You look really tired tonight. Why don't I let you get back to sleep? We'll talk tomorrow."

"Maybe you're right." Carly's voice was almost a whisper. Carly fell back into the pillows behind her.

Danie's chest tightened. Carly never gave up this easily. She hated going to sleep. Even at the ripe old age of ten, she still put up a major fuss about going to bed. She always made a joke about her illness. "I'll have time to sleep when I'm dead. Too much to see and do." *Until tonight.* To see her give in so quickly made Dani's stomach cramp. Nausea rose in her throat, and it wasn't from seasickness. Maybe it was a good thing she hadn't eaten. "Okay, Squiggles. I'll call you tomorrow."

Carly smiled and waved, then the screen went black.

A sob escaped Dani's lips. Carly hadn't even fought about being called "Squiggles." She was losing her battle. Her little body was giving up. Tears ran down Dani's face. She pounded her fists on the coffee table. She needed to work harder, faster. She needed to find a relative for Carly. Carly wanted to meet family. Real family. The software had to work!

The tears that had started slowly now raced in torrents down her cheeks, mimicking the rain outside. She was failing. For the first time in life, her talent wasn't enough. Her whole body convulsed with her sobs.

"No!" she said as she got to her feet and violently swiped at her cheeks. She would not give up. She would make it happen. She would fix the software and find Carly's birth family. They were out there.

Dani took a deep shuddering breath and walked to the bathroom. Her face was all blotchy and red. She was not one of those pretty criers. She was an ugly-cry kinda girl, and she was okay with that. Those pretty-cry people weren't really feelin' it as far as she was concerned. But Gage would soon be back, and she didn't want to answer any questions.

Her breath was still jerky from her sobbing, so she tried to calm down. She went out to her duffel and dug out a T-shirt and boxer shorts, her sleeping attire. She would grab a quick shower and get to work. She had lots to do yet tonight. As she turned and was walking back to the bathroom, someone pounded on the door.

Dani froze. Gage had taken his medallion. She'd been watching him in her peripheral vision. The pounding happened again. A muffled voice yelled, "I know you're in there."

CHAPTER EIGHT

"Hey buddy, what gives?" Gage asked. He'd seen this guy banging on the room door the moment he'd rounded the corner. His first instinct was to ditch the to-go containers in his hands and pummel the guy, but he held off. If this was one of the guys after them, he wanted an opportunity to talk with him before he reduced him to a pile of broken bones.

"Ah, whaaat? None of your fuckin' business, man." The guy started pounding on the door again. "I know you're in there. Let me in, bissshhh." The guy staggered back a step and bumped into the wall behind him. He turned and saw Gage again. Frowning, he tried to stand up straight. "I said leave me the fuck alone. Are you sshupid or somethin?"

"Buddy, I think you're a bit mixed up."

The guy turned full to face Gage. "You don't want to get in my faace, man. Thissh is between me and my girlfriend," he said while poking himself in the chest. Then he pointed at Gage. "You sshay out of it."

Gage took a deep breath. After the day he'd had—hell, after the last month—he really just wanted to bounce the guy off the walls and step over his body on the floor. It would be a great stress relief, but it wouldn't be a fair fight. Sometimes it sucked being a good guy.

He sighed and looked down at the containers he had in each hand. The food was getting cold. "Look, buddy, you got the wrong room. Your girlfriend isn't in there."

The guy looked puzzled. "How do you know?"

"Because that's my door you're banging on."

The guy looked at Gage and then turned and looked at the door again. He looked up and down the hallway. "Ssshit. I'm on the wrong floor. Sssorry, buddy." When the guy took a step forward, Gage promptly moved out of the way to let him by. The guy mumbled "sssorry" again and staggered down the hallway.

Gage waited until the guy had turned the corner before stepping in front of the door. He put both containers on one arm then opened the door. One look at Dani's face, and he almost dropped the food. Her eyes were golf ball-sized and filled with terror. Gage's chest felt like he'd taken a hit to his bulletproof vest.

"Are you okay? It was just a drunk on the wrong floor," he said as he set the containers on the dresser and turned back to Dani. It took everything he had not to wrap his arms around her. He wanted to make her feel safe.

Her color was gray, and her teeth were chattering. Her cheeks were all blotchy. Her body shook as she took a deep breath. Maybe he shouldn't have left her alone at all. From the looks of her, she'd been truly terrified. *Fuck*. He needed to do better. Protecting her also meant keeping her from being in a constant state of true terror. At least it did to him. No one should have to feel that. Ever.

Dani avoided eye contact with him. "I'm fine," she managed to get out, but her voice still sounded funny to Gage, like she'd been crying for a while. *Shit, how long had that asshole been banging on the door?* He deeply regretted not pummeling the drunk for terrifying Dani.

"He's gone. It's okay. You're safe." He gave in to his need to reach out to touch Dani and moved toward her with his arms rising from his sides. He saw her freeze. He'd noticed her turn to stone when her old landlord had hugged her as well. She obviously did not want to be touched. He stopped moving and dropped his arms.

"I was just going to take a shower," she said as she gestured toward the bathroom.

"Okay. I, ah, brought some food in case you were hungry."

She turned and glanced at the containers but made no move toward them. "Um, thanks. I think I'll take my shower and maybe eat after." She still avoided looking him in the eye.

Gage ran a hand through his hair. The old lady was right —this poor girl had been through the wars and was very much scared by it. His gut churned.

"You go ahead. Do whatever makes you happy. The food will still be here when you get out." He tried to give her a smile, but she didn't bother looking at him, just headed directly into the bathroom and locked the door.

Gage sat down hard on the chair he'd vacated earlier. Dani was a mess. She needed some help. Maybe more than he could give.

Deal with the problem at hand, he reminded himself. The best thing he could do for her was keep her safe until they got back to New York. She could finish the software there. Yup, that was the smart play.

He tried to distract himself by studying the room. The walls were off white with bright floral prints in bold colors. The king-size bed dominated the room with its pale comforter that had a colorful throw artfully tossed across it.

The TV on the dresser, a state-of-the-art flat screen with the remotes lined up underneath, was directly across from the bed. The food was getting cold, but he'd lost his appetite.

Finally, he grabbed his phone. He could stare at the walls all he wanted, but he needed a distraction and probably some help. He'd put off calling his brothers long enough. There was a mole for sure. It wasn't the first one they'd had to deal with and chances were good it was on Drake's end, not Callahan Security.

He listened for a moment to make sure the shower was still on. He didn't want to go out on the balcony; it was raining buckets. Hearing the water running, he hit the buttons on his burner phone to call his brothers.

"Callahan," the voice on the other end answered.

"Yes, but which one? You said we need to say our full names to identify ourselves clearly," Gage said. A small smile spread across his face at hearing his brother Logan's voice.

"Gage! Where the hell have you been?" Logan's voice was tight.

Gage laughed. "I've been all over the place. I'm exhausted. Sorry I didn't call sooner." He heard a click and some muffled sounds. "Are you still there?" Were they too far out of port now for the call? Had he waited too long? "Logan?"

"I'm here and—"

"I'm here too, bro. You had us worried!" his younger brother Mitch's voice boomed across the line.

"Yeah, I figured as much. Sorry about that. It's been a bit crazy."

"It only takes a second to send a text or make a phone call, at least according to my other half. She yells at me about it all the time," Mitch said with a laugh.

Gage grinned. No doubt Alex was keeping Mitch in line. She was a tough one. Gage loved her for it. "I know but"—

the smile slid off his face—"to be honest, a few things have happened, and silence seemed to be the best option."

"What do you mean?" Logan's voice had switched to his crisp lawyerly speak.

Gage hesitated for a second then mentally shrugged. "So, you know Drake didn't want to give me info about the hacker, Dani. Well, that's because he didn't have any. She kept him in the dark about her location and played him every chance she got.

"When I pressed him, and he gave me vague bits of information, like he thought she was in Berlin, or she'd mentioned Paris when they spoke, Drake was doing his best to help. I followed up on every clue and ended up running around Europe. Drake was pissed and so was I." Gage got out of the chair and peeled back the curtain with one hand. The rain pounded on the glass doors. He let the curtain drop.

"The thing is, I wasn't the only one there. A couple of times I thought I saw the same men. I thought maybe they were following me, but then I arrived at a location where her IP address had pinged, which of course, was another false trail, and they'd been there first. They weren't following me. They were tracking her, the same as me." Gage sat back down in the chair.

"There's a leak is what you're saying."

Gage was always impressed on how quick Mitch's brain worked despite his deceiving surfer style.

"That's my fear."

Logan said, "And you were worried it could be on our end."

"I like to think that's impossible, but I couldn't rule it out entirely unless I cut off contact and the guys still showed up."

"So the guys showed again, right?" Mitch asked.

Gage switched the phone to his other ear and ran a hand through his hair. "Yup, they showed up. In Juneau, Alaska, where Dani was hiding. They must have gotten to town right before I did, because they had already broken into her place and stole what they thought was the software."

"Oh, shit!"

"You said it, Mitch. And that's not all. Because they thought they had the software, they actually killed a woman they thought was Dani. Hit and run." There was silence on the other end of the phone. Gage didn't blame them for taking a beat. He heard his brother Logan curse softly.

"Is Daniella okay?" Logan asked.

That was a loaded question for sure. "Dani. She goes by Dani. She's okay for now." He hesitated and then shrugged. "I need you to do background on her, though. There's more going on here, and she's not exactly sharing any information. I think she might have a clue who's behind this. She said 'no' when I asked her, but I'm willing to bet she's not in the dark like she says."

He heard Mitch chuckle. "A woman not telling one of us the full story? No way! Couldn't possibly happen."

Gage laughed. After what his brothers had gone through with their significant others recently, he should know there'd be more to Dani's story. "Yup, it's shocking. Anyway, get me any details you can find on her so I am better prepared. Any luck on finding out who these people are? Did Drake or Janet come up with anything?"

He heard Mitch sigh. "Not so far. He's trying, Logan's trying, hell, we're all trying. Whoever's behind the attempt wants to keep a very low profile. It seems it's okay for some tech companies to have a basic facial recognition software, but they don't want the high-level stuff to be widespread.

Mitch sighed. "Only companies that deal in some sort of national security are allowed to have it. Airports, airlines, things like that. So I guess we can assume it's not someone involved in something above board."

"Sounds logical," Gage agreed.

Mitch continued. "We've been sort of asking around, but everyone is keeping mum on the subject. I get it. If you were trying to steal software that most governments have but don't want to share, would you tell the world? It would just put a big ol' target on your back." Mitch sighed again. "My question is, how did these people find out about Drake having the software?"

Logan piped up, "Which brings us back to a leak in Drake's company. Whoever the leak is will know who's after the software. Identify the leak and—"

"We identify the bad guys," Mitch finished his brother's sentence.

"Huh, well, I guess you two need to start investigating Drake's people. It shouldn't be too hard. I doubt he's telling the world about Dani. No more than a handful of people would have access to any information about her or the software."

"If that," Mitch said. "I've worked with Drake for a while now. There are very few people he would trust with this info. Maybe only three to five, tops. We'll start looking into this right away."

"Okay, sounds good. Email me what you can find out about our hacker and keep me updated on the rest," Gage said. "I'm not sure I'll have access all the time, but it should come through when we're in port." He glanced at the door. The water had stopped about a minute ago, so he wanted to get off the phone.

"Wait," Logan said. "Where are you? When are you flying home? Is there anything else you need?"

"I'm on a cruise ship, believe it or not. Nothing else was leaving port. We are in Ketchikan tomorrow, and then we get into Vancouver a day or two after that. I'll send you the info. It might be helpful to have backup when we get off the ship."

"Why are you on a cruise? Why not just fly home?" Logan asked.

"There was a storm, and I didn't want to wait since we were sitting ducks. This was the only thing leaving town."

"Well, it's certainly a novel take on making a quick getaway," Mitch said with a laugh. "At least it's a boat. You love boats."

"Sailboats. I love sailing. Cruising is not really my thing," Gage lamented "Too many tourists with selfie sticks snapping pictures all the time. People even take pictures of their food. Seriously."

"Nothing wrong with a picture of food if it's presented in an aesthetically pleasing fashion," Logan sounded slightly insulted.

"Says the chef." Mitch's laughter came down the phone line. "Could be worse, big bro. You could be in a fishing boat, having to sleep with the fish."

"Har har," Gage said as he shook his head, but he was happy. His brothers were worried but happy and, most importantly, getting along. That was what he promised his mother before she died. That he would take care of his brothers and make sure they got along.

Mitch piped up. "We'll be there to meet you in Vancouver. Have fun on your cruise. Take advantage of all the interesting things onboard. Think of it as a mini vacation of sorts."

Logan's voice was serious when he said, "Be very careful, Gage. We still have no idea what we're up against."

"Will do. Talk later." Gage hung up the phone. He felt better knowing he would have backup in Vancouver. Maybe Mitch was right. There was slim chance that anyone looking for them would find them on a cruise ship, especially after Dani had hacked in and changed their names. As long as his brothers didn't mention it, he could relax until Vancouver.

The door opened behind him and he looked over to see Dani standing in the middle of the room. She was all dewy faced with a lot more color in her cheeks. Her long dark hair was still damp and curling slightly as it hung over her shoulders and down her back.

She was wearing an old black T-shirt and a pair of boxer shorts with kissing lips all over them. Both of them clung to her every curve, and she had some amazing curves. To see them accentuated took his breath away. She was stunningly beautiful. He swallowed hard and cleared his throat.

"I…think I'll skip eating if that's okay with you," Dani said. Her voice still sounded rusty to him, but it was better than before.

"Uh, yeah. I kind of lost my appetite as well. It's getting late, and it might just be time to grab some sleep."

Dani glanced at the bed. Her eyebrows lowered a bit, and she nibbled her bottom lip. Gage couldn't help but notice. Those lips were so delicate looking, so delectable. He wanted to taste them. Her scent drifted to him, and he found himself surrounded by it. The wildflowers were back. *Shit*. He shot out of the chair, making Dani jump.

"Sorry, leg cramp." Jesus, he sounded like an idiot. "Don't worry about the sleeping arrangements." He passed her and walked to the closet by the cabin door. God, she smelled divine. *Get your shit together.*

He grabbed the extra pillows off the top shelf and then walked past Dani again, moving purposefully around the far side of the bed. "Here. We'll put these between us. That way we won't run into each other in our sleep."

Her glance flew between him and the pillows. Slowly, she nodded. "Okay."

Worry lines eased in her expression, but fatigue was taking over. Her shoulders were slumped and her eyelids droopy.

"Which side to you want?"

"Doesn't matter," he mumbled.

She nodded again and went to the side closest to the wall. She pulled back the sheets and slid into bed, pulling the covers up to her chin. Gage dropped the pillows behind her. Then he went around and turned out most of the lights.

He grabbed his gear bag and went into the bathroom. He braced his hands on the counter and looked in the mirror. The man staring back at him looked tired and pissed off. He was also horny as hell.

He closed his eyes. *Work the problem.* Protect Dani and get her back to New York. Any other problem she had wasn't his business. He did not need to make her feel safe. He did not need to make her feel happy. He did not need to make her feel anything. He opened his eyes. Then why was he so desperate to do just that?

CHAPTER NINE

Dani's heart crashed against her ribs as she sat bolt upright in bed. *What? Where?* She blinked a few times to clear the fog. There was a clatter and, suddenly Gage's head and upper body appeared around the corner and Dani emitted a tiny scream. Her hand flew to her chest. Where the hell did he come from?

"Are you okay?" he asked as he scanned the room.

"Er, um, yeah. Something woke me, I guess. I..." She glanced at his naked chest. His muscles flexed as he moved farther into the room. He was standing at the end of the bed, wearing navy gym shorts and nothing else as far as she could tell.

Smooth, tan flesh covered his chiseled muscles, from his shoulders to the top of his shorts and most likely beyond. Heat crept up Dani's neck to her cheeks. She had to stop staring. When she dragged her gaze from his chest to his face, she realized he was smirking at her. Caught, damn it.

"It's fine. You can go back to what you were doing now," she said as she flopped back down on the bed. What was he doing? Looking friggin' hot as hell was what he was doing. Seriously. *Get a grip.*

There was a loud thump, and Dani recognized it right away as the sound that had woken her up. Someone farther down their hallway had slammed their stateroom door. She groaned softly. It was time to get up. She had to figure out the problem with the software today. There was no time left.

She swung her feet over the side of the bed and stood up. She grabbed the wall as the room spun. *What the hell?* What was wrong with her? She didn't have time to be sick.

The ship wasn't moving. Fear shot through her. Why weren't they moving? Were they stuck at sea? When she let out a strangled cry, Gage popped back around the corner.

He stared at her. "Are you okay? You don't look so good. Are you going to be sick?"

She shook her head. Her tongue was suddenly three feet thick. She couldn't make it work at all. *Stuck out in the middle of the ocean. Surrounded on all sides by nothing but cold, black water.* She made another strangled noise.

Gage advanced toward her until he was mere inches away. He didn't touch her, but he studied her intently. "You're breathing. You're pale but not turning blue, so it's not physical. What's going on? You're terrified." His eyes narrowed. She realized he wasn't so much asking her as just speaking aloud.

She glanced toward the windows.

He followed her look. "You're afraid of the water. But you can't see the water now. So why are you frightened?" His eyes darted all over the room and then back to her. He opened and closed his fists. "What's making you so scared?" He looked around the room again but shook his head. "I'm missing it. Damn, Dani!"

She knew he wasn't yelling at her. How could she

communicate with him? She was frozen. Her body wouldn't obey her at all.

Gage walked over toward the window. He opened the curtain just a bit and let it fall. He turned back and said, "We're docked, but I still see water so I won't open the curtain.

Docked.

Relief flooded Dani's veins, and her legs gave way. She sat back down on the bed.

"Oh, shit." Gage quickly moved to next to her again. "You thought we were stuck at sea. I should have told you we're at port today." He reached out and squeezed her shoulder. "I'm so incredibly sorry."

"That's okay." Her voice came out as a croak. Heat crawled up her cheeks. What an idiot she was for panicking. She should have realized they were at port. If she'd thought about it for a moment, she would have. The panic had just set in so quickly. "I'm okay," she said.

His eyes were sad. He was blaming himself. It wasn't his fault.

"Really, I'm okay. It was just me being stupid."

"No. Fear isn't stupid. Fear is paralyzing and horrible. I'm so sorry I didn't think to go over the cruise schedule with you. My fault." He squeezed her shoulder again and then promptly dropped his hand.

"I'm just going to finish up in the bathroom and then it's all yours." He disappeared around the corner.

Dani flopped back on the bed and started taking deep breaths. She was trying to bring her heart rate down out of the stratosphere. Her fear was unreasonable, and she knew it, but she just couldn't control it.

The warmth from Gage's hand was still imprinted on her skin. He knew she didn't like to be touched. Last night he'd approached her but stopped after the drunk guy incident.

She'd appreciated it then just as much as she appreciated his touch just now. It had brought her back down to earth. It really helped calm her down.

It was weird how one minute he was a complete asshole with her and the next he was taking care of her. He'd closed the curtains immediately for her last night and gotten her food. Maybe he wasn't such jerk after all. Or maybe it was just part of his job—taking care of her so she reached New York in one piece. *Shit.*

She took one last deep breath and then got up off the bed. Her stomach growled so loud the people next door would have heard it if they hadn't already left their room. She needed food and about a gallon of coffee. That's why she was dizzy and her brain wasn't working. So, food first and then the software. She moved down to the end of the bed and ran straight into Gage's now covered chest. "Ack!"

"I've got you. You okay?" he asked.

She looked up. His frowning face was mere inches from hers. Before her freak-out of two minutes ago, she hadn't been this close to any man in a long time.

His eyes were even bluer than she'd first thought. His lips were fuller, too. When she licked hers in response to seeing his, his eyes followed her tongue. They changed color. Deeper blue.

"I'm fine," she said as she backed up away from him. "Really." She didn't like to be too close to anybody, but this guy set her nerves jangling. The fact that his navy T-shirt matched his shorts and hugged his chest didn't help either. Even his scent was intoxicating. Something woodsy with citrus.

God, she *was* losing it. She must be hungrier than she thought. "I just haven't eaten since yesterday morning. Um, if you're through in the bathroom, I'll just go get dressed."

Gage stepped sideways to let her pass. "All yours. I'm

going to the gym. It might be good if you joined me. We should stick together."

She grabbed her duffel bag and headed for the bathroom. "No, thanks. I'm good."

Ten minutes later, dressed in jeans and another T-shirt, this one red, teeth brushed and hair up in a ponytail, she was ready to go.

Gage had waited for her, which she wasn't so pleased about. She needed some space. From him. "So, I thought you were off to the gym?" She reached out, grabbed her backpack with her laptop in it, and then opened the room door. She'd given herself a pep talk in the bathroom. She could leave the room. Water was not going to defeat her. She moved into the hallway and then looked left and then right.

"Left," Gage said. He was right behind her.

She tried not to sigh. He was so insufferable somehow. She was hangry and she knew it. Best keep her mouth shut until she ate. She needed to get back to work on her software.

After turning left, she moved swiftly down the hall until she found the elevator bank. The doors magically opened just as she arrived. "Going down" someone inside said so she hopped on, but it was crowded. She took her backpack off and held it at her feet. Gage got on and stood beside her.

The doors closed, only to have them open again as someone else hit the button and then jumped on. She and Gage moved to the back of the elevator. He was standing in the back corner and she was pressed up against him.

The woodsy scent was back, and his breath teased the hairs at the nape of her neck. That, in combination with being backed up against his chest, was making her nether regions tingle. *Damn.* She needed to get away from this man. He was killing her senses.

"Do you even know where you're going?" he whispered in her ear, his breath tickling her earlobe now.

"Um, breakfast," she said, but her voice sounded funny to her own ears.

"We really should stick together."

"I have no interest in going to the gym."

The doors opened and, before she knew it, Gage had his arms around her waist and was maneuvering her out of the elevator.

"Wha—?" she sputtered.

"Don't worry, there are restaurants on this floor. There are restaurants on every floor. I just thought we should have a little chat first." He led her around the corner into a big open area, and they walked slowly along a promenade.

"I don't like the idea of you being alone," Gage said as they negotiated the crowds.

"I'm hardly alone." She rolled her eyes and gestured at the throng of people that surrounded them.

"You know what I mean. I would very much like it if you stayed with me."

"Then don't go to the gym. I'm getting breakfast." The tantalizing aroma of frying bacon made her mouth water. There was a restaurant off to her right. It looked like a buffet place. Worked for her. She just needed food and to get away from Gage for a bit. A group of people passed in front of them, speaking what sounded like Italian. She'd always wanted to go to Italy. Maybe one day she'd get there.

"What kind of food do you like?" Gage asked.

"What?" She glanced up at him and frowned. *What was he going on about now?*

"What kind of food do you like? You know, Italian, Greek…" He gestured at the Italian group that was walking away.

"For breakfast? Pancakes." Italian, Greek. Maybe he was hungry, and he just didn't realize it. He wasn't making any sense.

"Are you sure you want to eat right now? You could come with me to the gym, and we can eat after. There's always a restaurant open on the ship."

Dani shook her head. What part of 'I don't want to go to the gym' didn't he understand? "Nope. I'm all good. I want to eat breakfast now." She pointed down the hallway away from the restaurant. "You go do whatever it is you do at the gym, and I'm going to stuff my face and enjoy every minute of it. We didn't eat dinner last night, and I'm starving."

Gage started to laugh. "Point taken. Note to self, Dani gets very hangry when she doesn't eat." He smiled down at her.

She felt herself relaxing and smiling back. "Gym or breakfast? You have ten seconds to decide, and then I'm out of here. The smell is killing me. I need food."

"Under normal circumstances, I wouldn't let you out of my sight, but I figure there's no way the men from Juneau could have made it through the storm to Ketchikan last night. It's about a twenty-hour drive at the best of times, and with the storm, it would've been much longer. I'm hoping they still don't know we're on the ship, so I think you're safe for the moment. I'm not thrilled that we're docked here for the day. We'll have to be very careful as the day progresses, but— Are you listening?"

She'd been staring at the restaurant, thinking about what she was going to eat, when his voice snapped her back to attention.

His smile was gone, and his eyes were serious. "Please be aware of your surroundings at all times. Pay attention. If something seems off, then it is. Find a crew member as quickly as you can and call me." He handed her a burner phone.

"My number is programmed in. I took the battery out of your phone yesterday just in case someone is tracking it. I know I don't have to remind you to keep it out. Even if you need someone's phone number or some information on it, it's imperative your phone stay powered down."

Dani nodded and desperately tried not to roll her eyes. She wasn't an idiot...well, not a complete idiot. This morning's little fear-induced incident wasn't making her feel like her usual smart self. But she knew what she was doing and didn't want to be traced either. She wasn't giving up her laptop, though. She needed it to work, but she also needed it to contact Carly. No need to mention *her* just yet.

Gage continued. "I'll be at the gym for about an hour. I wouldn't go, but it's been almost two weeks since I worked out and I'm getting stiff. I need to move a bit to limber up. I will be back in the room in about two hours. If you aren't there, I'll call on that phone to check in. Answer it. And please be watchful."

When Dani nodded, Gage let go of her arm. After one last hard stare at her, he turned and stalked away.

She looked at the restaurant. Her stomach growled so loudly a woman walking by her turned and looked.

"Alien baby," Dani said. "They are quite vocal even when they're inside."

The woman blinked twice and hurried off, glancing back over her shoulder, a nervous expression etching lines into her face. Dani couldn't help but smile. She could've just ignored the woman, but where was the fun in that?

She walked into the restaurant and gave the crew member her medallion to scan. "Now, where to sit," she murmured. She walked to the end of the buffet and turned the corner. A glass wall was ahead of her where she could see the pier and the water. "Nope."

Then she spotted an empty table right at the end of the buffet. If she sat with her back to the water and faced the buffet, she'd be fine. She shifted her backpack and put the coffee she'd grabbed earlier on the table to mark her spot and then went to get breakfast.

She grabbed a plate and started toward the buffet. Within a minute, she had a stack of blueberry pancakes doused in maple syrup and a bunch of crispy bacon on her plate.

She went back to the table and hooked her backpack over the back of the chair and sat down. She took a quick sip of coffee and then cut into the stack of pancakes. She watched as the syrup oozed over the sides. "Ah, heaven." She took her first bite and practically moaned with pleasure. She really needed to avoid missing meals. It wasn't good for her. She grabbed a slice of bacon and started munching.

"All I'm saying, Dottie, is you need to watch what you're eating. Look at your plate. There's a lot of food on it all ready. Do you really need pancakes, too?"

Dani looked up to see two elderly women standing beside the buffet. One had a small bowl with what looked like a boiled egg. She was wearing a sweater with a graphic of a big red hat on it and a pair of leggings. Her hair was bright, brassy blond and coifed to within an inch of its life. She was in full makeup as well.

The other held a plate full of eggs and hash brown potatoes. She was wearing a T-shirt and a pair of old jeans. Her curly white hair was messy as if she'd been in a windstorm. She was shorter and quite a bit rounder than her friend. Dani figured they had to be in their seventies.

"Honestly, Ann. You are taking all the fun out of this cruise. I came to enjoy myself. What's a pancake or two?" She glanced down at the woman's egg. "Live a little. Have some toast with that." She turned toward the buffet and put a couple of pancakes on her plate.

"Dottie, it's really not good for you. You aren't helping anything. You said you wanted to lose a few pounds, and this isn't the way to do it." Ann sniffed as she looked down at Dotti's plate.

Dottie looked down at her plate, too, and her shoulders drooped. Then her face sort of crumpled. She looked so disheartened. Dani couldn't help herself. She spoke loudly. "Actually, she's helping the environment." Both women turned in her direction.

"Excuse me?" Ann said.

"The leftover food will go to waste and end up rotting in a landfill. That's horrendous for the environment. So, by eating more, Dottie is actually making a sacrifice and taking one for the planet. Way to go, Dottie." Dani gave her a big thumbs up. "What are you doing to help the environment?" She looked pointedly at Ann's single egg in her bowl.

"Well!" Ann sniffed again and walked away.

Dottie winked at Dani and then reached for the syrup. "I love saving the planet," she said.

Dani laughed and went back to eating her own pancakes. There was one in every crowd, she mused. Someone always wanted to suck the fun out of things. Her foster mother had been a prime example of that. But she wasn't going there. She didn't need to drudge up the past. It was over and done with. She never had to go back. She had Carly. Carly was her family.

She glanced at the phone Gage had given her. She didn't like how the little girl looked last night. Not at all. But it was too early to call. Plus, she wanted to work on the software. Maybe today was the day she would find where the code went wrong and was causing the memory leak.

The pancakes sat heavily in her stomach. She looked down at her plate. *Yeah, no more of that.* She got up, put her backpack over her shoulder, bussed her table, and then got a to-go cup of coffee.

She left the restaurant and started to go back to the stateroom but decided it would be nice to buy Carly something from the cruise. The tween would love a gift. Anything would do, but she wanted to get Carly something special. The girl deserved some joy.

Dani bit her lip. Walking around meant she would see the water. It was inevitable. She thought about Carly and all that she was facing. Dani could stand seeing the water. She was just being weak. She needed to be strong like Carly. She squared her shoulders and started off down the promenade.

CHAPTER TEN

G age coughed a couple of times and then wiped his face with the gym towel. He glanced at his watch. He'd only been working out for forty-five minutes, but it felt like he'd been at it for hours. His body hurt, and he felt a bit weak. Maybe he was getting too old to be on the road for so long.

Nah. What he really needed was to use a foam roller on his muscles and maybe a good massage. That would make him feel better. A solid dozen hours of sleep wouldn't hurt either. Even though he was exhausted, sleep had been a long time coming last night, and he'd woken at the crack of dawn.

He guzzled more water and looked around the gym. He couldn't get Dani's panic attack out of his head. His gut knotted at the memory. Pure terror had gripped her. It had been excruciating for him to watch. It had never occurred to him she would think they were lost at sea. It was his fault. He'd made her suffer simply by not thinking about her needs. He wouldn't make the same mistake twice.

Why did he care about her needs? Stupid. Just like it was stupid to circle back and watch her eat her breakfast. Not that he stayed long. Just long enough to see her settled and watch her help out the old lady with the pancakes.

Now he had proof. She was tough as nails on the outside but a softy on the inside. He'd witnessed it in Juneau as well. She might have turned to stone when Mrs. Williams went to hug her, but Dani cared very much what happened to her landlady. And Mrs. Williams cared about her. Enough to hold him at gunpoint.

So what if Dani brought out all the protectiveness in him? He obviously wasn't the only one. It was fascinating to watch her offer kindness or help to those she thought needed it. As long as it didn't involve physical contact or closeness, she was willing.

It made him think of his mother when she was dying. She would still talk with him for hours and offer advice on all kinds of subjects, including how to help his brothers get along, but he couldn't hug her. It hurt too much she'd said. He could hold her hands. Maybe that's where he could start with Dani. He could hold her hand.

Glancing at his watch again, he decided to end his workout right then. He'd done a decent run. It wasn't his normal couple of hours, but he didn't feel comfortable leaving Dani any longer than necessary. His body was also aching. He needed some downtime.

Time spent sailing. That would sort him out, and it would be relaxing. Sailing meant all he had to worry about was the thirty feet in front of him. Nothing else. It was exactly what he needed. He made a mental note to add some sailing time to his calendar as soon as he got back to New York and finished with Dani.

Dani. His thoughts kept returning to her. She made his head spin a bit. He'd needed to get away from her and breathe, remind himself this was just business, no matter how fabulous she looked when she'd just woken up. All tousled hair and swollen lips.

He frowned as he wiped down the equipment. *Get it together.* He walked out of the gym and made his way back to the room. He paused before he opened the door. Work not play. Only a couple more days, and this assignment, or at least this part of it, the part where he was in a confined space with Dani, would be over and he could have some solid time on his sailboat.

He hit the lock with his key and opened the door. Dani wasn't at the table where he'd pictured her. She wasn't back from breakfast yet. A small frisson went through his gut. She should have been back by now.

He glanced at his watch. It had been an hour. Not too long really. People took an hour to eat breakfast. She might have stopped to explore a bit, but she hated water, and it would be everywhere she looked. He stood there undecided for a second.

He picked up the phone and hit her number on speed dial. There was no answer. He wouldn't panic yet. She could have the phone in her backpack. He would take a quick shower and get dressed and then go look for her.

His shower lasted exactly four minutes. He hadn't even bothered to let the water get warm. He pulled on his jeans and a black, collared shirt. He grabbed his room key and was out the door eight minutes after he'd entered. Not that he thought Dani was in trouble. *Much.* He'd been in a low-grade state of unease since he'd left her, but now he was at Defcon 3. If he didn't find her in the next ten minutes, he was going to hit Defcon 5, and no one would be safe.

He stepped off the elevator and hit the Promenade. He walked to the restaurant where he had left Dani. After a rapid scan, he realized she wasn't there. He moved off down the promenade, looking in shops, trying to locate her. He never should have left her alone.

He tried to text her as he walked, but the text wouldn't go through. The reception was so damned spotty on the ship. He always brought a few extra burner phones on a job. They usually came in handy. This time, not so much.

He had just passed a couple of clothing stores and a high-end jewelry store when his gaze came to rest on two men ahead of him. Recognition shot through him. He'd seen one of the guys before, in just about every country he'd been in when he was trying to find Dani.

How the hell did they end up here? There was no way they could have made it down from Juneau. The weather had been too bad last night. Had they been waiting here for the ship to dock? How did they know Dani was on the ship?

Gage dove into the nearest shop and hid behind a sunglasses display. He had to find Dani fast before these men found her. And then he had to find a way to get them off the ship and back to New York.

DANI EMERGED FROM THE CUTE KNICKKNACK SHOP, BAG in hand. Carly was going to love the little gold locket. It had an Inuit design on the front and room inside for a picture. She knew just which one. There was a great shot of the two of them from the day she had taken Carly to the local fair. Carly had eaten too much cotton candy, so they had flopped down on a bench. Dani felt herself smiling. The weight on her shoulders lifted slightly.

She turned toward the elevator bank and saw Gage. He was standing about twenty yards up the promenade. Her heart hiccupped in her chest, and a warmth spread through her. Heat was in her cheeks. She glanced down, willing the blush to fade. She wasn't a teenager anymore. She needed to be in better control.

She looked up again. Gage was lurking behind a display of sunglasses, his steely gaze trained on something in front of him. Just the way he was standing, she knew there was trouble. She followed his gaze and immediately froze.

There were three Asian men spread out across the promenade. Sweat immediately broke out across her body. Her mouth went Sahara dry. They'd finally found her. They'd missed her by a hair yesterday.

She had been dreading this moment since Drake called her a few months ago and told her some unidentified people were after the software. He had no idea how they found out about it, but he warned her she might be in danger. Dani knew how these people found out about the software. It was because of her. Or what she'd done.

Swallowing hard, she looked around frantically. She turned on her heel and dove back into the shop. Was there a back door? It was a ship. No back alley. She went to the back corner of the store and paced frantically in the aisle. She turned and jumped when someone came around the corner.

"Hello, doll." Dottie came down the aisle. "Thanks for the rescue this morning. Sometimes Ann can have a bit of a stick up her butt, but she's only looking out for me." Dottie shook her head, making her white curls dance. "She needs to let her hair down a bit." Dottie grinned and then frowned. "You don't look so happy."

"I—" Her phone vibrated in her pocket. She grabbed it and stared at the screen. There were several texts from Gage warning her. "No shit," she mumbled. She looked up at Dottie and bit her lip.

"What's up? You look scared." Dottie's brows went up in a silent question.

"I— There are a few men out there looking for me. I need to avoid them."

Dottie's eyes narrowed.

Great. She thinks I'm a nutbar. Dani mentally kicked herself for spewing her troubles to the nice old lady.

"You're a spy, right?' Dottie whispered.

"*What*? No. I—I can't really explain it. Look, I'm sorry I said anything. I'll be fine. You just go about your day, and maybe I'll see you later." She started to walk by Dottie, but the older lady reached out and grabbed her sleeve.

"You don't have to tell me, doll, but I can keep a secret if you need to share." Dottie's eyes sparkled as she leaned toward Dani.

"You really don't want to be involved in this. Trust me." Dani gave her a half smile and moved down to the end of the aisle. She peeked around the corner but didn't see the men. She moved closer to the front of the store. She peered out the doorway.

"Which one are you trying to avoid?" Dottie asked as she peered over Dani's shoulder.

"Ahh!" Dani bit her cheek, trying to stop her scream. She hadn't heard Dottie come up behind her. She shuffled the elder lady back into the store. "You should just leave. I don't want you to get hurt."

"Lordy, doll, I'm just as likely to drop dead from a stroke at my age. Don't worry about me. Plus, this is exciting. So what can I do to help?"

Dani looked into Dottie's sparkling eyes and then glanced back out the door. If Dottie could just distract the men for a couple of moments, she could get by... "Are you sure you want to help? It could be dangerous."

Dottie nodded. "Of course. I'm up for the challenge."

Dani gestured for Dottie to stay back and then went to the store doorway again. Two of the men were much closer now. Only one store up the promenade. The third guy came out of the store next to his friends and moved to the store directly across the promenade.

Dani began to tremble. She swallowed hard. There was nowhere to hide from the men. She'd lied to Gage. She knew who was after the software, and they were scary as hell. She went back to the first aisle with Dottie. "I think it's too dangerous, especially by yourself. You need to go. Now. Before they find me."

Dottie dug in her purse and pulled out a two-way radio. "I've got friends," she said with a wide smile. "Now, who do you need to hide from?"

Dani shook her head but couldn't stop a small smile from appearing on her lips. "There are three Asian men," she said and went on to describe them. "If you want to help, you could distract them until I get past."

Dottie listened and then relayed the message to whomever was on the other end. Within seconds, Dani heard a disturbance. She peeked around the end of the aisle and saw Ann yelling at one of the men. She was joined by two other elderly ladies. Dottie buzzed on by her and joined the fray.

The men looked shell-shocked. They were blinking repeatedly, as if they couldn't quite understand what was going on. Dottie started tugging on one of the men's elbows, and he turned toward her and away from Dani. The other two men turned to face Dottie and Ann.

Taking a deep breath, Dani made a mad dash out to the promenade and walked quickly back toward the elevators. She was glancing over her shoulder when Gage appeared beside her and grabbed her elbow. "Don't look back. Just keep going." They walked quickly down the Promenade.

"Where do we go?" Dani asked. "If they found us

onboard, they might know our fake names, which means they know the room."

Gage grunted but kept quiet. They approached the elevators, but Gage kept propelling Dani past them and moving along until they were outside on the deck. They walked at a good clip toward the front of the ship. "We need a place to hide out. Somewhere out of the public space."

"Ya think?" Dani said as she rolled her eyes.

They came around the corner into a pool area. There was a bar in the corner of the deck and lots of deck chairs all around, but there were very few people. He walked them to the end of the accessible deck area and then through the doors at that end.

It was the ship's spa area. There was also another bank of elevators. There were benches and chairs set out for those waiting for an appointment. Gage walked them over to the chairs and gestured for her to sit. "Log on to your laptop and see if there are any open cabins."

Dani flopped into the chair and whipped out her laptop. She booted up and started the process to hack into the ship's system. She saw a woman approach, but Gage stood up and cut her off. "Hi."

"Can I help you?" the young, dark-haired girl asked.

"We're just taking a tour of the ship. Do you have a menu? I was thinking of maybe having a massage."

"Of course," she said. She reached back over the desk and selected a pamphlet. She handed it to Gage and gave him a megawatt smile. "We have lots of services, including many types of massages. Did you have a specific kind in mind?" She touched Gage's arm as she spoke.

Wipe the drool off your chin. Dani frowned as she looked at her screen. Seriously, this woman needed to get a grip. Gage had come in with *her*. Did she not see that?

Not that Dani cared, she reminded herself as she shifted

in the chair. She sneaked a glance at Gage. She couldn't blame the spa girl really. He looked amazing with his damp hair curling about his collar. The shirt was pulled tight across his well-muscled back. His butt looked fantastic in those jeans as well.

He'd been so kind to her this morning when she was panicking. Last night, too, when he'd closed the curtains and again, when he'd gone to get her food. *Yeah, but he'd been an asshole before that.*

Focus. She went back to looking at the screen. She clicked a few more buttons, and then a list of staterooms came up. She quickly went through the list. There was one room that was not occupied. She made note of the number and then backed out of the ship's computer system. She knew without Gage telling her that putting new names on it wasn't going to help them. It was better to remain under the radar. Names were hooked to pictures in the ship's system.

She contemplated deleting their pictures from the system and looked up to ask Gage what he thought. The girl was hanging off his arm now, blinking her big eyes at him, and he seemed to be lapping it up. She went back to her computer screen, and shutdown the laptop. What did it matter now about their pictures? The men were already on the ship. She closed her computer and slid it into her backpack. Then she stood up.

Gage gave her a slight nod. "Well, that all sounds great, Petra. I'll keep it in mind. Thanks so much for explaining everything in such detail." He turned toward Dani. "Ready to go, hon?"

Petra swiftly dropped her hands from Gage's arm. Dani smirked. She couldn't help herself. She beamed at Gage then turned toward the door. Gage said something else she didn't hear and then fell in step with her as she stepped out of the spa onto the deck.

He took a quick look around and then turned to her. "Is there an empty cabin?"

She had opened her mouth to answer when she caught sight of the water. Her knees softened, and she would've hit the deck if Gage hadn't caught her. "Are you okay?"

"The—the w-water." How had she not noticed it on the way over to the spa? How had she walked along the deck?

Gage led her to a chair and helped her down with her back to the water. He sat next to her and rubbed her back. "The adrenaline. You were so distracted by the men chasing you, you didn't notice it on the way over."

She tried to get her breathing to even out, but it was difficult. She concentrated on Gage's hand running up and down her back. Breathing became easier. She glanced around at the bar in front of her. There was just a smattering of people about. They were in port, so the ship had emptied out.

The heat from Gage's hand had worked its way into her bones. The cloud of panic had lifted, and she was able to focus again. She knew they had to move but sitting there in the warm sunshine with Gage rubbing her back, it was... nice. Nice didn't sum it up really. It was good. She hadn't felt anything but stressed in so long she'd forgotten what any other feeling was like. Gage's hand was so reassuring somehow. Strength she could lean on.

"We need to move. Are you okay to get going?" Gage asked.

She turned to face him. There were worry lines on his forehead, and his full lips were pulled into a frown. He took a swift measure of their surroundings and then looked at her again. The lines etched on his face deepened. He seemed to be worried about her. *Was that a good thing?*

"Yeah, I'm okay. I just don't want to look at the water."

He nodded. He helped her up and turned toward the

main deck area but then stopped dead. Quickly, he swung her around and started moving back to the spa.

"What?" she asked while trying to look back over her shoulder. "Is it them?"

"Don't turn around and just keep moving."

They entered the spa waiting area and hurried over to the elevator. Gage pushed the button with great force.

Dani shifted her backpack. "We have a problem."

"Yeah, I'm aware." Gage moved forward, hitting the elevator button again.

"No. Not them. I mean, yeah, they're a problem, but we have another problem."

"What? You're afraid of elevators now?"

And just like that, he was back to being an asshole. She clamped her lips together and ground her teeth. And just when she was starting to think he wasn't so bad. *Let that be a lesson to her.* "With the room. There's a problem with the room."

CHAPTER ELEVEN

G age stared at Dani. Her lips were clamped shut and colorless. Her whole face was pale, and her eyes were shooting daggers at him. He deserved it. The crack about the elevator was uncalled for. He'd known it as soon as it came out of his mouth. He hadn't meant to be a prick, but sometimes he just was.

His temper was short these days. And it was better to keep her at a distance. Rubbing her back and calming her down had stirred all these aggressive feelings of possessiveness and a fierce need to protect. It was great to protect Dani, but he needed to do it because it was his *job*, not because he wanted to protect her with every fiber of his being. He shook his head.

"We need to reprogram the medallions to open the new room door." She shifted her backpack off one shoulder and on to the other. Gage hadn't offered to carry it because he knew damn well there was no way in hell she was going to let him hold her laptop.

"Can't you hack in and do that?" he asked as she glanced

at the elevator numbers. What the hell was taking so long? No one was on the ship. They should have come right away.

"Of course, I could *if* I had the right equipment, but I don't have a chip reader with me. I must have left it back at my lab." She rolled her eyes.

He raised an eyebrow at her. "Funny. How was I supposed to know you're a hacker, not a computer programmer with a lab? It wasn't like you or Drake bothered to share that information."

Dani sniffed. "Whatevs. We have to go to a registration or concierge desk to get them reprogrammed. And we can't exactly ask them to do it because they'll look us up in the system, and we're not in that room. I can switch us to that room, but I'm betting the guys after me have access to the system, too, so it would defeat the purpose."

Gage nodded and ran a hand through his hair. "What the hell is taking this elevator so long?"

Just then the doors opened.

"Jeremy!" Gage said. "Just the man I wanted to see." Gage grabbed Dani's arm and moved her into the elevator, blocking Jeremy's exit.

Jeremy's smile faltered. "Ah, this is a crew elevator. The regular elevators are back that way." He pointed toward the other end of the ship.

"No worries, Jeremy. We're just going to borrow this elevator and you for a couple of minutes." Gage hit the *close door* button.

"Um, Mr...?" He waited for Gage to fill in the name but when he didn't, Jeremy continued, "What can I do for you?" His eyes flicked back and forth rapidly between Dani and Gage.

"Jeremy, we're in a bit of a difficult situation. You see, we came on board to avoid seeing some people, but they seemed to have found us. We need to switch to a different cabin."

Jeremy's face cleared. "Oh, well. I'm not sure we have any empty ones, but if we do, they can help you at the main desk on deck eight." His smile was back.

"See, the thing is, Jeremy, we can't book it under our names. We can't have those people finding us again."

"Um, I'm not sure what I can do to help." Jeremy's eyeballs were back to flicking from Gage to Dani at lightning speed. His face went pale. *This kid was going to either pass out or puke at the rate he was going.*

Gage shifted his stance so he wasn't leaning over the kid quite the same way. "Relax, Jeremy. We just need you to do us a small favor. We already know which cabin is free. We just need you to reprogram the medallions to open the door."

"But they can do that for you at the main desk."

The elevator doors opened, but Gage shifted his weight again to block Jeremy's exit. No one moved. The doors closed silently.

"I know that, but as we explained, we can't have our names attached to it. So if you could just program the medallions to open the door and not add our names, that would be great."

Jeremy's eyes grew to the size of golf balls. "Ah, um, I can't do that. I'd lose my job. I mean…if anyone caught me, that would be the end. I need this job. I send money back to my family. They need me to work. I j-j-just can't."

Dani cleared her throat. "How much money?"

Jeremy looked at her. "W-w-what?"

"How much money do you send them?"

"Um, well…" Jeremy swallowed.

"Thirty thousand dollars. Sound about right?" Dani asked.

Jeremy made choking noises.

Gage swung around to stare at Dani. *Shit.* He didn't have

that kind of money. He was thinking a few hundred. Was she crazy? "I—"

Dani said, "I know how little cruise lines pay. That's more than you could send home in a year or even two years. I'll transfer the money to your family, and you'll help us. Deal?"

Jeremy's Adam's apple was bobbing like a piston in a hemi engine.

"Thirty grand. Yes or no?" Dani's voice was ice. Gage had to admit he was impressed with her nerve. *She has serious balls.* He just had no intention of giving the kid thirty grand.

"Ah, y-y-es," Jeremy stammered and then nodded several times.

Dani leaned over on her side of the elevator and put her finger over the keypad. "Which floor?"

"Deck four."

Dani hit the button. "Okay, do you have the bank information for your parents?"

"Yes." Jeremy's voice was getting stronger. He was getting used to the idea. *Or he was making a plan to sell them out,* the voice in the back of Gage's head reminded him. The elevator doors opened on deck four. He told the voice to shut up and followed along behind Dani and Jeremy.

"Give me the numbers." Dani handed Jeremy her phone, and he started typing.

"You're taking us somewhere to program the medallions, right, Jeremy?" Gage asked.

Jeremy nodded but kept on writing. Dani got her laptop out of her backpack and handed the pack to Gage. She booted up as they walked. Jeremy handed her the phone.

They turned right and then made a quick left. Jeremy walked them through a rabbit warren of hallways and then stopped at an office door.

"How do I know you'll do what you promised?" Jeremy asked. He eyed them as his hands curled into fists.

"Deal!" Jeremy offered his hand, an ear-to-ear grin splitting his face.

Dani grabbed his hand but held it still. "Just remember…there's no money if we get busted."

He saluted her and grinned again. "Aye, aye. No worries. I'll bring you dinner in a bit. In the meantime, there's snacks and stuff here in the suite. See you later." Jeremy gave a half wave and left the suite.

Dani finally closed her laptop and looked at Gage. She must have seen something in his face because uncertainty flashed across her own. She took a quick step to the right. He tried to block her, but he was too late. She took in the glass wall and the view. The blood drained from her face, leaving it chalk white. She turned and deliberately placed her laptop on the table in the entry way, stumbled back a step, and then slowly sank to the floor.

CHAPTER TWELVE

Dani's lungs stopped working. Her legs were as useless as pipe cleaners, unable to hold her weight. Her entire body shook with a ferocity that was painful. *Water was everywhere.* She was surrounded. She was going to drown. Her body was desperate for oxygen but not getting any. Her vision was closing to small circles of light.

Suddenly, she was jerked to her feet and her head was pushed down between her knees. Her entire weight was resting on a steel band around her hips. It hurt. She wanted to shift her weight, but her legs still wouldn't hold her. Slowly, her vision was coming back. Her lungs expanded fully for the first time in what seemed like forever.

She registered that someone was rubbing her back and making soothing sounds. Gage. The steel band was his arm. He was holding her. Helping her so she wouldn't pass out.

Heat crept down her neck to her cheeks. It was mortifying. She was a strong woman. Tough. And yet she damn near passed out at the sight of…water.

She'd chosen Juneau on the spur of the moment. It was remote and surrounded by mountains. Also it was cold, and she liked the idea of living in a small cozy cabin with a fireplace. She'd known it was on the water but figured she could work around that, and she had. She just looked down. A lot. Her strategy included not leaving the house unless she had to. Now she was on a ship surrounded by water. She seriously needed to do more planning next time. If she lived through this. *Shit.*

"I'm okay," she said as she struggled to stand.

"Are you sure? Gage asked as he continued to rub her back.

"Yes." Dani half turned and swung herself up so that she was facing him head on. But her knees had other ideas and started to buckle.

Gage caught her and held her to his chest with the arm that had been around her hips. His eyes roamed over her face as he casually rested his other hand on her hip. "You're still pale."

"I—I'm fine. Really." But she made no effort to move. She couldn't move even if she wanted to. Her legs were still too weak to hold her. A tremor went through her. Gage slipped both arms around her and held her more tightly.

"Maybe just give me a minute," she managed to mumble. Mortified that she needed this long to recover, she couldn't look up at him, so she placed her forehead on his chest.

It's only water. You drink it. You shower in it every day. She'd been telling herself these things for years. Never really made a difference, though. She bit her lip and tried to focus on something else. Running lines of code in her head usually calmed her down, but it was damn hard to do with her body pressed against Gage's.

The urge to run her hands over his chest made her palms itch. His woodsy, citrusy scent was intoxicating. The hardness of his body against her softness. They seemed to fit together perfectly. She looked up to find him staring down at her.

Her mouth was parched. When she licked her lips to relieve the dryness, his eyes followed her tongue. They changed color, turning a deeper blue, and his pupils dilated.

She tilted her head a bit more and studied his lips. She wanted to know what they would feel like on hers, what they would taste like. Her glance went back to his eyes, and their gazes locked. Dani slowly raised her lips and brushed them softly against his. She froze, waiting for him to react. He made no move, as if afraid she'd bolt if he made any sudden movement.

She brushed his lips again, this time lingering. Finally, when she was about to give up, he lowered his head and captured her mouth with his. He touched her lips with his tongue and traced their outline. She willingly opened her mouth, and he responded in kind, their tongues meeting in a slow dance that made Dani desperate for more.

She moved one hand to fist the back of his hair while wrapping the other around Gage's back where she spread her fingers wide, trying to feel all of him at once. She flattened her body along his. His hard plains against her soft ones excited her.

Gage wrapped his arms tightly around her. One hand moved to cup her butt and lifting and pressing her against his length. His other hand tangled in her hair and held her head in place. He deepened the kiss.

Her belly somersaulted. Gage's skin was hot beneath her fingers. She wanted to rip the man's clothes off and have him right there on the carpet.

The wave of desire that washed over her was so incredibly intense it scared her. She'd never been like this. Not once in her life. She'd had sex before with a few different partners and never had she ever wanted anyone like this. She stiffened as that thought echoed around in her head. *What the hell was going on? Was it because she'd been so afraid?*

Gage realized she had stopped responding and pulled back, searching her face. "Are you okay?"

"Ahhh…" She blinked. "Yes." She stepped away from Gage and stumbled a bit but managed to avoid his arm when he reached to help her. She saw his expression change from open to wary. He ran a hand through his hair.

She cleared her throat. "I'm fine now." She was having a problem meeting his gaze. The heat was creeping back up her neck and cheeks again. She started to turn but caught site of the windows and whipped back around quickly.

"Um, can you close the blinds, please?"

Gage shook his head. "No."

Dani blinked rapidly. "What do you mean, no? You have to close the blinds."

"No, I can't close the blinds." Gage who had been leaning against the wall took a step forward toward her and frowned.

She promptly stepped away and glared at him. "Why the hell not? You want me to be sick and helpless? Is that what this is? Take advantage of me?"

Gage reared back as if she'd slapped him. "Just what kind of guy do you think I am? I just stopped you from passing out. You were the one who kissed me, remember?" His eyes were stormy, and his jaw closed with a click.

Damn. She'd forgotten she was the instigator of that little interlude. The flush of her embarrassment bloomed on her cheeks. "I—"

"I won't close the blinds because we're not supposed to be in here, and the quickest way for someone to come and find us is for us to go around changing how this room looks from the outside. We have to lay low. The blinds stay open. And no lights, even when it gets darker later. We just have to make do as is."

Gage walked around Dani into the room. She closed her eyes and swore a blue streak in her head. She'd forgotten all about being seen. Her terror over something as simple as water made her forget everything. *No. Kissing Gage had made her forget everything.* The water had just given her a panic attack.

She turned slightly to her left and grabbed her backpack off the table. She needed to sit down and get herself together. A cup of tea might be good. Her stomach rumbled. Breakfast had been a while ago, and Jeremy wouldn't be back until dinner. Where did he say the mini bar was?

CHAPTER THIRTEEN

G age strode through the living room area. It contained a beige couch with blue throw pillows, a couple of matching chairs, and a coffee table. A dining area with a table and six chairs in a similar beige tone lay to his right.

To the left was the rest of the living room along with a huge deck on the other side of the wall of glass. There was also a "floating" stairwell, as his brother Logan would have called it, leading up to the sleeping area.

Gage crossed the room and took the stairs two at a time. When he reached the top, there was a huge king-size bed in the middle of the loft. The comforter was yet another shade of beige. The headboard rested against a fake half wall with the master bath situated behind it.

Gage entered the bathroom and firmly closed the door behind him. He leaned against it and rubbed his eyes with the heels of his palms. He could not believe he let his guard down that way. Kissing a client was so far out of bounds it wasn't even on the field. It was in the damned parking lot. Jesus, what had he been thinking?

He hadn't been thinking. He'd been feeling again. One

minute, Dani was tough and being a hard-ass and the next she was all vulnerable and needed help. He didn't know which one appealed to him more. Either way, it had to stop. It didn't matter that she was a smart, sassy, beautiful woman. She was out of bounds.

He stood up and started pacing back and forth. The fact that the bathroom was big enough to pace in did not leave much of an impression on him. He slammed his fists into his thighs. Stupid! It was the cardinal rule. Never get involved with a client. Not that they were involved. It was one kiss, never to be repeated.

What about her being a hacker? It went against everything he believed in. He'd just witnessed it. She'd given Jeremy money she had stolen. She just admitted as much. Why didn't that bother him the way it should? Because he could still feel Dani's body against his. Her scent was still in his nose and the taste of her lips still on his tongue. He was getting hard just thinking about her.

He flexed his fingers as he continued to pace and tried to focus on other things. He could not let himself give in like that again. He'd tried to resist, but she'd been so gentle, yet persistent, that his defenses had been defeated. Who was he kidding? He'd folded like a dirty shirt, but who could blame him with her curves and those haunted dark eyes? He'd been hers from the first "Hey, asshole."

He stopped pacing and ran his hands through his hair. He coughed and the room seemed to spin a bit. He must be angrier than he thought. He leaned on the vanity and took a deep breath. Then another. *Work the problem.* The room righted itself, and he switched his thinking to deal with the problem at hand, namely how to avoid the men stalking Dani.

He reviewed what had happened that morning and stopped suddenly. He tilted his head and narrowed his eyes.

"Oh, she has some explaining to do," he said as he moved across the bathroom and out into the loft. He took the stairs two at a time down to the main living area. Glancing around, he didn't see her. Had she left?

"Dani?"

"Over here," came the somewhat muffled reply.

He walked over to the cabin door and looked left. There was a short hallway with a bathroom at the end of it. Dani was sitting, propped against the wall by the bathroom door, her laptop open in her lap.

"We need to talk," Gage said as he stalked down the hallway to stand directly in front of her. Reaching out, he flicked on the bathroom light. She looked up from her screen, blinking in the sudden brightness.

"How did you know you'd been found?" He knew he'd practically growled at her, but he was pissed. She wasn't telling him the whole truth, and he was tired of lies.

Dani looked up at him, eyebrows raised. "What? When? You mean at the garage apartment? I put a hair in the door-jamb every time I left. I knew they'd been there because the hair was gone and, well, my place had been ransacked."

Gage ground his teeth. "Here on the ship. How did you know to hide in that shop? How did you know to avoid those men?"

"Um…" Dani swallowed. Fear flickered in her eyes, but then she looked down again. "I saw them in Juneau in the van that hit that woman."

He snorted. "Liar. They couldn't have made it down here from Juneau. They had to be here already, or they flew down this morning. The storm is just starting to hit here. It's been between here and Juneau all night, and with the amount of hail being reported in the news, there's no way in hell they got here from Juneau. Besides, I thought you said you didn't get a good look at the men in the van."

His gut knotted. He hated being lied to and, even more, he hated that it was Dani doing the lying. He needed to stop trusting her. Stop caring about her more than just a client. It wasn't worth the misery she was putting him through.

Gage fisted his hands on his hips and leaned over her. "So, I'm going to ask you one more time, and you better tell me the truth or being surrounded by water will be the least of your worries. How did you know who those men were?"

Dani closed her laptop and stood up. "I saw you, and you looked all serious, so I looked where you were staring and saw the men. I figured they must be after me, so I went back into the store."

Gage took a step closer to Dani. She moved slightly backward, bumping into the wall.

"Stop with the bullshit. If you know something, you sure as hell better tell me, or so help me, I will walk out that door and let them have you."

Dani frowned and her eyes narrowed. "You're bluffing. You will not. Drake is your client. You have to protect me." She raised her chin and glared at him.

"My brothers and I have been putting everything, including our lives, on the line to protect Drake and now you. If you know something that can help with that and don't tell me, then it's your own fault if this goes sideways."

Gage moved closer until he was towering over Dani. His short fingernails dug into his palms. "And if one of my brothers gets hurt or worse, I will hold you responsible. So you better own up now, or it's going to get very real for you."

Dani's expression faltered. Her eyes were darting around, and she was trying to surreptitiously wipe her palms on her jeans.

"Look, it's a long story, and I'm hungry." She crossed her arms over her red T-shirt. I'll explain it all later maybe, but first I need to eat."

Gage wanted to slam the wall with his palms and make her talk right there, but there was a risk she'd bolt if he did that. He clamped his jaws down hard, gave her one final pointed look, and then turned and left the hallway.

"Come on. You can sit at the dining table with your back to the windows. I'll get the food from the snack bar, and you can eat and tell me the whole story."

He stopped dead when he realized she wasn't behind him. Turning, he saw she was at the edge of the short wall. He bit his tongue and started counting to a hundred. He was all out of patience. He and his brothers had been busting their asses for months on this job, all of them almost getting shot at one point or another, and this woman refused to help. He took a deep breath.

He walked back and, cursing up a storm in his head, he took her gently by the arm. She stiffened at his touch. *Nice.* He tried to ignore it. She had been soft and yielding a short while ago, and he'd been the one who'd been stiff. *Focus.*

"Just look at the carpet, and I'll guide you." He helped her over to the table and sat her with her back to the windows. She didn't say a word, just stared at him.

He went around to the snack bar by the windows. The bar was fully stocked, and God knew he could use a shot of scotch right now, but instead he grabbed two bottles of water and an assortment of snacks, including a banana, just in case she preferred fruit.

Rain lashed the windows, and the wind started to howl. The room had gotten dark because of the storm. He started to flick the light switch with his elbow and then remembered that lights were off bounds.

He went back and set all the snacks and one bottle of water down in front of her. He then walked to her right and picked a seat a far enough away he couldn't get his hands on her easily. With the light behind her it would be hard to see her face, so he'd picked a chair that gave him a better view. It still wasn't great, but it was better than nothing.

"Spill it." Gage leaned back in his chair.

Dani reached out and fiddled with the packages in front of her. She even reached out and touched the banana but brought her hand back empty. She looked up at Gage and then grabbed a bottle of water. She opened the cap and took a long swig. She set it down again as she swallowed.

She shrugged and then started speaking. "Drake had put it out that he wanted someone to take on the project. He wanted facial recognition software that would work even if the person was wearing a beard or had different hair. Even if the person had aged twenty or thirty years."

She shrugged again and looked around the room. "I thought it sounded like fun. A real challenge. I mean, why not? I could make a pile of money and make something useful. What could be cooler?"

Gage hoped his expression was blank. He didn't want her to know that he knew she wasn't telling the truth. Well, at least not the whole truth. She tended to let her eyes roam around when she was lying. It was her 'tell.'

"Then what happened?" he asked.

"Well, I made a deal with Drake and started on the project." She paused, taking another large gulp of water.

"So, here's the thing. Drake's timetable was a little… intense. I didn't have a lot of time to create the software. I looked around to see who had a good product that I could build on.

"A lot of the fancy computer companies have some facial recognition software, but the current bunch of software is crap. Just look at social media. There're all kinds of stories where a person is told someone posted a picture of them online, only to see it's their sister or cousin. Or try using facial recognition to open your laptop and then grow a beard.

Your own computer won't recognize you. What Drake wants is total cutting-edge stuff."

She drummed her fingers on the table, and there was a vibration. Probably her knee hitting the table leg as she bounced her foot on the carpet. "A few countries have something going on, but it's still not great. There was one place where I knew I could get a base code to build on so Drake could get what he wanted. They weren't ever going to be willing to share it, so I…" She shifted in her seat and started playing with her hair. "I went in and borrowed a copy of the basic code, and then I used that to develop Drake's software. I'm almost finished, and I know it's much better than anything out there."

Gage's hands curled into fists again, and his gut churned. He knew what she was about to tell him, and he couldn't believe it.

"The guys on the promenade. I've never seen them before, but since you were staring at them, I knew they were probably after me." She glanced over at Gage, most likely to calculate his reaction at her next words. "The fact they were Chinese pretty much guaranteed it."

Gage remained motionless. He was having a hard time breathing, let alone speaking. Finally, in a voice that sounded strangled even to his own ears, he said, "You stole code from the Chinese government to build the software?"

Dani met his eyes. "Yes."

CHAPTER FOURTEEN

"The Chinese fucking government?" Gage leapt out of his chair. "Son of a bitch!" He slapped the table with his hand.

Dani jumped, flinching at the sound.

"We're all damn lucky to be alive. I've got to call my brothers," he said as he paced back and forth. "Jesus! No wonder we've been outgunned from the start."

Dani shifted again in her chair and laced her fingers together. Her heart was pounding in her chest. She closely followed Gage's every movement. She didn't think he would be violent towards her but all this pacing and yelling had her on edge.

The Chinese had the best code out there. Why would she start anywhere else? Seemed like a no brainer to her.

Gage was staring at her. "You—" He turned and walked away, digging his cell out of his pocket as he went.

Dani got up from the table and walked with her head down back toward the little hallway. Rain pelted the windows and ship swayed under her feet. She rounded the corner and put her hand on the wall, using it to guide her to the bathroom. When she saw the carpet end at tile, she looked up and walked into the small bathroom. She closed the door behind her and locked it. Then she sat down hard on the toilet seat cover.

Rubbing her chest, she tried to slow her thundering heartbeat and ease the hollow feeling. She hated seeing anger and disappointment on Gage's face. He was thoroughly pissed with her now, and she couldn't blame him. She should have told Drake from the beginning. It never occurred to her the risk that Drake and his people, including Gage and his brothers, were facing.

China had the best, so that's what she used because she needed the best. It had to be absolutely perfect so she could find Carly's birth family. Nothing but the best would work. She hadn't thought about the consequences of her actions. She thought only of Carly.

She ran shaking hands through her hair. A tremor went through her body. Her breath started coming in gasps. She bit her lip. She had been an idiot and had endangered lives. Now she was risking Gage's life. Her heart skipped a beat in her chest. *Oh God, what had she done?*

There was a thumping at the door. "Dani, you need to come out here. We have to talk about this," Gage said.

She swallowed the unshed tears blocking her throat. Even through the door, she recognized the steel in his voice. Saying "no" was not an option. He'd probably just knock the door down. She imagined he could be very Neanderthal when he wanted. She'd seen him come close. She'd thought he was going to throw her over his shoulder when they were back on the pier and carry her on to the ship like a sack of potatoes. Not very attractive in a man. Until she met Gage. He was attractive even when he was yelling at her. She sighed and ran a couple of lines of code in her head. She needed a moment to gather herself.

He thumped the door again. "Dani."

It was her last warning, and she knew it. She stood up, squared her shoulders, and opened the door. "What?" she said with all the false bravado she could muster.

Gage towered over her, his fingertips white around the cellphone clutched in his hand. "You're on speaker. We have questions."

"Fine." She folded her arms across her chest and glared at him. "Fire away."

Gage frowned but didn't try to move her back to the dining room. The voice on the phone asked, "Are you sure it was the Chinese government that you borrowed the code from? Sorry, I should tell you this is Logan, Gage's brother."

"Yes. I took a copy of their code and used it as a starting point for my software."

"But weren't you worried they would come find you? The Chinese government doesn't share well, and isn't exactly known as the most forgiving of groups."

She could hear the incredulity in Logan's voice. She thought for a second. "The truth is I thought it might take them a while to find me— which I want to point out, it has —and I was thinking I would give them a copy of my software if they ever tracked me down. I know they have some great facial recognition stuff going on, but I doubt they're at the point where they can find someone in a crowd from a twenty-year-old photo. My software can do that. I just figured they would be more interested in the software than me. Plus, when I upstage people, they usually attempt to hire me."

"People try to hire you when you steal stuff? Sorry, this is Mitch."

"You don't have to sound so surprised. Yes. They always offer me jobs when I beat their systems. They want me to work for them so I can stop anyone else from doing it."

Logan's voice came through the line again. "And you *thought* the Chinese government would do the same?"

Dani crossed her arms in front of her chest. "Sarcasm much? It wouldn't be the first time the Chinese hired out. I know people who worked for them before."

"Is that how you got the code in the first place?" Gage asked.

Dani looked up at him. Was he going to yell at her for stealing? But Gage seemed to be genuinely curious. "No. I got it another way, but the hacking community does share things occasionally, depending on what it is, what someone is looking for, and why they want it."

Gage snorted. "Yes, because all hackers have a conscience. I'm sure the 'why' matters."

"Hey, asshat, why don't you ask yourself where certain information that hits the media comes from? You think all those CEO's voluntarily release their salaries? Think again." Dani smacked the wall with her hand. "Ask yourself next time something big gets leaked, who benefits.

"A lot of things just mysteriously end up in the inboxes of journalists all the time." She sucked in a breath. "Just because we don't stand up and say 'Yoo-hoo, over here. Hey look at me! Look at all the wonderful things I did' doesn't mean all of us are out there poking around in your business and stealing from you.

"Some of us are trying to create positive change in this digital age where most of the governments have the means to shut down anything they don't want out there." Dani had started pacing back and forth in the hallway as she spoke. She liked to move when she was angry. It made her feel more in control.

"So, you don't steal people's info or hold companies' information hostage or steal from banks?" Logan's voice floated down the hallway.

She turned around and moved closer to the phone. "No, I don't. Most of us don't do that stuff." She heard a grunt and looked up at Gage, who was watching her. The heat crept up her neck into her cheeks again. *Damn*. She'd told him she stole the money for Jeremy from a bank. She was busted.

"Look, all that stuff doesn't matter. What matters is I used the base code from the Chinese and wrote the software program off of it. They clearly seem to want it back." She moved down the hallway a little bit. She needed space and even a foot or two would help. She didn't want to look at Gage just now. He'd give her that look. The one that made her feel like he could see her soul.

"Right," Mitch said. "So, what do we do about this? How do we handle it?"

Gage cleared his throat. "I think we have to lay low until we hit Vancouver, and the rest is the same. We have to get back to NYC so Dani can finish the software. Maybe talk to Drake one-on-one so the mole doesn't know we know what's going on. He might have some contacts he can connect with and maybe come to some sort of deal. Any news on the mole?"

"Maybe," Logan said. "We're running through all of Drake's closest employees. Anyone who might have had access to the information about the software, his whereabouts at certain times, and your location. There are about five altogether, but there's one that stands out. We're checking to see if he had access to all the right information. It will take time to do a deep dive on this guy and on everyone else."

"Who is it?" Gage asked.

"Devon Michaels. Do you know the name?"

"I don't. What about you?" he asked Dani.

She shrugged. "Wait, isn't he the head of IT? I know there were some issues with him. Janet let it slip one time when we were talking about her dead son. Devon's an addict. His vice is gambling."

"What's that got to do with Janet's dead son?" Gage asked.

Mitch spoke up. "Janet's son died not too long ago. He was a drug addict. Janet put him in rehab a few times, but he just couldn't kick it. Ended up OD'ing."

"Janet said Micah, her son, was almost clean when something happened. She didn't elaborate, but I got the impression it had something to do with Drake," Dani said. "It was when they were in Macao."

Logan's voice came down the phone line. "Sounds like we should poke around a bit about their time spent in Macao and see about Devon. He could be the key."

"Sounds good," Gage said.

"How are you doing on your end?" Mitch asked. "No real vacation time, huh?"

Gage grinned. "No, not really. Trying to lay low and stay outta site. I thought it would be easier to do on a cruise ship, but I gotta say, they have these things pretty much locked down these days. We're managing. I'll feel better when I see your ugly mug on the dock and we can head back to NYC. We'll be in the day after tomorrow."

Gage heard Mitch laugh. "We'll be there, and my mug is better lookin' than yours, big brother."

"And I'll feel better when you're here, Gage, but at least now we know what we're up against. Mitch and I will put our heads together and see what kind of game plan we can come up with for meeting you and getting you here. I know once you're further from port, cell service will be sketchy. Call when you can." Logan's voice sounded worried to Dani, and she didn't even know him.

They were freaking her out about the Chinese thing. It

sounded crazy, but it never had occurred to her they would want to kill her.

Yes, they would track her down and probably take the software, but why kill her? Wasn't she more valuable alive? She couldn't count the number of clients she'd acquired this way. They all threatened to prosecute her, but then they hired her to fix their security issues or adapt their software. She vaguely heard Gage sign off with his brothers. He seemed calmer at least.

Just then, there was a knock on the door right beside Dani's head. "Ahhhh," Dani yelled and then quickly covered her mouth with both hands. Gage put his finger to his lips to tell her to be quiet.

Well, duh. It wasn't like she'd planned on screaming. She just hadn't been expecting a knock. Gage was in front of her now, gesturing for her to go into the bathroom and close the door. She moved down to the bathroom and pushed the door closed until there was just one small crack she could see through. Gage approach the door from the side as quietly as possible and took a quick glance through the peep hole. She saw his shoulders relax, and he opened the door.

Jeremy entered with his huge smile. Dani opened the bathroom door. "Jeremy, man, you can ditch the fake smile. It weirds me out." She shuddered.

Jeremy blinked and then frowned. "Sorry. My smile gets me lots of tips. It becomes a habit."

Dani nodded. "I bet the old dolls just love you with those dimples of yours and your muscles."

Grinning, Jeremy nodded. "Not to be immodest, but it does help." He winked at Dani, and she had to smile back.

"I'm Dani, by the way, and this is Gage."

Jeremy nodded.

"Why are you here, Jeremy?" Gage growled.

What's his problem? Maybe he gets hangry, too? Dani's stomach rumbled loudly.

Jeremy looked at Dani and grinned. "Ah, I…um, brought food. It's outside around the corner." He looked back at Gage, who was practically leaning over him, glowering. "I didn't want to attract too much attention or anything…" Jeremy swallowed hard.

"That's great, Jeremy. I'm starving." Dani tried to smile to encourage Jeremy, but he was still staring at Gage. "Um, maybe you can get it?" she asked.

Jeremy's gaze finally swung over to her. "Right." He turned quickly and pulled the door open before Gage could check to see if it was safe to do so.

Gage's teeth were clamped together so tightly Dani could see the pulse in his jaw. Whatever his problem was at the moment, he'd just have to wait because she was starving and hadn't eaten a proper meal in so long she couldn't remember. Jeremy had better've brought something good, or she was going to lose it.

Dani heard the room service cart, so she didn't bother to wait for the knock. She reached over to open the door, but Gage grabbed her hand and held on to it. He shook his head and motioned for her to back up again.

"We have to be safe. We can't take any chances."

Dani rolled her eyes but said nothing.

Gage opened the door and let Jeremy in with the cart. "Take it over to the dining room table."

Jeremy pushed the cart around the corner and through the living room area, or at least Dani assumed he did. She stopped at the end of the wall. It was getting darker now. The storm was getting stronger as well. She could hear the rain and the wind. That was good. It would mean she wouldn't be able to see out the windows to the water.

She grabbed the edge of the wall and took a deep breath,

but in the end, she just couldn't propel herself around the corner. Instead, she turned around and went down the hall into the bathroom. She threw some water on her face and washed her hands. She was walking toward the door when she heard Jeremy and Gage coming back.

"So, if you need anything, um, well…" Jeremy frowned. "There's no real way for you to reach me. Cell phones don't work. You can't call from here because the suite number will show up on the screen with no name, and people will know you're here and start asking questions."

Gage leaned against the wall. "How about you just come back and check on us if you get the chance? If not, just bring us breakfast tomorrow morning."

Jeremy nodded. "Okay, I can do that. See you later then." He gave Dani a half wave and then started to open the door. Gage quickly put a hand on the door to stop him and checked the peep hole. Then he nodded and let Jeremy open the door and push the cart outside again. Gage closed the door.

"So, how about dinner? I'm starving." With that, he walked around the corner and disappeared.

Dani gritted her teeth. She needed food. She needed to be able to move around in the suite. She needed to get over her irrational fear of the water. But knowing all that didn't make it happen. She walked to the edge of the wall and closed her eyes. She took a deep breath. Sweat immediately broke out on her forehead and upper lip. Her breaths rushed in and out.

Stop it! She'd already walked across this room twice. She could do this. She wiped her palms down the front of her jeans and tried again to make her feet move. Her stomach tied up in knots. Her toes curled up in her sneakers. She wiped her palms again. But she just couldn't do it.

"Fuck!" she said as she hit the wall next to her with her fist.

"Hey. Go easy there."

Her eyes flew open to see Gage standing right in front of her. "I—I was just…"

"I know. It's hard to overcome fear, and it usually doesn't happen when we try and force ourselves. You have to take it slowly."

"But I've already walked across this room. Twice!"

Gage nodded. "And you were upset and thinking about other things both times. The only thing driving you at the moment is your hunger, and no matter how hangry you get, it's not enough to distract you from thinking about what's on the other side of that wall of glass."

"It's so damn frustrating." Dani tried to blink as tears pricked her eyes. "You're not helping!" A single tear trickled down her cheek. She brushed it away violently with the back of her hand. She never cried. Never.

"I'm going to eat, sitting at a table like a normal human," she said through clenched teeth. She saw a hint of a smile on Gage's lips, and her eyes narrowed. "Are you laughing at me?"

"No. Not at all. I'm admiring your spirit." The smile was bigger now and genuine. "I'm going to help you."

She tilted her head. "How?" Her stomach twisted. *What the hell did he have up his sleeve?*

"You're going to give me both of your hands, and I'm going to lead you across the room. I'll walk backwards. You just look at me and don't worry about anything else."

"I'm not sure—"

"I know. Just trust me. You'll be fine." He offered his hands.

She looked down at them. They were big, strong man hands. They'd brought her food when she was hungry. They'd rubbed her back when she was upset. They were hands that did not hit her. But, she didn't like being touched. She hated having someone hold her hand. It made her feel trapped. The only person she'd ever let hold her hand was Carly, and that was because she'd been frightened watching a scary movie on Halloween.

If she didn't do this, she wasn't going to eat. She needed to prove to herself she was strong enough. Maybe she even wanted to prove it to Gage. Great. Now she was starting to care what he thought. She swore again and then dropped her hands on top of his.

"Look at me," he said, and she did. *This is stupid.* He moved slowly backwards, tugging her along. She started to withdraw her hands, but he held onto them gently but with a firm grip. She looked down at their hands. "No. Look at my face. You're doing fine."

She looked back up into his eyes. She could see they had passed by the wall and were now in the living area. Her breath was starting to come quicker. "I don't think—"

"Exactly. Don't think. Just trust me."

She focused on his eyes. They were so intense. Even in the growing darkness, they sparkled. His eyes expressed what he was feeling. She'd noticed it before. They also seemed to be able to see right through her. It made her nervous on a whole different level.

Her gaze dropped to his lips, and she remembered how they'd felt pressed to hers. Was it getting hot, or was it just her? She was sweating now but not out of fear. His lips were curving into a smile. She looked back at his eyes, and they were sparkling. He was laughing at her. Not at her phobia but at what she was thinking. How did he know? *Damn him.*

CHAPTER FIFTEEN

"We've made it," Gage announced.

Dani glanced around, and her shoulders dropped. She let out a big breath she must have been holding. They were at the dining room table. She promptly let go of his hands and made her way to the seat that had her back to the windows.

Gage had already laid out a plate at her spot and the food all around it, so everything was in easy reach. He wanted her to be as comfortable as possible. He wanted her to relax. They had lots to discuss. This China thing was big, and he wasn't sure she'd really grasped what it all meant. He needed her as calm as possible.

"So, Jeremy did a great job. There's all kinds of stuff to choose from. Chicken, fish, meat and veggies just in case. I think there's even pasta."

"I see that. Good thing. I gotta say, I'm starving."

Gage grinned. "I know. I've been listening to your stomach rumble all afternoon."

"Hey! That's not fair," Dani complained, but she was smiling, too. "I've only had one real meal recently. I'm not one of you exercise freaks who eats a piece of lettuce and feels full. I *need* food, *real* food to keep my brain going."

"Well, help yourself and dig in." Gage moved to the other side of the table and sat down. He reached out and lit a small candle in the middle. "I think this isn't enough light to attract any attention. Besides, I'm not sure anyone is on deck in this monsoon."

The rain lashed the windows, and the wind howled. Dani shivered.

"Are you cold?" Gage asked.

"Not really. We can turn up the heat though, right? That shouldn't trigger any systems to let someone know we're in the room."

"That should be fine," Gage agreed. He reached over and pulled a beer out of an ice bucket. "Jeremy also brought beer and wine. Would you like something?"

She shook her head. "Not much of a drinker, but you go ahead."

"Don't mind if I do. I'm only going to have one. It won't affect my ability to protect you." He opened his beer. "I just need some normalcy at the moment. This is a first for me. I don't ever remember being in such a tough spot and being surrounded by so much luxury. It's kind of weird."

Dani had just put a huge forkful of food in her mouth so she couldn't talk. She nodded her head rapidly, though.

Gage took a swig of his beer and then set it down. He picked up his plate and started helping himself to dinner.

Dani grabbed some more French fries. "It's kind of creepy, hiding out in this cabin. It feels so cut off from everything else, which is also good in a way. I used to dream about being cut off from everyone and everything. I always thought it would be a relief. Now, I'm not so sure." The worry lines on Dani's forehead deepened, and her full lips had turned into a frown.

"It's fine. We're okay. My brothers will be there to help us when we dock, and we'll be fine in this cabin. Just enjoy the solitude."

Dani ate a French fry. "Tell me about your brothers."

Gage shrugged. "What do you want to know?"

"Start with what they look like," she said, then popped another fry in her mouth.

"Well, Logan looks quite a bit like me, or I guess I look like him since he's the oldest. We have the same dark hair and we're about the same height. He's a bit leaner than I am. He's also a control freak. He's a lawyer by trade and the CEO of Callahan Security. He likes to boss me and Mitch around."

Dani snorted. "I'm sure you love that."

Gage grinned. "I'm used to it after all these years. I ignore him mostly."

"What about Mitch?"

"Mitch," Gage laughed. "Mitch is a pain in the ass. He's a 'shoot first and ask questions later' kind of guy. Loyal as hell, though, and excellent at every sport. He's slightly shorter than me with lighter hair. He's sturdier. Wider shoulders. I have to say I miss talking to them. We've only recently been in constant contact. It's been great. I was just happy I could get them on the call earlier. Now I know we'll have backup for sure when we hit Vancouver."

"I wish I could contact someone," Dani mumbled as a shadow crossed her face.

Gage wasn't sure she realized she'd spoken aloud. He debated asking her about it, but decided against it for the moment. There were other things to get to. He ate slowly, keeping an eye on Dani. When she started slowing down, he decided it was time. He cleared the last few bites of food off his plate, chewed quickly, and swallowed.

"Would you like tea or coffee? I think I can make either." He gestured toward the kitchen area.

"Tea would be great. Thanks."

Gage got up and made his way over to the kitchenette. He filled up the kettle and plugged it in. He told her the tea choices and, once she made her selection, he put the tea bag in a mug for her. "Is there anything else you need?"

"You mean besides a hot shower and some clean clothes? Oh, and something to sleep in?" She smiled. "Nope. Doing just fine now. Think I will start working on the code again. Now that my stomach is full, maybe my brain will work better."

"I might be able to get Jeremy to track down some clothing if he comes back, or I can go out and get some. I—"

"I'd rather you didn't," Dani said quickly. Her hands went to her hair and then back to the napkin in her lap. She was biting her bottom lip.

"No worries. It's probably better not to take the risk anyway." Gage watched as her hands stopped fidgeting and her shoulders relaxed. "Can I ask you something?"

"How can I take showers, but I can't stand seeing the water?" Dani sighed.

That hadn't been the question he was going to ask, but since she'd brought it up, he was game. He didn't say anything, just let Dani continue in her own time.

"I'm not afraid of water by itself, just large bodies of it. My foster mother… Even though we lived in Maine, she used to take me to the beach all year round, no matter the temperature." Dani's voice cracked. "The shoreline was rocky but not many waves. She'd make me go barefoot into the water. She would wear rubber boots."

Dani's hands were back picking at the napkin, and her shoulders were up around her ears. "She would tell me that if I didn't listen to her and do exactly as she said, she would make me undress and go out into the deep water until I drowned. I was only four the first time she took me. I never learned how to swim, so I was always terrified."

Gage's gut was tied up tighter than Dani's napkin. Bile rose in his throat. Jesus Christ, what kind of a sick mind would do that to a small child? He clenched his hands into fists. He was glad the kettle chose that moment to boil. He had to turn away. He was having a hard time keeping his anger in check. If he ever met Dani's foster mother, it might end up being her last day on earth.

He poured the water into the cup and brought the mug to Dani. She was lost in thought and didn't acknowledge it. He placed his hand on her shoulder and squeezed.

He wanted to do so much more. He wanted to haul her into his arms and kiss her until she forgot every single bad memory. He wanted to love her until nothing else mattered. *Jesus where did that come from?* He blinked.

Yup, too much time alone with Dani was not a good idea. She was a hacker. *Just remember she's your job. She's not available in any way, shape, or form.*

She cleared her throat and sat up straighter, dislodging his hand. "So anyway...I don't like water." She reached out and started to play with the tea bag in the mug.

Gage returned to his seat and sat down hard. He grabbed his beer and took a long swig. He swallowed and then leaned forward. Trying to pull his shit back together could qualify for an Olympic sport, it was just that hard. *Work the problem, dammit.*

Dani's eyes were black in the candlelight. He could feel her gaze on his face. He wanted to look at her, but he was afraid if he did, he might frighten her off. He knew his eyes would be dark and stormy, as his mother used to say. He also knew the desire he was feeling for Dani would be there as well. He didn't need her to know how much he wanted her.

"So why do the job for Drake?" This was the question

Gage really wanted the answer to. She'd given him the brush-off before, but there'd been something there. Something more. Something else driving her.

Dani shifted in her seat. "You know, it's a chance to go up against the best and see if I could create a great software that works." She took the tea bag out of her mug and dropped it on her plate.

"There's more to it," he prodded.

"Nope. Just the idea of competition and, well, the money, of course. The money always helps." She took a sip of the hot tea.

"Dani." Gage leaned back in his chair. "I haven't known you long, but I know when you're lying. You have a tell. You're lying now. Or at least not telling me the whole truth. I'm putting my life on the line for you. So are my brothers."

She started to speak, but he held up a hand. "Yeah, I know Drake is paying us, but he's not paying me enough to want to die for him. I'm here protecting you because there's the very real fact that several men on this ship at this moment want your laptop and want you dead. There's a real possibility they are going to want you dead even after you finish the software and give it to Drake.

"China is known for being very patient and waiting years to get what they want. It's all a game of chess to them. They'll wait a long time if they have to. Saving face is a big part of the Chinese culture. You've embarrassed them. They're not ever going to forget that. Even when all this is said and done."

Dani swallowed hard. Her hands were shaking as she covered her face. She then pulled them down so they covered her lips. Dani stared at him with big, wide eyes.

She had no idea what she'd gotten herself into. Gage knew it as soon as she'd admitted what she'd done. She was young. Street smart but not worldly. She'd had no idea what kind of fallout could come from her actions.

Gage sighed, leaning forward again. He placed his beer bottle on the table. "I promise I will help you, even when the job is over. I'll find you a new identity, a new place in the world. I'll continue to protect you. I will not leave you alone to face this. But you have to tell me the whole story. It's the only way I know to guarantee your safety. Lies are opportunities for things to go wrong."

Dani was pale. Fear and sadness danced at the edges of her eyes. He knew she hadn't considered the long game. No one ever really did when they started out.

"I, ah, I appreciate that. I didn't think...about the Chinese government not letting this go. I just figured..." She knotted her hands together around the tea cup and lifted her shoulders. "I don't know what I thought. I guess I didn't, really. I guess I thought I'd be on my way when I was finished."

"Dani, why are you doing this? Why didn't you give up at the first sign of trouble? Drake isn't paying you that much, is he? Is your life worth it?"

Tears filled Dani's eyes and spilled over, streaming down her cheeks. He wanted to go to her and wipe them away, but he needed her to tell him what was truly going on. What the hell was driving her?

"My life isn't worth it, but Carly's is." It came out barely more than a whisper. "I'm doing this for her."

Gage's gut twisted. He didn't want to ask her questions that made her cry, but he needed answers. "Who is Carly?"

She swiped at her tears with the back of her hand and then took another sip of tea. "Carly is my sister."

"You have a sister?"

"Not by blood. She's my foster sister. My foster mother brought her home one day. She said she needed another daughter to make her life complete. I tried to be mean to Carly at first. She was so much younger than me and I didn't want to get attached to her because I couldn't be sure I could protect her from our foster mom. Carly is so sweet, though. She just wormed her way into my life, and now I can't imagine it without her."

Gage needed to do something with his hands. He was having a hard time not taking Dani into his arms and just holding her. "Is she still with your foster mom?" he asked as he stood up slowly and made his way back to the kettle. He turned it on again and then faced Dani.

She shook her head. She was staring at her nails. When she looked up, her eyes darted over to the picture on the wall, but then she went back to staring at her nails. She was looking anywhere but at Gage. That was probably best for both of them. Gage could tell this was hard for her to talk about, and he wasn't sure he could take seeing the pain in her eyes.

Dani rolled a napkin between her fingers. "After Carly was with us for about six months, she became sick. Our foster mom, Lydia, took her to the doctor, and they ran some tests and then some more tests. Turned out Carly has a tumor in her brain. Medulloblastoma—brain cancer." More tears trickled down Dani's cheeks.

"Lydia couldn't deal with it. That meant Carly would be too much work. She wouldn't be able to perform to the high expectations Lydia had. She wouldn't be the top of her class at school, nor would she excel at ballet or the piano. She was a disappointment. That's what Lydia called her, a *disappointment.*

"Carly needed treatment, so Lydia took her to the hospital and left her there. I tried to go back for her, but I couldn't do it on my own. I wasn't old enough." The napkin was balled in Dani's fist and her knuckles were white.

"We kept in touch, though. Carly bounced from one family to another and then was placed in a group home. I aged out of the system and got the hell away from Lydia, but I went back for Carly. Then I wasn't 'stable enough' to take her in as my foster kid.

"Eventually, Carly ended up in the hospital permanently while she got treatment. I was with her every day. And then Drake came along. I said no at first, but Carly asked me to find her a family member, a real actual DNA-sharing member of her family.

"We tried all the ancestry sites, but her DNA doesn't seem to match anyone out there. She does have an old family picture of her mom when her mom was about fifteen, but I haven't had any luck finding her. It's like she dropped off the face of the earth. I thought if I could build the software, maybe I could find her mother using the old family photo, so I finally said yes to Drake."

Dani looked at Gage, tears still streaming down her cheeks. "But I'm running out of time. Carly isn't doing so well, and the software isn't finished. I-I don't think I'll be able to m-make her dream come true." The dam broke, and now Dani's body was wracked with sobs.

Gage couldn't take it any longer. He turned off the kettle and went over to Dani and gathered her into his arms.

CHAPTER SIXTEEN

W hen his arms closed around her, she stiffened. She couldn't help it. She took a deep breath and tried to control her tears, but this day had already been too much. The storm inside her had built to hurricane force. All the fear and sadness and guilt that she'd been jamming down inside came burbling to the surface all at once.

Sobs wracked her body and, for the first time in years, she stopped trying to control it. She leaned into Gage's embrace and accepted the comfort he offered. She needed him in this moment, but needing people was always bad. She tried again to dial down the storm, but her body wouldn't have it. She shook as tears streamed down her face. Her breath came in great gasps. She was ugly crying and it was mortifying, but she had no control.

Gage's hands rubbed up and down her back as he pressed her to his chest. After a few minutes, she caught her breath. The storm inside was passing. Thank goodness, the one outside was not.

The room was still dark. She kept her head bent. The heat in her cheeks only increased as her tears stopped flowing. She had no interest in looking Gage in the eye at this moment. She rarely allowed herself this level of breakdown, and the fact she'd had one in front of Gage was the biggest of all sins. It went against every fiber of her being.

The loud thump was so unexpected, Dani screamed a bit. Gage whirled around, placing himself between Dani and the windows.

"W-what was that?" Dani asked. She wanted to look over Gage's shoulder, but they were facing the water and it was still light out. Damn these long Alaskan summer days!

"Not sure. Gage took a few steps forward. "I think a plastic cup hit the windows. There's one caught down below on the ledge. The wind is powerful. Someone probably forgot to bring it inside, and the wind took it."

Dani said a silent thank you to whoever left the cup outside. It gave her the chance to collect herself. She moved toward the kitchenette, looking for something to wipe her face. She tore off a paper towel, mopped her cheeks and then pulled another.

She needed to blow her nose. Another embarrassment. What choice did she have? She blew her nose and threw everything away. Then she washed her hands in the sink. She threw a bit of water on her face and used yet another paper towel to dry it. *So much for being environmentally friendly*.

"You okay?"

She hauled in a deep breath and turned, leaning against the counter. Gage rested his butt on the dining table, his legs crossed at the ankles, the pose deceptively casual. She met his eyes but only briefly.

"Um, yes. Sorry about that. I just needed—"

"Don't worry about it. That's a hell of a lot to keep bottled up inside. Everyone needs to let loose occasionally." He crossed his arms over his chest and cleared his throat. "So, all this is to save your sister."

"Yes." Their gazes met again, but she couldn't hold his. Crying in front of him. Jesus, it didn't get worse than that in her world.

"Good reason. I'd do anything for one of my brothers."

He approved? Wait. Why did that matter? Her brain was a mess. She needed to move. To work. That would sort it all out. She glanced at him and then away again. "Well, anyway. I need to work on the software. I need it to work."

She moved away from the counter and started toward the living room but then the rain let up a bit and she caught sight of the water. Her body went cold. She couldn't breathe. Gage was suddenly in front of her.

"It's fine. You're fine." He gently pushed her hair off her face with his finger. "The water is out there, and you're in here. You're safe. I've got you." He put his hands on her arms and rubbed them softly up and down. She looked up at him. Their gazes locked. The ice in her body melted. As suddenly as the cold had come on, it was gone. In its place, fire. A slow burn was starting between her legs.

She was aware of Gage, of the heat from his body, his scent surrounding her, his closeness. Her hands had somehow moved to his chest. His heart beat strong and steady under her palms. A glance at his face confirmed her desire was mirrored in his eyes. She flexed her fingers on his chest and parted her lips.

He swooped down and claimed her mouth. She opened willingly. Their tongues danced while their bodies came together.

His flesh was hot under her hands, even through his shirt. She longed to touch bare skin. He pulled her hips against his. It felt so good she moaned. An immediate hardening in his groin was the response. She moaned again at how good it felt. He walked her backward toward the table until she bumped up against it. Then he picked her up and placed her on top. His lips found hers again.

The kiss deepened, and she wrapped her legs around his waist. God, she wanted him. Wanted *this* so much. She was running her hands down over his shoulders when he suddenly broke off the kiss.

She opened her eyes, puzzled.

"Dani, I want you. I want to do this, but I need to make sure you're okay with it. That this is what you want, too."

A flush clawed its way up her neck into her cheeks. "Was I not obvious enough? Should I be moaning and calling your name every two seconds?" she managed to get out between clenched teeth. She tried to twist away from him, but he held her in place.

"It's my job to protect you. Having sex with you is breaking every rule in the book. It could be said that I'm in a position of power over you. I don't want you to feel like you're being forced into this—that you have to have sex with me. I need you to say you are okay with this. With us having sex."

She blinked. Once. Twice.

No once. Not once had anyone ever been so clear about sex. About consent. It was mortifying in one way, but sexy as hell in another. Damn. He'd managed to make her go from vulnerable to in charge with the uttering of a few words. Heat shot from her core. She wanted this man like she had wanted no other.

"Gage Callahan, I want to have sex with you. I want to touch, taste, and feel every single part of your body. I want to feel you inside me. I want you to make me moan your name over and over again. And I want to make you yell mine." She grinned. "Clear enough for you?"

He didn't speak, only nodded but pulled her hand down to his crotch. He was as hard as rock. He cleared his throat.

Once. Twice. "Condoms," he managed to choke out. "I have one in my wallet." He pulled the wallet out of his back pocket and threw it on the table.

"Only one?" she asked, making her eyes as big as possible and blinking hard at him.

He groaned and bent down to capture her lips again. She fisted her hands in his hair and deepened the kiss. His tongue joined hers in a now familiar rhythm. She wrapped herself back around him.

He ran his hands down her thighs and gripped her tighter. She lifted her hips and moved back and forth across his crotch. When she reached for the button of his jeans, she heard his breath catch. She grabbed the bottom of the T-shirt she wore and pulled it over her head. His eyes went down to her breasts and then came back up to lock with hers.

THIS WOMAN WAS GOING TO BE THE DEATH OF HIM. SHE tasted so good, felt so right against him. He was powerless to say no. He wanted to be a professional and stop this insanity, but he saw the naked lust in her eyes, too. It was his undoing.

He dipped his head and captured one of her nipples in his mouth through her bra. He sucked and pulled at it, her groans spurring him on. He switched to the other breast. When she arched against him, he pushed her back on the table and laid her down slowly. He then moved from her nipples down her body, leaving a trail of kisses across her stomach. He moved back to her nipple and sucked some more. Then he undid her bra and slipped it off. She moaned when his tongue found her bare nipple. He swirled his tongue around it again and again.

Her hands moved over his shoulders as she arched up to

meet his mouth. She tugged at his shirt, so he took it off over his head and then went back to her nipples. He trailed more kisses down her belly and then paused only to undo the button of her jeans. She helped him, lifting her butt so he could slide them off. She was wearing the barest scrap of purple lace. He kissed her belly along the edge of her underwear. She fisted her hands in his hair and lifted her hips again. He slid the underwear down over her knees and dropped it to the floor.

He paused above the apex of her legs. Glancing up to make sure she was still with him, he saw her bite her lip, but then her hands reached for him.

He gently pushed her hands away and dropped his mouth over her hot center. She moaned in response. He slowly moved his tongue in little circles, alternating licking and nipping her sensitive area. Her breath was coming in small gasps. He used his fingers in tandem with his tongue. Her breath came faster. He heard her nails scrape against the table.

"Gage," she gasped. "Gage." She repeated his name over and over, faster and faster, until he felt her core tighten and then release.

She lay back relaxed on the table as he made his way back up her body, dropping kisses along the way.

She smiled up at him and ran her hand down his chest. "Hmm, not bad."

He chuckled. "High praise from you. Don't worry, I won't let it go to my head." Then he trailed his lips along her neck. He touched her breast, tenderly flicking his thumb over the nipple. She bit her lip again. He was so hard it hurt.

She sat up on the table and then reached down, and he felt the button of his jeans go. He helped her push them down. She grabbed his boxer briefs and pushed those down as well. He shifted his weight to one foot and tugged every-thing off.

Then he stood up straight again and pulled her close. He continued to rub her nipple while nibbling on the hollow of her neck.

She reached down and closed a hand around him. He groaned. It felt so good he couldn't help it. She moved her hand slowly up and down his length. He claimed her lips again, and she immediately deepened the kiss. The blood thrummed through his veins as the tempo of her hand matched the movement of her tongue.

He broke off the kiss. "You're killing me," he growled.

"Good. Turnabout is fair play." Her smile was sexy and filled with promise.

"Just hold that thought." He grabbed his wallet and got the condom he had there. He tore it open and started to put it on.

Dani brushed his hands away. She took the condom and rolled it slowly over him. It was the sexiest thing Gage had ever experienced.

When he pulled her hard against him, she laughed. She then kissed him, nibbling on his lips and moving down his jaw. When she bit his earlobe, he hissed. She was driving him crazy. Her hands were everywhere, and her tongue was leaving a trail of desire in its wake as she moved down his chest.

She licked first one nipple than the other. He tried to bring her lips back to his, but she refused. He moved to pull her hips to his, but she shook her head. Then she smiled.

She shifted her weight and moved to the edge of the table. Then she locked her legs around his waist and pulled him inside of her. He was rock hard. "You're so tight. You feel so damn good."

Her movements were slow at first, but she gained speed

until he couldn't stand it. He grabbed her hips and picked her up off the table. He turned and leaned against the edge of the table as he guided her down on top of him. his hands on her hips, guiding her. Faster, harder.

She opened her eyes, and their gazes locked. He knew, at that moment, he would do everything in his power to keep her safe. She was his and his alone. She called his name, and her core squeezed the length of him. A couple more thrusts, and the force of his release almost buckled his legs, his voice raw as he called out her name. He turned and rested her butt on the table and leaned on her as the two of them sat there gasping for breath.

"That…was…incredible," Gage managed to huff out between breaths.

"Uh huh."

"I feel weak," he admitted.

Dani pushed away from his chest. "Does that mean there's no round two?"

New energy surged at her invitation. He grinned. "Not on your life," he said and then picked her up and carried her over to the sofa. Her yelp of surprise ended in a fit of giggles. It was music to his ears.

CHAPTER SEVENTEEN

D ani lounged against Gage's chest, her fingers tracing the outline of a scar on his ribs. "How'd you get this one?"

"A knife fight in Egypt." His voice rumbled out of his chest, vibrating in Dani's ear.

"Sounds interesting. What happened?"

Gage chuckled. "I could tell you, but then I'd have to kill you."

Dani smiled. "What about this one?" she asked as she ran her finger across an odd-shaped scar on his lower abdomen. Gage stayed silent. She heard him sigh and felt the muscles in his chest tense up under her head. The silence went on, and she was about to give up on him answering when he finally started speaking.

"It was caused by a piece of shrapnel." He went silent again.

Dani didn't want to push. Hell, everyone had their secrets. She certainly did, but at the same time, she sensed the memory of the injury caused Gage pain. Her curiosity got the better of her and she asked, "Was it from an IED?"

"No." His response was clipped, and his voice was flat. She'd hit a nerve of some kind. Better to leave it alone. But she'd revealed so much to him, she was a bit hurt he didn't want to share back. In truth, it was making her uncomfortable. She hated being vulnerable, and yet she'd been open with him. Now he was shutting her out.

He must have sensed something because he started speaking again. "It was a Stinger. Someone shot a Stinger missile at a building that was across the road and down the block a bit from where I was, and some shrapnel hit me."

"Oh." She chewed on the inside of her cheek. She shouldn't have asked. She was way out of her depth.

"The building, a café, was hit…I was running towards it. Someone I worked with"—he paused, and she felt him swallow—"a friend was there, and I was trying to warn him." Gage's voice was soft. "He wouldn't answer his phone. He was at a meet. I was too late." His voice cracked on the last word.

Dani found Gage's hand with hers and squeezed hard. There were no words.

"My friend, his name was Joel, Joel Cutter, was a great guy. From California." Gage's words tumbled out faster now. "He had this talent. He could do impressions of everyone. Famous people, regular people. It was amazing. And not just their voices, but he'd do the actions, too. He'd turn into them. He would've been a big star in Hollywood if he'd made it back.

"Joel was big on giving people second chances and believing that everyone had good in them. Even after everything we'd seen, he still believed in people. It was amazing." His legs shifted restlessly. "And it was his downfall.

"We had a new commanding officer. Roderick. He was green and in over his head. We all hated the stupid mistakes he made. I've never reported to anyone who made such poorly informed decisions. Putting guys where they shouldn't be. Haphazardly planned ops based on shitty intel. He was in a hurry to make a name for himself."

Dani pressed her palm over Gage's heart, dreading what had to be coming in his story.

"I wanted to complain through back channels. The brass had to know it was only a matter of time before this guy got some of us killed. But Joel, he said we should give the guy a break. He was doing his best. Just give him a bit more time to sort himself out. Joel even went and talked to Roderick about chilling out.

"Roderick didn't take it too kindly. He retaliated by assigning Joel every shit job for a week. Roderick was some higher-up's son. Someone with stars on their collar. There was a lot of pressure on him. Joel thought Roderick would smarten up if we just gave him a break."

Gage stopped speaking. His breaths increased. His muscles tensed under Dani's cheek. When she squeezed his hand again, he continued.

"There was a meet. We'd been working this guy, an informant, for a while. He'd given us some good intel in the past but there was a problem. We'd heard rumors that command had been hacked. There was a good chance the Taliban knew this guy was feeding us info. We all balked at going. It was too risky. Not worth it."

Dani's stomach dropped. Her heart slammed in her chest. A hacker was responsible for his friend's death. Gage's hatred for her work and hackers in general made so much more sense now.

"Roderick didn't care. The informant said he had details on the location of a high value target. One of the top enemies on the list. One that would make Roderick's career if he bagged the guy. So he sent Joel.

"We got confirmation after Joel left for the meet that

Command had been hacked. Roderick, that asshole, knew before Joel left. I tried to get to the meet. I tried to call. We all did but, in the end, we were too late. Ten people died in that cafe, Joel being one of them." Gage ran a hand through his hair and then down over his face.

"I lost it. When I got back to the base, I went after Roderick. I beat him 'til he was almost dead. I probably would've killed him if the guys hadn't hauled me off him." He swallowed. "I should've been court martialed, but Logan got me off. I have no idea what he told them, but I even got an honorable discharge. I'm guessing Roderick's father pulled strings. He wouldn't want his son's fuckup to get out."

She lifted her head off his chest. "I'm sorry Gage. So, so sorry." Their eyes locked, and she shivered. She'd known from the beginning he'd had hands that hit. Hands that could hurt.

He said nothing for a long moment. Then he looked away and said, "Thanks. Joel was a good man who didn't have to die. If we'd had a better system, a secure, impenetrable setup, he'd still be alive."

It was as if he'd slapped her across the face. Her breath caught. She put her head back down on his chest while her heart thudded against her ribs. What was she supposed to say to that? That she got the message? People like her were the reason his friend was dead. Better not to say anything at all. It would just lead to a big fight, one she knew she couldn't win.

Dani sat up and covered her chest with her arms. "I really am sorry about your friend. Life sucks most of the time. Nothing is more brutal than watching someone you love… die." Dani swallowed hard as she blinked back tears. She wasn't going to cry again, not in front of Gage. Not after what he'd just said.

She started to climb over Gage. She wanted off the sofa and back in her clothes now.

Gage locked his arms around her so she couldn't move. She struggled a bit against him, but he refused to let her go. "You're right, life does suck sometimes, and it's very hard to watch people you care about die. I hated what happened to Joel almost as much as I hated watching my mom waste away. Both were awful."

Dani made the mistake of looking at Gage. His beautiful blue eyes were full of pain. She wanted to resist. She wanted to get up and move away from him. They couldn't be together. It wasn't good for either one of them. But she couldn't move.

He'd been kind to her. Helping her with her phobia and taking care of her. She needed to help him. No, she wanted to help him. She wanted to make him forget his pain. She wanted to tell him everything would be fine but she had never ever known life to work out that way. There was always a curve ball coming.

CHAPTER EIGHTEEN

Dani woke with a start. *Where was she?* She sat up and blinked several times. Her heart thudded against her rib cage. The flash of lightning lit up her surroundings. *Right, the cruise ship.*

She looked around in the inky darkness. Gage was asleep beside her. She could scarcely make out his bare chest in the ambient light. She didn't even really remember moving to the bed. She sure as hell remembered everything else, though. It had been amazing. Right up until she found out Gage's best friend had died because of a hacker. A tremor ran through her. She needed some space. It was all…so much.

She shifted and swung her legs over the side of the bed, stifling a groan when her feet hit the floor. She was sore all over. The "I've had amazing sex" kind of sore. Still, everything hurt. She got up slowly. *Where were her clothes?* All over the suite if she remembered correctly. Damn.

She swallowed hard as images of their intimacy flickered like a high-speed camera through her brain. She shook her head. It wasn't so much the physical intimacy as all the sharing about Carly and her own feelings.

She moved silently down the stairs. She really didn't want Gage to wake up. She wasn't ready to face that. What if he regretted what happened? Or worse. What if he just didn't care either way?

No, he cared. Gage was the type of guy who cared about everything to one degree or another. She just wasn't sure he cared about her in a positive way. She swallowed the lump that was rapidly forming in her throat.

He'd been so kind to her. All her pent-up worry about Carly had come flying out in an avalanche of emotion and she'd needed to be held, but in the cold light of day, there was no doubt in her mind he was going to regret it. Regret her. He'd already said as much. She was a hacker, a criminal, and he'd been hired to protect her. She was his job, and he'd crossed a line. In the cold light of day, she was certain he would kick himself for the choice he'd made.

She walked over to the dining area and picked up her jeans and her bra, carefully avoiding looking out the windows even though it was pitch dark. It took a moment to find her red T-shirt and her lace panties but, at last, she had it all in a ball in front of her.

She went back toward the front door and then around the wall to the bathroom tucked into the end of the hall. Showering here was a safer bet than upstairs by Gage. She needed a bit of time to collect herself.

She needed to rebuild the wall she'd so carelessly torn down last night. She was going to do a reset. Keep her distance. She just had to make it off this ship and back to New York. Then she would be able to put real distance between her and Gage. Distance she so greatly needed right now.

She almost tripped over her laptop in the hallway. Cursing quietly, she turned on the bathroom light and brought the bag inside with her before she closed the door.

She put the toilet seat down, threw a towel over it and a towel around herself, and then sat down and opened her laptop.

Glancing at the clock on the screen, she noticed the time. 4:00 a.m. It would be too early to call Carly. She needed another couple of hours for her sister to be awake. Guilt flooded her chest. This was the first time in a long time she'd missed their nightly call.

When she tried to launch a browser, she realized she probably couldn't have called anyway. The internet was sporadic at best since they weren't at port anymore. It was an excuse, and she knew it.

Carly was counting on her. That little girl deserved to meet a real flesh and blood family member after everything she'd been through, and it was up to Dani to make it happen, but she was no further ahead on the software. She drew in a shaky breath and then closed her laptop. The only thing to do was grab a shower and then get back to it.

Dani put her laptop down and leaned it against the wall. Then she stood and grabbed the clothing that she'd dumped on the floor. She rinsed out her underwear and then looked around for a hair dryer. After finding one under the sink, she took the risk of waking Gage and flipped it on. It didn't take more than a couple of minutes to dry her stuff. She'd have to live with the T-shirt and jeans, but at least she'd have relatively clean undies. She turned on the shower and let out a groan of pleasure when she stepped into the warm spray. Twenty minutes later, Dani slung her backpack over her shoulder and opened the bathroom door.

Gage was standing directly on the other side of it. She opened her mouth, but he quickly put a hand over her lips and put a finger to his own.

Dani glared at him. Was he trying to give her a heart attack? Why was he standing right outside the door? Why was he only half dressed? She was eye level with his chest. The urge to touch him was intense.

He made a small sound so she looked up. He gestured toward the door to the cabin. She listened. Someone was on the other side of the door in the outer hallway. Her knees got weak and sweat broke out on her palms.

Gage gestured for her to move down the inside hallway toward the living room. Dani moved but stopped at the end of the wall. It would be getting light out soon, and she would start to be able to see the water. She looked at Gage.

He cocked his head as if he was listening. Then he grabbed her hand and pushed her head down gently so she was looking at the carpet. He pulled her into the living room.

Dani strained to hear, but didn't detect a sound. Frowning, she realized the rain had stopped. The weather was finally silent. Then she heard a faint click. The door lock.

Gage stopped moving. She looked up. He motioned for her to go between a chair and the wall. She squatted down, pulling her backpack with her, and slid into the spot.

Gage moved over and flattened himself on the floor in front of the sofa. She could just see his head peeking around one end, and the blackness beyond the back of the sofa.

Dani's heart was beating double-time in her chest. Surely, it was just Jeremy. She listened intently but still heard nothing. Maybe it was a mistake. Maybe something else had clicked in the suite. It could be anything.

But then she heard the soft tread of a foot on carpet. She didn't dare look. It wasn't Jeremy. He would have called out by now. Her heartbeat went to stratospheric levels. Sweat trickled down her back. She labored to keep her breathing quiet. Her lungs were on fire. The roaring of blood in her ears muted all other noise.

Suddenly, a shadow moved behind the sofa. It turned to

her left and then back to her right. It started to move toward the stairs to the loft when a second shadow approached and turned toward the dining room. There were two of them!

Her breath hitched and stopped altogether. Fear crawled up her throat and tried to claw its way out. She clapped her hands over her mouth to stifle her scream and tried to focus. She glanced at Gage. He was still. Unnaturally so. What was he—?

Gage shot to his feet, then picked up the end table and threw it at the guy next to the stairs. The shadow let out a yelp as the table hit him square in the chest. He fell back against the stairs with a crash. Gage turned toward the other shadow, but it was gone. Where did he go? Dani searched the darkness, straining her eyes, until at last she saw the shadow charge toward Gage from his left. She was about to yell, but Gage had seen him, too. The shadow jumped, and the two of them hit the coffee table and crashed to the floor.

"Dani, run!" Gage yelled as he fought with the shadowy figure.

Dani scooped up her backpack and made a mad dash for the door. The guy untangled from Gage and grabbed her foot as she ran by. She crashed to the floor. Gasping to catch her breath, she tried to get back up, but he still had her ankle. Gage was struggling to get him to release her, but he wouldn't let go.

Dani let loose with an almighty yell and kicked the guy square in the face. His grip loosened enough for her to get away. She was on her feet, running for the door. She pulled it open and flew into the hallway where she barreled directly into an elderly gentleman, knocking him into the wall. She felt badly for hitting him, but she couldn't stop. Her life depended on it. Hers and Carly's.

THE BITS OF COFFEE TABLE CRUNCHED UNDER GAGE'S back as he struggled with the intruder. He managed to get a good punch in. The man's nose crumpled under his fist and the warm spurt of blood covered his knuckles. He followed up with another punch, and while the intruder was disoriented, he rolled them both over so he was on top and hit the other man once more. When the intruder's head bounced off a coffee table leg his body went limp. He was out cold.

Gage stumbled as he picked himself up off the floor and started toward the door. He looked out the peephole, but the hallway was empty. He put the metal triangle across the lock so no one could open the door again, berating himself for forgetting to do it after Jeremy left.

He'd been distracted by Dani. She looked so cute when she was arguing with his brothers about stealing the code from the Chinese. Fuck. This is why sleeping with the client was always a bad idea. It was a distraction, and that distraction had almost gotten them killed.

He leaned against the door for a moment and coughed. He was more winded than he should be. Too much fun time with Dani and not enough sleep. He needed to get home and get some serious rest.

Gage walked over to the table and grabbed his shirt. After pulling it on, he picked up the candle they'd left burning. He carried it over to the end table and set it down. He walked back to the men and started searching them. He noticed a tattoo peeking out from under the collar of the first guy's shirt when he was checking for a pulse, but the guy had no ID. Not surprising.

He did the same to the other guy with the same results. This guy had tattoos on his arms as well as his neck, but nothing else Gage could use to identify them. He didn't have a camera to take pictures of their faces and tattoos to send to his brothers, and his burner phone didn't have the capability.

Both men were out cold but still breathing. They would have serious concussions when they woke up, but they would live. Too bad.

Gage walked back to the door and checked the peephole. The hallway was still empty. He flipped the metal bar and opened the door. He stepped out and closed it quietly behind him. As he walked down the hallway, he heard stirring behind some of the doors. People were waking up. Good. He could blend better. Now he just had to find Dani.

He heard the elevator ding, and a phalanx of security stepped into the hallway. They turned and started walking toward him. An elderly gentleman was with them.

"She hit me and then she took off down this hallway," he said as he half-walked half-ran to keep up with the security guards.

Gage kept his head tilted down and moved to the side to let them pass. It was all bad if they noticed his swelling lip or the blood on his knuckles. They moved passed him, taking no notice.

He picked up his pace to catch the elevator. Once safely onboard with the doors closed, he let out a pent-up breath. This reprieve was only temporary. They would check the security cameras now that there had been a complaint and discover who was coming and going from that stateroom. His face would show up and so would Dani's.

Jeremy. Shit. He was there, too. Gage had to find him and warn him as well.

CHAPTER NINETEEN

Dani walked down the hallway as if she did it every day. It was the key to success. She'd learned it from a hacker buddy. Sometimes physical access was needed to hack things. He'd taught her if she dressed like everyone else and made an effort to look comfortable, like she belonged, chances were good no one would ask questions. He'd been right.

Dani had used that approach a time or two. Now was no different. She glanced at her hand where she'd written a few directions. The hallways in the crew quarters were much more maze-like, and she'd needed a few helpful reminders to find Jeremy's room. Pretending to be staff on a cruise ship was infinitely easier than pretending to be a worker on an oil rig. She shuddered at the memory.

Jeremy's quarters were just ahead, after the next right. She looked up from her hand and saw a guy coming down the hallway. She gave him a smile and kept going. He just nodded and didn't bother to stop. He'd probably just come off some shift since he was in work clothes, or he was just starting. Either way, he looked half asleep.

Dani made the right and knocked on Jeremy's door. She was worried he wouldn't be in his room. Or that he'd have roommates. Either one could be a problem. She knocked again. "Come on, come on," she pleaded in a whisper.

The door opened, and Jeremy's surprised face filled the doorway. "What are you doing here?" He stuck his head out into the hallway, looked both ways, and then pulled her into his cabin. "Are you trying to get me fired?"

Dani hissed, "Some men broke into the cabin and attacked us. Gage told me to run."

Jeremy's eyes bulged out of his face. "Is he okay?"

"I don't know." She bit her lip. "I have to check the security video to know for sure. Where are the repeaters located on the ship?"

Jeremy blinked. "The what?"

There was a loud snort, and Dani jumped. Her heart sank as she noted another bunk in the room. "Who is that?"

Jeremy gestured over his shoulder. "My roommate, Dale. Don't worry. He wears a face mask and ear plugs so he can't see or hear you. Plus, he sleeps like the dead. Now, what are you looking for?"

"The things that provide the internet. Where are they located? I need to get service 'cause I've gotta make a call." *Or two,* she added silently.

"Oh, right. Well, you can access it here in my cabin. It almost always works in here. I'm not sure about anywhere else."

Dani looked around. The cabin was tiny. Her eyes had adjusted to the dim lighting and she noted a third bed. Two were against one wall, bunkbed style, and the other was against the opposite wall but was built up high with a desk underneath. "Is this guy likely to wake? Or will your other roommate show up soon?"

"Dale will sleep for hours. He just went to bed not too

long ago, and the other guy left altogether. He couldn't take life on a cruise ship."

"Okay. I'll log in here. Where are you going to be?" Jeremy was dressed in his work uniform.

"I've got to start work." He turned around and opened a closet door. He reached in and pulled out a radio. "Here. Click once so it squawks, and that will be the signal. I'll change mine to channel eighteen. You do the same. Then you can speak to me when you need to. If you hear one squawk, it means I'm trying to reach you."

Dani nodded. "Good. I'll find the best place for internet access, and then I'll squawk once I leave." She looked at Dale, who grunted as he rolled over. "Once we change the channel, I'll let you know where I'll be. Keep your eyes peeled for Gage." She couldn't even think about the possibility the men had Gage and he was hurt. Or worse.

"Okay. Good luck. Talk soon." Jeremy slid quietly out the door.

When Dale snorted again, Dani about jumped out of her skin. She'd forgotten he was even there. She took a deep breath and immediately regretted it. The cabin smelled like stinky boy. Yuk.

Dani sat down gingerly at the desk and pulled out her laptop. She put her backpack on the desk and her laptop on top of it. No need to touch too many surfaces. She booted up and logged on to the internet. Jeremy was right; he had great signal.

She checked the video feed and saw that Gage made it out of the cabin. Her shoulders sagged with relief. She immediately set to work erasing the video from the hallway. She also deleted the video of them entering the cabin the previous day and the clips of Jeremy bringing them food. Then she picked random clips of video and erased them.

When security looked at the system, it would look like there was some kind of glitch.

Dani then took a quick look at the schematics and found where a repeater was located in the passenger area of the ship. There were a few, but the ice-skating rink looked like the best choice.

She grabbed the radio and squawked once. Then she turned to channel eighteen. Jeremy responded in seconds. She told him that Gage was on the promenade and she'd be in the rink. "Oh and tell him I'm calling Janet for help. He'll understand."

"Roger that," Jeremy said, and then she turned the radio back to its original channel and turned the volume down so she could just hear the chatter.

Dani backed out of the ship's systems and stared at her screen for a second. She bit her lip and then tried Carly. She wanted to speak to her little sister badly. No answer. She was probably off getting treatment or tests or something.

She sighed. She would feel much better if she could reach Carly. It would just have to wait. She made another video call. This one was answered. "Hi, Janet. It's Dani Pierce."

"Dani. This is a surprise. Is everything okay? You usually email."

It was true. She emailed Janet when she needed anything per Drake's instructions. They'd only spoken a few times on the phone. Once when Dani wanted to run a trial of the software at one of Drake's hotels. Another time when Dani was looking for Drake to discuss a time extension. That was when she and Janet had fallen into a discussion about what it was like when Janet lost her son.

He'd been struggling with drug addiction and, according to Janet, almost beat it, but in the end, he overdosed. Janet had been crushed as any mother would be, but she had also seemed so angry. Dani remembered feeling uncomfortable confronted by Janet's rage. She could understand it, though. She'd been wildly angry about Carly's diagnosis in the beginning, but the little girl was always so upbeat and full of sunshine that she made Dani promise to let the anger go.

"Everything is…going." She didn't want to get into details. "How's everything with you?" She could see brochures on Janet's desk. She quickly asked, "Going on vacation?" She had no interest in seeing Janet rage about her son again. Best stay away from that topic.

Janet laughed. "Thinking of retiring actually. It might be time."

"That's uh, good, I guess." Retirement. Dani knew nothing about that type of thing. Janet wasn't young, but Dani didn't think she was yet in her mid-sixties, but maybe it was time. She couldn't get over losing Micah. "Good for you for going while you're young." She'd heard one of her teachers at school say that to another one who was leaving. Young was relative. The teacher had white hair.

"Yes, I want to travel and enjoy life. I've certainly earned my golden parachute."

"Um, cool." Dani nodded. "So, anyway, do you have cell numbers for Gage's brothers? I need to talk to them."

"Sure, dear." Janet flicked through some rolling paper thing on her desk and pulled out a little card. She read the numbers off and then put the card back.

"Well, thanks. Take care. Enjoy your parachute and your retirement."

Janet laughed. "I will."

Dani clicked off and then opened another app on her computer. She tried calling the cell numbers, but neither call would go through. It was a bit odd, but maybe they were in the air already on the way to Vancouver. Dani shut her laptop. It was time to get to the rink. She stood up and put her laptop in her backpack. She grabbed the radio and tucked it inside as well. She went over to the door and put her ear to it. She heard nothing so turned the knob.

"No!" Dale yelled.

Dani let out a squeal. She whirled around and stared at Dale. He turned restlessly in his sleep and mumbled something. Dani swore and pulled open the door. She turned left and started down the hallway. She needed to get to the rink, but first she needed the restroom. She'd damn near peed herself when Dale yelled.

CHAPTER TWENTY

Gage got off the elevator on the promenade deck and walked toward the shops and the restaurants. It was still pretty empty, but it wouldn't be for long. He tried to figure out where Dani would go but had no idea.

He ran a hand through his hair. God! He needed a shower. He could still smell Dani on his skin. He had grabbed his T-shirt on the way out the door so at least he was covered, but he was looking rough. He tried to fix his hair again. The last thing he needed was to attract more attention. He sighed. His sailing vacation seemed to be getting farther and farther away.

He checked for Dani in the restaurants that were open, but nothing. The shops weren't open as yet so unless she'd broken in, she wasn't there.

As he searched, his stomach churned with guilt. He'd crossed a line last night. His only job was to protect her. Sleeping with her muddied the waters and made his job difficult but, *damn*, he just didn't care. That woman had burrowed under his skin and he had big plans for a repeat performance of last night's adventures.

He worked his way to the other end of the ship and then stood in front of a map, trying to figure out where to look next. Jeremy appeared out of nowhere and stood beside Gage. "Can I help you find something, sir?" he asked loudly. Gage turned to look, and Jeremy whispered, "She's with me. She's down in my cabin. She said to tell you she's talking to someone named Janet, asking for help."

"How did—? Never mind. Did she tell you what happened?"

"Yes. I'm sorry." Jeremy had guilt written all over his face. "I guess I wasn't as discrete as I thought. They must have followed me."

"Don't worry about it. To be honest, I'm not sure how they found us. They seem to be one step ahead all the time. Not sure it was you that tipped them off." Gage continued in a low voice. "Besides, we have bigger things to worry about at the moment. Dani hit some old guy on the way out of the cabin so now security is up there checking it out."

"Oh boy." Jeremy wiped his forehead with his shirtsleeve.

"Yeah," Gage grunted. "By now they'll have found the two unconscious men and a pile of broken furniture. They'll question the men and probably get nowhere, and then they'll watch the video of the hallway. They are going to see me and Dani and you coming in and out of that cabin."

Jeremy blinked and swallowed hard. He pointed to the ice rink on the map. "I think this is what you're looking for, sir." He glanced around and then said, "She said to tell you she'll meet you in the rink and not to worry about the cameras. Apparently, they have been going out all over the ship at random times in random hallways." He grinned. "She's good."

Gage's shoulders sagged. *That's my girl!* He grinned back. "Yes, she's amazing."

"Go to this door to enter. It will be unlocked." Jeremy

pointed at the map again. "I gave Dani a radio. Just make sure you change it to an outside channel so no one on the ship hears you if you use them. We worked out a channel to use to communicate and times for me to check in."

"Jeremy, I can't thank you enough for his," Gage said.

"Dude, I'm getting paid big time for this. It's totally worth it." Jeremy's big smile was back in place. He winked and left Gage standing at the map.

Gage chuckled and shook his head. Then he sobered up and checked the map again for the location of the rink. He strode to the nearest set of elevators and punched the down button. It took a few minutes for an available elevator to arrive.

Dani. They were bad together. He couldn't stand that she was a hacker. She probably couldn't stand that he liked law and order...*when it suited him*. It was just bad on all kinds of levels. And yet his relief at finding out she was okay was profound. She was bold and intelligent, sassy and all kinds of sexy. And he loved every bit of her.

He closed his eyes. *Just work the problem.* Keep both of them alive until they get back to NYC. He'd figure out the rest then. He opened his eyes.

Activity was picking up. People were hungry and hitting the decks. Gage kept his head on a swivel. There was at least one more guy onboard that they knew about. Chances were good there were more.

Finally his elevator arrived, and he got on. Fortunately, no one else was in the car, so the ride to the floor with the ice rink didn't take long. He moved down the hallway to the door Jeremy had indicated. He pushed, but nothing happened. Panic started in his gut, but then it hit him. He pulled on the door, and it opened easily. He cursed his stupidity and entered the rink.

A cool blast of air hit him. It was dark except for a few

small spotlights above the theatre seating and a couple above the ice. He gave his eyes a moment to adjust. He looked around but saw nothing but the red theatre seats.

"Gage." A waving hand appeared directly under the light in the back corner. He walked down the stairs to the rink and then around the outside wall. He wasn't about to walk across the ice. No doubt he'd go flying. He went up the stairs on the other side of the rink and stopped next to the row where he'd seen Dani's hand. About five rows back, Dani was just sitting down again in a corner seat.

"Thank God, you're okay," he said as he took the remaining stairs two at a time and then moved swiftly down the row. When he came up beside her, he picked her up out of her chair and gave her a big hug. She gave him a small hug back. *Progress.* He squeezed her harder.

"Ahh. Easy, that hurts."

He pulled back and held her at arm's length. "Where? What hurts?"

She looked up at him. "My ribs. I think I bruised them when that guy grabbed my leg."

Gage ran his fingers over her ribs, and she winced. "You're right. Bruised but not broken. Are you hurt anywhere else?"

She shook her head. "You okay?"

He nodded.

"The men, are they…?"

"They'll have bad headaches when they wake up and a few broken bones but no permanent damage."

Dani nodded again and sat back down. She pulled her laptop into her lap and opened it up. The screen seemed really bright in the darkness, but Gage knew it was quite dim. He sat down, too. "Jeremy said you've been busy."

She nodded and smiled. "Yes. The ship's security system seems to be wonky."

"Wonky. Is that a technical term?" he asked with a grin.

"As a matter of fact, it is. They'll have a hard time figuring it all out, and they certainly won't be able to fix anything until we hit Vancouver, so we should be fine." She shifted in her seat and winced.

He ground his molars. Those goons had hurt her. He could kill them for it. His hands curled into fists. She shot him a look so he uncurled his fingers and rolled his shoulders. He needed to let that anger go and focus.

"Work the problem," he said under his breath.

"Exactly," Dani replied.

He swore silently. He hadn't meant for her to hear that. He sighed. "So, why are we in the rink? And how did you find Jeremy?"

"I found a spot with decent Wi-Fi and hacked the system again. Then I looked him up to see where his sleeping quarters were located. In the end, I just got lucky and caught him as he was coming out to start work. And we're in the rink because it has the best Wi-Fi on board." Dani leaned back and gestured with her head. "There's a repeater behind this wall."

"You are impressive. Have I mentioned that?"

Her fingers stilled and she cleared her throat. "Thanks." The keys clacked softly again. "I figure we'll stay here as long as we can. It's safer that way. We'll move when we have to." She held up the radio. "Jeremy will check in with us to give us an update if there's anything going on."

"Looks like you've got it all sorted. Now I just need to find a way to call my brothers. I think I should update them on what's going on and find out if they have anything new for us. I sure as hell like to know who the spy is in Drake's office and how the guys found us on this ship."

He wasn't going to admit it out loud, but he also just wanted to hear his brothers' voices. He'd always been the one who held the family together since his mom died. Logan and Mitch hadn't made it easy, but they were getting along better these days, and since he lost Joel, he'd found himself more shaken up by scenes like the one in the cabin. He looked at Dani. He knew very well how he could lose everything in a heartbeat. *Enough of those thoughts.*

"I called Janet, and she gave me your brothers' numbers, but I couldn't connect with them. Not sure the cell service is working well. Do you want to send them an email or text? We could try a video call if you want." Dani's fingers had been screaming across the keyboard at lightning speed, but she stopped typing. "Wait. You don't think the men followed Jeremy to the cabin, do you?"

"No. A random purser on the ship? They picked him out of the crowd? Even if he was in our hallway, that wouldn't be enough to make them suspicious. There are pursers all over the place. No, I think they found us another way. I think there's a distinct possibility they hacked into the ship's system as easily as you did and watched the video feeds until they found us."

Dani grimaced. Then he watched as she rapidly closed what she had been working on and brought up the ship's software again. "Let's see. They might have left a trail if they did. We might be able to trace it."

"Wait, will they be able to trace you?"

The look she gave him could only be described as pitying. "Seriously," she said as she shook her head.

Her fingers raced across the keyboard, and what seemed like seconds later, she smiled. "You're right. Here they are." She pointed to the screen as the door to the skating rink opened and the third man from the promenade walked in.

CHAPTER TWENTY-ONE

D ani froze. *How the hell did he find them?* There was no way he tracked her online. No. Way. She left no trace. Her lungs were on fire. She drew air deeply into her lungs as she slowly closed her laptop.

With the main lights off, he couldn't see them. There were only the few downward pointing spotlights, and as long as they stayed directly out of them, they couldn't be seen. She knew that from when Gage entered, but if he turned on the lights, they were done for. Gage was still beside her. Sweat trickled down her back, and she longed to wipe her palms on her jeans.

The man peered into the darkness and then walked over to the wall. He appeared to be looking for light switches, at least that was her guess. Gage's, too, apparently because he nudged her and pointed to the floor.

Slowly, carefully, they slid to the edge of their seats and then knelt down on the floor. Dani held her laptop in her right hand while keeping her seat down with her left. The seat would pop up as soon as she let go. Had it squeaked when she first sat down? For the life of her, she couldn't remember.

Gage was facing her. He let his seat up very carefully with no sound. He glanced at her and raised an eyebrow. She motioned to the seat with her head and then shook it. His lips compressed. She glanced back over at the guy. He was walking to the other side of the door, presumably still looking for the light switches. She turned back to Gage. He put his hand on her seat and motioned for her to move hers. Then ever so slowly, he let the seat rise. She turned back to watch the man. He was moving his hands along the wall when suddenly he stopped.

She whipped around to tell Gage, but he was already watching the guy. Gage pushed her head down with his left hand and used his right to let go of the seat at the same time as the lights came on. The seat made a slight squeak. She held her breath. Maybe the man didn't hear the squeak. It had seemed deafening to her.

Dani couldn't see anything, but she knew Gage could see the guy between the seats. She noticed a scant bit of tension leave his body. The man hadn't heard. The rush of relief was short lived. They were still stuck in the rink with no way out.

The seconds seemed to stretch into hours. Her legs were cramping. Her palms were slick. *Was he searching the whole place row by row?* She tried to catch Gage's eye, but he was totally focused on the guy.

Gage had come around the arena when he had walked up to see her, but the ice was positioned directly between the guy and their location. She heard what she thought was the door leading onto the ice open. Was the guy going out on the rink? She heard it slam closed again.

An eternity later, she heard one of the main doors to the skating rink close. Her breath left her lungs with a whoosh.

She started to stand up, but Gage caught her and held her tight. He shook his head.

What now? she mouthed at him, but he remained watching through the seats. Her leg muscles were screaming at this point and her ribs were starting to pulsate with pain. What the hell was going on? She needed to stand, to sit, actually. She also needed coffee, about a gallon of it. She heard the door open and close again.

Gage held her arm for another ten seconds and then let go. "Okay, you can stand now."

Dani slowly stood up. She pulled her seat down and placed her laptop on the cushion. Then she shook out her legs a bit and gingerly stretched her arms. "What was that about? Why did you hold me down? Did he come back?" she asked Gage as she massaged her legs.

"He didn't leave. I guess he figured if we were here, we might not be able to see him, so he pretended to leave to see if we'd pop up. He searched the rows on the side and then started across the ice but started sliding, so instead of walking around the ice, he just went back and played with the door. Lazy."

"Doesn't that seem a bit strange? Wouldn't he have been better trained than that?"

"Yes. It's weird."

Dani shrugged. "Well, I'm glad he was. It would have been ugly otherwise."

Gage nodded.

"Now what do we do?" Dani asked.

"We go over and sit on the other side of the rink." Gage walked down to the end of the row and then turned down the stairs. Dani grabbed her backpack and her laptop and followed him.

She frowned. "I have no idea how he knew we were here.

I swear to you I covered my tracks. There is no way he could've traced me to the access point we're using."

"He didn't," Gage said over his shoulder. "If he knew you were using this specific Wi-Fi access point, he would have searched more thoroughly. He's just checking every area with a repeater because that's where the signal is the strongest."

They hit the bottom and were walking around the ice. "How does he know where the strongest access points are? He didn't have a laptop with him."

"Yes, and that tells us there are definitely more bad guys on the boat. It also confirms they've been hacking the boat's systems as well. These guys seem organized and well equipped, but yet they are slightly sloppy. They are making mistakes," Gage said as they started up the stairs on the other side of the rink.

At the top row, he turned in and went to the corner seat again, but this time there was a walkway behind it. Gage sat down. "Not ideal, but it will do. We can sit here and blend in with the skaters and watch the shows."

"What mistakes?" Dani asked as she settled next to him.

Gage frowned at her. "What?"

"You said they made mistakes, but what mistakes did they make?"

"Well, the guy should've searched the entire rink. He should've walked around and checked each and every door to make sure they were all locked."

Dani nodded as she got her laptop back out of her backpack. "What else?"

"When they came to search the stateroom, they should've had at least one guy in the hallway just in case, and if they were smart and had the manpower, at least one more guy with them when they entered the suite."

Dani's fingers found their familiar spots on the keyboard

and then took off at full speed. "Maybe they don't have that kind of manpower."

She saw Gage shake his head out of the corner of her eye. He was looking around the rink. "I think they do. There has to be at least four of them, right? The three we saw and someone with a laptop somewhere. You saw at least two more in Juneau, so that's six. The Chinese government has lots of agents. I'm guessing they sent at least ten." Gage's voice petered out.

Dani glanced over at him. "You sound unsure. You think there's more than ten?"

Gage shrugged. "There could be a hundred. What do I know? But that's not what's bugging me."

"So what's the problem?" Dani asked as her fingers flew along the keyboard.

Gage shook his head. "The mistakes. Not very professional." He paused and shook his head again. "That's not true either. They are sort of professional."

He finally turned to face her. "They're good, but not quite at the level I would have expected, and that makes me nervous."

Her fingers stopped typing. If Gage was nervous, she should be terrified. He knew a lot more about this type of stuff than she did. Her breath caught in her throat. She sat back and wiped her palms on her jeans. She trusted Gage. Not something that happened, like ever, really. Trust usually took years for her to build, and she'd only known Gage for a few days.

Had it really only been a few days? She was tired. More tired than she'd ever been. She blinked rapidly to keep the rush of emotion from spilling down her cheeks. She didn't want to cry in front of him again.

She glanced at Gage. Her heart fluttered. It was definitely too late. She trusted him. Well, she'd had to. He was sent here to protect her. To save her life. But it was more than that, and she knew it. Deep in her heart, she felt it was more, and that had her wiping her sweaty palms on her jeans yet again.

The trust had been built when she wasn't looking. It had happened when he didn't press her on things, when he accepted her word. When she'd told him about her foster mom, and he understood. It'd happened when she cried about Carly and he'd held her. It'd happened when they'd had mind-blowing sex.

She swallowed hard again and closed her eyes. It was bad. Trust was bad. Once she trusted someone, they could disappoint her, and she'd get hurt. Getting hurt was just not something she wanted to go through again. She'd fought long and hard to come back from the pain her foster mom had caused. Trust was a painful word for her.

One of the great benefits of being a hacker was she rarely had to deal with anyone face to face and the only person she had to trust was herself. It was a dream job for an introverted, trust-deficient person like herself. Or it had been.

Rebuild the wall, she reminded herself. *Keep your distance.* This wasn't going to end well for her. Gage didn't want a criminal in his life, especially a hacker.

"What are you working on?" Gage asked.

She cleared her throat. "I'm using their tactics against them. I figured out their access point, so I know their general vicinity. Then I went back into the video logs and captured pictures of the three guys. I ran them through my software. They are staying in a cabin on deck eleven. They are using the repeater on the bow to get the best signal.

"Now, I think if we watch the last couple days of video feed of the hallway the room is in, we can figure out how many guys there are and what they look like."

Gage whistled softly, as though impressed.

Dani shifted in her chair. "Also, if you want to, we can send pictures to your brothers to see if we can get some kind of identification on them. Not sure that's going to help any since we know they're Chinese government." She shrugged.

"Your software can't identify them?" Gage asked.

"I don't have anything to compare them to so my software is not helpful here. The software can only identify someone if it has something to compare it to. If you have an old picture, it can say yes this person that walked across the street is the person from the photograph. But picking random people out of a crowd and identifying them can only happen if there is another database to compare it to. I could work on hacking some of the Chinese military databases if you want." She flexed her fingers and smiled.

Gage was staring at her.

"What?" she asked.

"You're amazing. Don't ever believe anything different, but let's not hack anything else by the Chinese government. Let my brothers see what they can dig up after we send them the email." He leaned in and gave her a quick kiss.

She needed to stop this. *No kissing. Keep your distance*, she tried to remind herself, but it wasn't working. Heat crawled up her neck and was advancing into her cheeks when he leaned down and kissed her again. This time it wasn't so quick.

She broke off the kiss and went back to her laptop, making a silent vow to avoid letting Gage get close to her again. Panic pooled in her belly. Each breath she drew felt like oxygen was in short supply.

If she continued to be close to him, to fall for him, it would kill her when this was over and he left. She was already in danger of losing Carly. She just couldn't take anymore hurt. She needed to focus on Carly and the software. Carly was the only thing she was absolutely one hundred percent sure of in this world, and she wasn't going to let that little girl down.

CHAPTER TWENTY-TWO

"So what are you going to do after this?" Gage asked as he watched the skaters move around on the ice. He glanced at the clock in the corner of Dani's screen. The rink officially opened twenty minutes ago, but it was filling up fast.

"After? What do you mean?" Dani asked. The clacking keys on her keyboard sped up.

"After you finish the software for Drake. What are you going to do?"

"Go see Carly."

Gage ran a hand through his hair. "Yes, but after that. What are you going to do? For a living?"

The sound of fingers on the keyboard stopped. He looked over at Dani, and their eyes locked. She blinked and then went back to her keyboard, but not before he saw a strange look flit across her face. One he couldn't name. His gut knotted.

"There you are." Jeremy appeared just behind their row. "I have the stuff you asked for." He held up a bag.

"Thanks, Jeremy." Dani tried to smile but Gage saw her

smile was tight. She turned back, shut her laptop lid, and then stood up.

Gage stood also and eyed Jeremy. "What stuff is that? I thought you were busy today."

"Dani radioed me a while ago and asked me to pick up some hats and T-shirts." His smile faltered as he looked back and forth between the two.

"You were in the restroom," Dani said.

Gage reached for the bag, but Dani took it out of Jeremy's hand first. She opened it and handed Gage a dark blue T-shirt. He held it up. It had *ALASKA* in bright white across the front. "Not the best to blend in."

"Beggars can't be choosers," Dani grumbled. "Thanks again, Jeremy." She whacked Gage in the chest with a dark blue ball cap that had *Juneau* on it.

Obviously, he'd done something to piss her off. He grimaced. It was going to be a long afternoon. He shrugged and shook his head. Jeremy smirked.

"Yes, thanks Jeremy." Gage glanced at Dani. "I'm assuming you think this will help us blend in so we can move more freely around the ship?"

She took a navy sweatshirt out of the bag and pulled it over her head. It had *Ketchikan* in small letters over her left breast. "I don't know if you've noticed, but there's a repair guy over there by the corner camera. I can only stall them for so long. Once they turn the camera on, they'll be looking for us."

She reached up and pulled her hair into a bun at the nape of her neck, then used a scrunchie she'd pulled out of the bag to tie it up. She yanked a black ball cap out of the bag and put it on.

Dani sighed. "As you know, most facial recognition software can't recognize you unless you look directly at it. Since you haven't shaved in a couple days, the beard you have is enough to fool most laptops. These guys don't have much in the way of cutting-edge software, so this should do it."

She adjusted her sweatshirt one more time and then picked up her backpack. "Jeremy, you should get going. The software is going to come back online in a minute or so. You need to be somewhere else."

He gave her a nod. "Just remember the doors will open tomorrow morning at six. Be there at about 5:30 so you can be in the front. It will help get you off the ship quickly."

Dani and Gage both nodded.

Jeremy waved, did an about-face, and then was gone in seconds.

"Maybe we shouldn't stick so close together. They're looking for a couple. Be better if we split up," Dani suggested.

"No," Gage growled. He wanted to yell, "Oh, hell no," but didn't think she'd respond well. "That's not an option. We stick together. It's my job to protect you and the software. You will not be alone."

She sighed before lifting her shoulders and dropping them swiftly. "Fine. Let's go."

Gage spent the rest of the day moving them from spot to spot all over the ship. He tried to stay with the crowds and keep them out of direct line of site of the cameras.

Dani was getting more and more agitated as the day progressed. He noticed her try to connect to the system and make a video call a few times, but it wasn't going through. She wouldn't say much, but her hands were curled into fists and she constantly gnawed her lip.

He managed to get an email out to his brothers with the shots of the guys that were after them. He was hopeful they would have them identified by the time they arrived in Vancouver in—he glanced at his watch—a little more than six hours. He yawned again. It was just before midnight.

"You want to see if we can find a place to crash for the night?" Gage looked over at Dani. She was sitting with her eyes glued to her screen. The library was going to close shortly. They had to move.

"Sure," she mumbled. She closed her laptop and slid it back into her bag. She stood up and took off for the door.

Gage got to his feet and followed her. He stifled another yawn and stretched his arms above his head. She'd stopped talking to him hours ago. Asking about her future had been a mistake. He was pushing her. He really wanted her to stop hacking, but what he wanted wasn't what she wanted. Another reason they weren't meant to be. No matter how much he loved her spunk and her smile.

He opened and closed his fists and rolled his shoulders. He tried to make his body relax, but he wasn't having much luck. This cold shoulder thing was really pissing him off and she knew it, but he wasn't going to give in to her game. He could be silent, too.

They walked down the main hallway with the promenade one floor below. Gage glanced over the rail and saw security doing a sweep. Then he looked up and saw more security guards on the walkway like theirs but on the other side of the ship. They were moving away from the bow of the ship.

Gage grabbed Dani's arm and kept them moving past the elevators and toward the bow. He turned her away from the promenade and down the hallway. She glanced up at him and pulled her arm out of his hand.

He stopped her and pointed to a door on her left. Captain's lounge was written in bold letters. "We can hide out in here." He tried the door, and it was open. He walked in and then signaled Dani to follow.

It wasn't a huge room, but it was created to give people the best view. Two floor-to-ceiling glass walls met in the far corner of the room. One wall looked out over the ocean and the other looked out over the top deck of the ship. It had a view of the deck below with the pool and the bars all lit up.

"Fuck," Gage growled. He'd been looking for a quiet space to hide in, but this was like being in a fishbowl.

Dani climbed onto a stool that faced the bar that was along the nearest wall. No one was behind it thankfully.

"Are you sure we can stay here for the night? Not exactly low-key." She didn't bother to turn around when she spoke.

Gage ground his teeth and counted to ten. "No, it's not the best, but if you have any other ideas, I'm all ears."

Silence. He closed his eyes and regretted being snarky. The situation and Dani's attitude were getting to him.

He sighed. "It stands to reason they've already searched here since they came from this direction. Not to say they won't come back, but hopefully we'll have a few hours, I'm sure. We only have to stay hidden for five hours. Jeremy said to be the first ones at the exit," he reminded her.

He checked out the furniture. Overstuffed couches in shades of brown with navy throw pillows were strategically placed around the room to provide the best views. Gage swung one around until it faced away from the windows. "Here," he said. "You can sleep on this one."

Dani shot a quick glance over her shoulder. "I'm fine where I am. I need to work." She opened up her laptop.

"Then work here so you can be comfortable and maybe catch some shut-eye." Gage shoved another couch that had been against the inside wall, turning it to face Dani's couch. This set up gave him a good view of Dani *and* the door.

"I'm fine thanks," she replied.

Gage ran a hand through his hair. Exhaustion was wrapped around his shoulders like a blanket. "Dani, I need you to work on the couch so I can see you and the door at the same time." He was taking great pains to be polite but it was costing him dearly. "Please, take a seat on the couch," he said through clenched teeth.

Dani slammed her laptop lid and slid off the barstool. Keeping her gaze glued to the carpeting, she hurried to the couch, sat down, and curled her legs up. She opened her laptop with a little more force than necessary.

He was driving her crazy. She'd been doing her best to push him away all day when all she really wanted to do was crawl into his lap and have him hold her. She'd never *ever* wanted that before in her life. It just added to her general sense of all-out panic.

She looked up. "You know, this room doesn't seem like a great idea. There's only one door." She started typing.

Gage rolled his shoulders trying to get them down off his ears. This woman was so damn frustrating. "I'm aware, but it's raining again so we can't sleep on the deck. Most areas are starting to empty out of travelers and close up. We don't have a room to go to that won't get us killed, and we need to avoid security. You've played with the ship's systems too much, so if you play with the cameras again, we're bound to get caught. If you have any other suggestions, I'm happy to hear them, but I think we're stuck with here for now."

Dani rolled her eyes. "You don't have to get testy. And I didn't *play* with the ship's cameras. I did what was necessary to save your ass. Besides, they aren't good enough to catch me."

"Really? My ass." He'd had it with her attitude. "Who is it they're trying to find? The only reason the guy in the ice rink didn't see us is because he was lazy. You are not beyond being caught. No one is.

"Eventually, even if the ship's crew doesn't figure out

what's going on, the men chasing you will. I suggest you do *not* access the system again with that thing." He pointed to her laptop. "You'll just be asking to be caught. We only have a few hours left on this ship, and I would like to survive, so why don't you grab some shut-eye instead of playing with your laptop?"

Playing? Is that what he thought she was doing. She imagined steam coming out of her ears. "I am trying to fix the software," she said through clenched teeth.

Gage cracked his knuckles. "Software you stole, which is why we're in this situation to begin with. If you'd built it from scratch like a normal person, then everything would be fine. No one would even know about you or the software. Stealing part of it from the Chinese government, of all places, wasn't the smartest move. It was lazy. But I forgot. You're a hacker. That's what you do. Hack things. The hell with the consequences."

"What would you have me do? Start from day one? Work on a team in a lab? That would take years, and I don't have years. Carly doesn't have years!"

Gage sat down on the couch. "But don't you want more than this? What are you going to do after you're finished with this job?

"Go back to what I do best. Hacking. This was only a contract job. I don't do nine to five. Like ever. *So* not my scene." She shook her head but kept her face averted toward the screen.

"You never want more? You could put your talents to good use. I'm sure—"

"I *am* putting my talents to good use." Her fingers stopped moving and she started hitting the backspace key with serious ferocity. *Damn him.* He was distracting her and she was making mistakes.

"I know you have money, but wouldn't you like to do

something more? You could work for the government. With your talent, you could really help. Cyber security—"

"Let's just get this straight right now. I have *made* all of my money, including the money I gave to Jeremy, *legitimately*. I do not steal money. And I will not be working for any government. I do *not* want to specialize in cyber security. I am perfectly content doing what I do on my own terms, in my own time."

Gage's shoulders stiffened. "But you could make a difference."

Why couldn't he understand? "I do make a difference. In my own way. I'm not interested in working for a government that wants me to 'make a difference' in their way." Her fingers were flying now.

"Wiki Leaks for example, or the group Anonymous. It's a bunch of hackers who pick a wrong in the world that they want to right, and they work on it. Doing what they can to make it better. Or at least it used to be. Now it's different."

She stopped typing and looked up. "Now it's all state sponsored. A government decides who they want to target, and the hackers go after them on social media etcetera, or they do a deep dive and bring out personal stuff about a politician in hopes of influencing elections. Wiki Leaks is a whole different animal now than when it first started. So is Anonymous."

She closed her laptop lid with a distinct click. "I have no interest in being a tool for the government to use whenever they feel like it, for whatever project they deem necessary, only to have it all go to hell when the next government comes in and decides that project isn't valid anymore."

She lifted her laptop and uncurled her legs. "I choose my own work, like this contract with Drake. I still make lots of money, and *I'm not hurting anyone*."

Gage pushed to his feet. "You don't think this software can hurt people?"

"I am creating a software to help Drake find his sister and help me find Carly's mom or another relative. Anything that happens with it after that is up to Drake and his conscience. I'm not responsible for what happens in perpetuity."

Gage snorted. "Passing the buck. Nice."

Dani's eyes narrowed. "Not passing the buck. Being realistic. Is Henry Ford responsible for all the accidents that have happened in a Ford vehicle? Are the Wright Brothers responsible every time an airplane crashes? No. They came up with the idea and made the first one of the items, but what happened to cars and airplanes after that is not up to them. I am making a tool. How the owner of that tool uses it is beyond my scope."

Gage crossed his arms over his chest and grimaced. He sat back down on the arm of the sofa.

Guilt washed over her. It was her fault he was in pain. If he didn't have to protect her, he wouldn't be in this mess. She didn't want him to be hurt. She'd do almost anything to stop that from happening. *Almost* anything. Abandoning the project that she'd worked so hard on, it was out of the question. Carly needed her and she had to come first.

"Still seems like a cop-out to me," Gage growled.

Dani raised an eyebrow. "But if I said I would give it to the FBI, you'd be all for it. Then it would be okay."

"Well, that's different. They are law enforcement. They should have a tool like this."

Dani snorted. "Because, God knows, the government has never misused a tool ever." Dani rolled her eyes. "You think in black and white, but really the world is a bunch of shades of gray. Not every soldier is a good person just because they're a soldier."

She jumped to her feet. "You know one of the biggest

problems the army has at the moment? Gang infiltration. They get trained in combat and take that training back to the gang. Does that mean everyone with combat training is bad?" Dani locked gazes with Gage. "Is that the army's fault?"

Gage ran his hand over his face and then through his hair. "I get what you're saying, but it's hard to reconcile that idea with hackers. If they hadn't broken into the system, Cutter would still be alive. If you or your kind worked for the military and were there when the hack happened, Cutter wouldn't be six feet under.

"Instead, it was *me* racing against the clock to get there, to warn Cutter, and I failed. Cutter died. Other people died as well. Not to mention all kinds of ops were blown because we didn't know how much they knew about the informant.

People like you, hackers, need to step up and do the right thing!" Gage was on his feet now, too. "I know you were in the foster system, so maybe the government is not your favorite thing, but you have the kind of talent that could help stop other governments from influencing our elections and from crashing our systems."

Dani shook her head. "Do I strike you as the type of person that's going to sit in an office and have some boss tell me what I can and can't do? Do you see me dressing in business suits and punching a clock? Does any of this seem like something I would remotely want to be a part of? I'm sorry, have we met?"

"You're wasting your talents." He fisted his hands again. "You could be more than just some hacker. You could be better than—"

Dani's eyes narrowed. "You better be very careful what you say. Better than what? Better than just some no-good black hat? Better than just some two-bit hacker? You still don't get it. I don't want to be 'better.' I'm completely happy the way I am. I don't need your approval or anyone else's. I like who I am, and I live by my own code. I don't need to conform to your rules just to make you feel good."

Dani's body was shaking. She was pushing back hard. Way too hard. She knew he was trying to look out for her in his own way, but it wasn't her way. She had lived by another person's rules before, and she'd vowed never to do that again.

Gage just wasn't getting it. Maybe he never would. She had to do what worked for her no matter how much it cost her. No matter how much she cared about him. If he cared about her, he should understand that.

Gage growled. "Conform to my rules? How about the law? How about conforming to that?" He pointed at her. "You could actually save people's lives by keeping important information safe. Instead, you choose to subvert the law. Why?" He raised his palms upward. "What does it give you other than money? You don't have a code. If you did, you wouldn't be a hacker. You could be doing good on a daily basis."

He was back to pointing again. "You could be shoring up our system, making sure intelligence stays out of our enemy's hands, but instead you tear it down. It's not sustainable. You can't always live like this. You must see that."

"You know what I see?" She was done trying to convince him. Dani moved to stand directly in front of Gage. "I see a man who is lost. Who felt cheated by the system and feels he let down his friend and then got kicked out because he couldn't handle it. You lost your friend, and that sucks. But I'm trying not to lose mine. I won't work in the system because it always lets you down. Suck it up, buttercup! Get over it."

She was pushing him to the breaking point. He would either see it her way and accept her for who she really was, or he would walk away.

CHAPTER TWENTY-THREE

A mask came down over his face. She might as well be yelling at a wall. He wasn't listening. His hands kept fisting and opening again. His shoulders were rigid. He didn't want to hear it. Well, tough shit. The truth sucks sometimes.

"You want everyone to do things your way because you think it's better. Safer. Well, here's reality. It's not better. You're an asshat just like everybody else. Get over yourself. Who died and made you God? You don't get to call the shots."

She could hear his ragged breathing now, but she didn't care. Someone had to tell him the truth, and it might as well be her.

"I absolutely love how you think that if, in your mind, it's all justified, then it's okay. It was okay for me to be a hacker when we needed to hide from the cameras or needed a room to stay in, but it's not okay that I'm a hacker when it comes to stealing the software.

"Your ego is out of control. I'm not some problem that needs fixing. I'm a woman who needs loving, and you obviously are not the man to do that. Too bad because I thought you were different. Stronger." She squared her shoulders. "I'm done here. You can take your sanctimonious crap and shove it. I can take care of myself."

He stared stonily at her, his blue eyes icy. *Like what runs in his veins.* His whole body seemed to be made out of a slab of cold marble.

"Dani," his voice was soft, too soft. She'd expected him to yell at her. It scared her how quiet he was. "You're just another wannabe badass who makes excuses for committing crimes when you really just get off on the thrill of it. You're no different from any other harlot getting paid for services rendered. To hell with the consequences."

Pain filled her chest until drawing a breath was impossible. She'd finally fallen in love, and it was with the worst man for her. It shouldn't have surprised her, but it did. She'd been so careful until now. She swallowed hard. No way was she going to cry in front of the bastard.

"Fuck you, asshole!" She whirled around, grabbed her laptop and jammed it into her backpack. Then she ran out the door. She moved quickly down the hallway, determined to get away from Gage. Not that it mattered, she realized a few steps later. He hadn't bothered to follow her.

Searing pain radiated out across her body, and she gasped. The hallway spun as she stumbled out into the area in front of the elevators. She put her hand out and reached for the wall. She staggered and crashed down, leaning on the wall. Her breathing was labored, and her chest was on fire.

What was wrong with her? Was she shot? Drugged? Her vision was becoming blurred and shrinking. It was all going dark. She pushed up the baseball hat onto her forehead. It was so hot.

"Well there you are, doll. I was hoping I'd run into you again before we docked tomorrow."

She knew the voice, but it was too hard to focus. She felt

a hand on her arm. She wanted to pull her arm away and run but couldn't manage it.

"Breathe, just breathe. Long, slow breaths."

She clung to the voice. She did not want to lose consciousness.

"That's it. Follow the sound of my voice. Deep breath in and then release slowly. And again."

Her vision started to clear. Her chest was no longer on fire. Her heartrate, although still elevated, was not stratospheric. "Wha—what happened?" She tried to focus her eyes. She looked up from under the brim of her ballcap to see Dotti bending over her. Relief flooded her system. "Oh, thank God! Dottie, it's you."

"Yes, doll. Who'd you think it was?"

Dani bit her lip.

"Never mind. It's all good. Now, let's get you up on your feet. Maybe you can help me straighten up. I shouldn't bend over at my age. There's a definite risk I could stay that way." She winked.

Using the wall for support, Dani pushed her way to her feet. Her knees were still a bit wobbly, so she stayed leaning as Dotti used her arm for leverage to straighten herself up.

"What happened?" Dani asked. "I was fine, and then I couldn't seem to move or breathe."

"I'd say you had a panic attack. My niece gets them occasionally. She stayed with me for a bit, so I've seen them up close and personal quite a few times." Dotti peered at her. "You've never had one before?"

"I…" Dani wiped the palms of her hands on her jeans. Her heart was still beating erratically in her chest. She swallowed hard. There was no water in sight, and she'd still had a panic attack. That had never happened before.

"I— It's been…" Her voice petered out. She cleared her

throat and tried again, "I haven't had one until recently. I'd forgotten all about the strength of them."

Dottie hit the elevator button. "Well, something triggered it. You'd better find out what it was, so you won't be caught off guard next time."

"Um, right." Gage had triggered it. Or more accurately, Gage crushing her heart and soul had triggered it. Trust and love. Two things she needed to avoid in the future. She gave Dotti a half-hearted smile. "I'll have to work on it. So, what are you doing up at this hour?"

Dotti laughed. "I'm old. We don't need as much sleep as you young folks do. I was just on my way up. What about you? Why aren't you all tucked up in your cabin with that handsome man I saw you with the other day?"

"Ah, I'm not with—that is, we're not—I'm by myself." Her stomach knotted and her knees trembled.

Dottie gave her the once over. "You okay?"

"Um, sure. Just a passing thing. The panic attack. Much better now."

The elevator door dinged then opened. Dottie put her hand out, blocking the doors. "That's not what I meant, hon. You're looking a little rough, like you haven't had any sleep or a shower in days."

"No. I'm fine. Really," she said as she pulled the ballcap down to shield her face and started backing away. God, what if she smelled? Yuk.

"Huh. Don't think so."

Dani glanced over Dottie's shoulder and saw a security guy coming in their direction. "Ah, I've gotta run."

Dottie turned to look and then swung back to face Dani. "Get in the elevator."

"I—"

"Get in," Dottie said firmly and pointed into the elevator.

The security guard was getting closer. Dani moved around Dottie and went to the back of the elevator. Dottie stepped all the way in, and the doors closed behind her. She was facing Dani. "You're going to come to my room and have a shower and a nap 'til it's time to go. I even have snacks."

"Um—"

"I won't take no for an answer, young lady. You are coming with me. You need a friend at the moment, and I'm it."

Dani bit her lip and then sagged against the elevator wall. Dottie was right. She did need a friend, and if she was being honest, she'd kill for a shower. "Deal." She smiled. "Thanks for rescuing me again."

"That's what fairy godmothers are for!" Dottie said as doors opened.

Dani followed Dottie to her stateroom. She kept the hat pulled low so the cameras wouldn't see her face. When Dottie opened the door, Dani heard a loud, low rumbling. She paused in the doorway.

Dottie saw her standing there and waved her in. "Don't worry. That's just my roomie, Ann."

Dani raised an eyebrow but stepped in and closed the door as quietly as possible.

"You don't have to worry about being quiet, doll," Dottie said in a voice loud enough to make Dani jump. "Ann took out her hearing aids, so you could throw a party in here and she'd never wake up."

"Um, okay."

"Why don't you grab a shower? I'm just going to get ready and crawl in with Ann. You can have the other bed. It's clean. I had them change the sheets this morning. I like clean sheets every day when I'm on vacation because I'm too lazy to do it at home. This is my one chance." She winked again.

"There's some snacks in the bag on the other side of the

room, between the bed and the wall." She grinned. "I wait 'til Ann's asleep and then I turn on the TV and snack away. She'd yell at me if she knew. Lecture me about my health. I know she's right, but it's vacation!" Dottie chuckled.

Dani couldn't help but laugh. "Thanks. I'll grab something if I get hungry."

"The only thing I don't have is clothing that you'd want to wear." She pointed to her clothes. "Old lady stuff, I'm afraid."

Dani grinned. "I don't know… I bet you have some cool clothes hidden somewhere. You seem too hip to have only old lady stuff, but don't worry. I can rinse out my underwear, and my clothes can last one more day."

"I may have a thing or two in my closet." She waggled her eyebrows, and Dani snickered. Then Dottie said, "Oh, and don't worry about waking me. I'm putting in my ear plugs and using my sleep mask." Dottie held up the items, one in each hand. "So I'm good to go." Then she frowned.

"I feel bad I don't have a set for you. Ann's loud." On cue, Ann's snoring reached a fevered pitch. She snorted and then held her breath and rolled over.

"Um, I'll be fine. I can always put the pillow over my head."

Dottie pointed at her. "Good thinking! Okay then, enjoy your shower."

Dani nodded and went into the bathroom, closing the door behind her. There was no way she was going to sleep, so the snoring didn't matter, but it was sure nice to be alone for a few minutes in a safe place. And there was a shower. She leaned over and turned on the hot water. She peeled off her clothes and rinsed out her underwear.

She stepped into the warm spray and let out a groan of relief. Her shoulders slid down from her ears as the water cascaded over her body. She tried to relax and not think, but it was impossible. Gage was gone. Her protector. The man she'd foolishly let in had wanted her to be something she wasn't. He's made it obvious she wasn't good enough. She was all alone again.

Tears crawled up her throat. It was okay to be alone but, damn, it hurt. She'd fallen for Gage. She'd let him in, and now he was gone. She didn't try to stop the tears. It hurt too much. The last few days had left her feeling raw and exhausted. She let her tears carry the hurt and anger down her cheeks and mix with the drops from the shower to flow down the drain.

CHAPTER TWENTY-FOUR

Gage glanced at his watch as he leaned against the wall in the stairwell by the exit door. Dani should be here by now. His stomach knotted to go along with his shoulders. He was stiff from sleeping in a chair. Not that he'd slept after the fight he'd had with Dani.

Jesus. He'd called her a *harlot*. He wasn't even sure where that had come from. She was never going to forgive him. He'd just lost it. Saw red, heard nothing but roaring in his ears and completely lost his shit.

She'd hit every single one of his buttons, and he hadn't been able to control his rage. All those times he'd fought with both his real brothers and his brothers in arms, nothing had compared to the rage Dani had triggered in him. He'd scared her, he was sure. Well, hell, he'd scared himself as well.

He was supposed to be the moderator of the family. The most even-tempered guy who dealt with everyone else's shit. Maybe that was the problem. He'd never dealt with his own shit. Dani had been right for calling him on it, and he'd attacked her in the worst way possible.

He wished with all his heart he could go back and unsay

the horrible words. Or had chased her after he'd been such an ass. But he'd frozen in place. He'd had no idea how long he'd stood there, staring at the empty place where she'd been.

Now he needed to find her. His only job was to protect her, and no matter what had transpired between them, he wasn't going to let his brothers down by failing his part of the Drake contract.

He rolled his shoulders again. He'd give his left testicle for a shower and some clean clothes. He was damn tired of wearing the navy ALASKA T-shirt, and he was pretty sure his jeans could get up and walk away on their own at this point. He hadn't had to wear the same clothes this long since his days in the military.

He shook his head. Worry was eating a hole in his gut. He'd sure as hell like to know where she disappeared to. Job one had been to protect her and he'd blown it spectacularly. Not since he'd failed to save Cutter had he blown an assignment so badly. He ground his teeth and not for the first time, cursed a blue streak in his head.

After he'd come back to his senses, he'd gone through as much of the ship as he could, but finally gave up and sat in a chair on deck that he'd pulled under the eaves so he didn't get wet.

He shifted position against the wall, trying to avoid clocking an elderly lady in the head with his elbow. He hadn't expected so many senior citizens would be so excited to leave the ship. They were jammed in like sardines, and he stood out like a sore thumb.

He glanced around for the umpteenth time looking for Dani, but nothing. She was either blending really well or she wasn't here yet. Jeremy had been specific. They had to be there when the door opened so he could check them off the ship. Dani had her passport in her bag, but Gage's was lost in the state room the bad guys were casing. Jeremy said he'd do his best to get it, but Gage had doubts he could pull it off.

There was a loud bang and some clicking and then people started to move. "Shit. Dani, where are you?" Gage mumbled as he was forced forward in the crush. He'd wait for her outside on the dock, but it would be risky. At least his brothers would be there. That thought was the only thing that kept the panic that was growing in his stomach from coursing through his whole body. Maybe she was stuck somewhere and couldn't get here without seeing the water. Not likely, but possible.

Gage turned the corner and saw Jeremy standing there, saying good-bye to all the guests. He caught Gage's attention and gave his head a slightly negative shake. What did that mean?

Gage took a closer look at Jeremy. There were two men standing beside him. They weren't checking people out. They were surveilling the crowd. *Fuck*. Ship security. They were looking for Gage and Dani.

Gage tried to slow down and shift out of the human tide, but it was too difficult. He was at least a head above the rest of the crowd. There was no hallway to turn down. He couldn't do an about-face and run. He was going to have to hope for the best.

Jeremy glanced his way again. He flicked his eyes to the security guys and then back to Gage. Gage nodded slightly. Jeremy looked around and then back at Gage. He raised an eyebrow. Gage let out a string of mental curses. If Jeremy was looking for Dani, then that meant he hadn't seen her either.

Gage's heart was double-timing in his chest, matching the churn in his gut. He had to make it off the ship and find Dani. He took off his hat and ran a hand through his hair. He put his hat back on and tried to look bored. He uncurled his hands and willed his shoulders to relax.

He had to look like there was nothing wrong. He worked on his bored expression while at the same time watching the distance between him and the doorway grow ever smaller. He took one last look around, but still no Dani.

Suddenly, he was next in line. Jeremy reached out as if to take his exit card and his passport but bent down as if he'd dropped something. "Sorry about that, sir," he said as he stood back up with Gage's passport in one hand and the exit card in the other. He ran them through the system and handed the passport back to Gage. "Here you go. Have a pleasant flight home."

Gage nodded and headed out the door, thanking his lucky stars the two security guys let him go. He had started down the gangplank when a hand landed on his shoulder. "Excuse me, sir. You need to come with us," a voice said into his right ear.

He was tempted to make a run for it. He looked down at the pier. There were two security men coming up the ramp. He looked over and saw there were more security guards on the pier.

"Sir. You have to come with us now, please." The voice was more demanding in his ear and a hand now gripped his arm firmly.

He searched around one last time, hoping to see Dani. Instead, he saw his brothers. Logan and Mitch were walking along the pier in his direction. He was tempted to yell to get their attention, but he didn't want to upset security any more than he already had. At least they were here. He uncurled his fists and relaxed his shoulders before he turned around.

"What seems to be the problem?" Gage asked.

A larger security officer had joined the first two. He was obviously the man in charge as the other two gave way to him. "We need you to come back on the ship, sir. We have some questions we'd like to ask you."

"Of course. No problem." Gage shot one last look over his shoulder but his brothers didn't see him. He ground his teeth. He was stuck. Hopefully his brothers knew what Dani looked like and would keep an eye out for her. If only he knew where she was? What the hell was she thinking?

CHAPTER TWENTY-FIVE

Ann stepped back to admire her work. "You look sensational, if I do say so myself."

"She looks like an old lady. Nothing sensational about that," Dottie retorted from the other side of the cabin.

"That's the entire point!" Ann huffed as she shook her head. "I need to use the restroom." She shot Dottie a look and went over to the bathroom.

Dottie grinned at Dani. "I can't resist winding her up sometimes. But I have to say she did an amazing job. You look just like one of us. Ann was always a whiz at makeup. She worked in the theatre for years. We rely on her to make us all look much younger when we go out to the local dances. I also made her promise to do my makeup for my funeral. I hate how people look so blotchy and..."

"Dead?" Dani asked.

"Yes!" Dottie laughed. "It was also a good thing Elenore brought her fancy wig. Sometimes she doesn't travel with an assortment, but for the cruise, she went all out. I think the dark red suits you."

Dani turned and looked in the mirror. Dark red. More

like deep maroon, but who was she to complain? With the ball cap over the wig and the bright floral muumuu she was wearing, no one was going to notice her lack of wrinkles. The sunglasses, big oversize round ones, would cover most of her face anyway.

She hitched up the muumuu, put her backpack on in front of her, and then pulled the muumuu down over it.

"Not bad," Dottie said. She leaned over and adjusted the backpack a bit. "Hunch over a little bit." Dani did as she was told.

Ann walked out of the bathroom. "Nice touch." She gave a nod of approval. "You'll pass for sure." She walked over and gave Dani's wig one more slight tug. "I'll tell you a secret. No one notices old people. In fact, people stop noticing women when they get in their fifties. People just stop seeing you. It's weird."

"She's not lying," Dottie said as she bent down and pulled her suitcase off the bed. "Once you're not young and cute, no one looks anymore. I could walk in and rob a bank, and all they'd be able to say is an old lady did it."

"I'm sure it's not that bad—"

"You're wrong." Dottie shook her head. "Younger people everywhere are conditioned to think that an old person equals no danger. Especially old biddies like us."

Ann gave her hair one last quick brush in the mirror. "But that's not necessarily a bad thing," she said and winked at Dani. "There are a great many things we can get away with because of it." She turned and glared at Dottie. "Bank robbery is not among them."

"Spoilsport," Dottie mumbled under her breath.

Dani laughed. She'd been laughing a lot this morning. These ladies were great fun. When she'd asked Dottie to help her get off the boat without being seen, she'd had no idea what a hoot it would be. Dottie had enlisted a whole crew of women to help. Many wigs and muumuus later, they finally had the look. Now she just had to pull it off.

There was a knock at the door. "That must be Elenore and the girls." Ann walked over and opened the door. The "girls" were all there in the hallway. There were too many to count and not one under the age of seventy. "We picked up a few more recruits," said Elenore. "You girls ready?"

Dotti pulled the handle of her small wheelie bag and started for the door. "All set." She moved into the hallway and turned. "What do you think?"

The ladies all studied Dani from head to toe. She made sure to slouch forward so she looked like she had a rounded back.

Elenore clapped her hands. "Well done. She looks like my neighbor's sister, Eugenia. She's going to blend right in."

There were murmurs of assent from the others. "It's the wig that does it, I think," said Dottie. Elenore beamed. "Okay, girls. Does everyone remember what to do?"

There was a chorus of "yeses" and a few thumbs-up. Dani mentally crossed her fingers that this would work. There was no other way off the ship without passing security, or at least none that she could use. And she wasn't about to find Gage to ask him for help. He'd made himself damn clear on how he felt about Dani. Her heart kicked viciously. She swallowed the tears that had instantly blocked her throat. She wasn't going to think about it or him. Gage was the past, and it was done.

"Lead the way, ladies. And in case I don't get a chance to tell you later, thanks for the help."

The women moved en masse down the hallway to the elevator. One arrived in record time, and they all piled on. Dottie leaned over and whispered in Dani's ear. "You're going to be alright. You're a survivor. Remember that." Then she winked.

Dani swallowed hard again. Before this trip, she couldn't remember the last time tears had run down her face. Now she seemed to be crying every day. She needed to knock it off because tears would ruin Ann's incredible makeup job, not to mention she'd look like she was straight from a horror film.

The doors opened, and they merged with the throng of people heading toward the exit. The girls shuffled around so Dani was in the middle of them, protected on all sides. She had to grin. Protected by the granny brigade. Whatever worked.

They moved slowly down the hall to the wide staircase. As they started down, there was a commotion. Dani glanced to see what the holdup was. Her heart started thumping in her chest, and she rubbed her palms on her muumuu. She did not want to get caught. Not when she was so close to freedom. She craned her neck to see over the crowd and saw Gage being escorted upstairs, flanked by three security guards. She bit her lip and quickly looked down.

Sweat started running between her shoulder blades. She wiped her palms again. She tilted her head so she could see him out of the corner of her eye. Gage passed by her not two feet away and didn't give her a second glance. Her heart pounded against her ribcage. It was on the tip of her tongue to call his name, but what good would it do? Then they would both be caught. No, she needed to go so she could finish the program and see Carly. She needed to know Carly was okay.

Gage would figure a way out. He always seemed to think of something. *With her help*. Ridiculous. He'd gotten this far without her. He didn't need her help now.

She looked up again after Gage was long gone. She and the "girls" were almost at the door. She caught a glimpse of the pier and tried not to think about being close to the water again once she was out.

Jeremy was there, but his smile wasn't so big. He must have seen the whole Gage thing and now was freaking out. He had to be wondering if he was going to get caught, too. She felt badly for him. He was really going to wish he'd been assigned another cruise.

Jeremy turned to Dottie. "Your card and your passport please."

Dottie slowly pulled her passport out of her purse and handed it to Jeremy. "Here you go," she said loudly.

"Um, I need the little card with the number on it as well. It lets us know you're off the ship."

Dottie frowned. "I don't remember a little card. Do you know about the card, Ann?" She was practically yelling at this point. Ann had her hearing aid in, but the ladies thought it would be better if they pretended they couldn't hear.

"I have mine, dear. Where did you put yours?" Ann yelled back.

Dottie shrugged. "I don't know."

"Did you put it in your bag?" yelled Elenore.

Dottie looked down at her wheelie bag. "Maybe I put it in my bag." When she started to lean over to unzip it, Elenore grabbed her arm, making it appear as if Dottie was unstable.

Jeremy looked at the other crew member with panic on his face. The line behind the ladies was growing, and there was a rumble of dissatisfaction building. "Um, ladies, maybe you can step to the side so you don't block the doorway." Jeremy gestured to his left to try to move Dottie.

Dottie completely ignored him and unzipped her bag. Underwear immediately started falling out. Very large, colorful underwear. One pair was white with pink lips all over it. The underwear plopped on the floor directly in front of the door. "Well, now look what you made me do!" she scolded Jeremy. She rooted around in the bag while still leaning on Elenore.

"What am I looking for again?" she yelled at Ann.

"The fob thing with the number on it."

Dottie nodded and rooted around some more. The crowd was getting more restless. When Ann nudged one of their gang she started to complain loudly about the holdup.

The one next to Dani yelled out, "Are we going to be stuck here much longer? I'm going to miss my bus to the airport." There were calls of agreement from the crowd. A young man and his partner came out of nowhere and tried to push past the girls, causing them all to sway to one side. Dottie almost toppled over for real this time.

Jeremy was in full panic mode. "Okay, ladies. That's okay. Why don't you just close the bag. We can check you out using your passport." He bent down to help Dottie put her underwear back in her bag, but he stopped short. It was obvious he didn't want to touch it.

This was Dani's cue. She clamped her jaw shut. *Don't look at the water.* She moved around Ann and helped Dottie to put it all back in the bag and then zipped it up. Dottie took her passport back from Jeremy and latched onto Dani's arm for balance, and they walked down the gangplank together. Dani's heartrate was stratospheric, but no one stopped them. No one even noticed her. It was awesome! Ann was right. There were benefits to being ignored.

"That was wonderful. You were incredible, Dottie," Dani whispered.

"Ah, shucks, doll. Thanks. It was marvelous fun. I haven't enjoyed myself like that since I lifted Mike Pritchard's wallet at the Christmas party."

Dottie gave Dani a wink. "He deserved it. He complains about the snacks every year but won't donate to the party fund. He said he is an atheist, so he doesn't have to. Ann and I helped him make a small donation. That's all. He never noticed. Thought he lost more at poker than he realized." She winked again. "Sometimes life is fun."

Dani grinned. *Sometimes life was fun.* She looked up and saw three Asian men with lots of tattoos moving past them toward the very end of the pier by the water. They went and stood next to some crew members from the ship.

And sometimes life wasn't. The smile was long gone off her face. She wanted to get out of there as quickly as possible. Those men were probably looking for her, and she did not want to tempt fate by hanging around.

They quickly made their way over to one of the customs' tents that were set up in a long row along the side of the pier. They had to cross through the tents to get out onto the rest of the pier.

"Oh my God. Your face!" Ann said while blinking furiously.

"What? What's wrong with it?" Dani asked.

"She means the make-up, doll," Dottie said. "How are you going to go through customs looking like one of us? You sure don't match your passport picture now."

Ann moaned, "We didn't think about that part."

Dani raised a hand to touch her face and promptly dropped it. If she had the time and the materials she was pretty sure she could fake a decent passport but she had neither. There was only two people ahead of her in line.

"You could take everything off. Then you'd match the picture," Ann offered.

"Yes," Dottie agreed. "I'm sure they would only hold you in customs for a few hours or maybe a few days. That wouldn't be suspicious at all."

Ann glared at Dottie and smacked her gently on the arm. "You're not helping."

Dottie chortled. "No. Probably not." She sighed. "I'm sorry Dani. I'm all out of ideas."

Dani looked at both women and then looked at the man waiting at the table in front of her. It was her turn. "I guess I'll just have to tell the truth."

"Passport," the customs officer said, lifting his hand as Dani approached. He was older, probably in his fifties with silver hair and kindly brown eyes. His name tag read B. Walsh.

"Here you go." Dani handed over her passport. She smiled and took off her sunglasses.

Officer Walsh took it and opened it to the picture page. He glanced at the photo and then did a double take. He looked at the photo and then held the passport up next to Dani's face. His kindly brown eyes turned piercing. A small frisson of fear snaked down her spine.

"You don't look like your photo at all. Are you sure this is yours? Do you have other ID?"

Dani fished her wallet out from her jeans underneath her muumuu. The customs officer's eyebrow went up and then immediately dropped into a frown when he saw her driver's license photo.

"You're going—"

"I can explain," Dani said in a rush. She said a silent prayer and launched into her story. "You see there was this guy onboard and he wouldn't leave me alone." *It was the truth.* Gage wouldn't leave her alone. At least until she'd taken off on him.

"I didn't want to get him in trouble because he seemed really nice. So, I didn't report him to security, but I wanted to avoid him today. He wanted to take me around, show me the sites and I just didn't have the heart to be mean." *Yeah, right. Liar liar, pants on fire.*

"The ladies"—she pointed behind her and the officer

looked over her head. Dottie, Ann, and the rest of the ladies all waved—"took me in and helped me with my disguise. Ann's a former theatrical make-up artist and the others lent me clothing and a wig." She reached up and moved the wig so the officer could see a bit of her real hair.

"I swear officer I really am just trying to avoid this guy." Dani blinked and tried to look as small and defenseless as possible.

"Uh huh."

"Problem, Bruce?" Another officer came to stand beside the first. His name tag read T. O'Reilly.

"This young lady is giving me some song and dance about trying to ditch some guy by dressing as," he glanced at the 'girls' again, "an older lady. Apparently, the ladies over there helped her."

"I see." Officer O'Reilly looked over at Dottie and the rest of the ladies. They all waved at him. He gave Dani a once over. His pale blue eyes were like chips of ice. "I think you should make them all step out of line while we look into this."

Shit. This was bad. She'd been doing her best to not look at the men at the end of the pier, afraid her anxiety would show on her face. The last thing she needed was to get into some long battle with Canadian customs. Who knew what would happen? She'd never see Carly at this rate.

She looked up at Officer Walsh and silently pleaded with him. He studied her, his face impassive. Then he glanced at his watch and back over her head. He turned to his computer and typed something. Officer O'Reilly stood beside him, reading over his shoulder. Time ticked so slowly. Sweat trickled down Dani's back and front. Her backpack was hurting her chest.

Officer Walsh turned back to face Dani. He studied her

once again. Then he grabbed his stamp and stamped her passport. He handed it back to her. "Welcome to Canada."

"I... I— Thanks," she stammered as she took her passport and then stepped out around the table and through to the pier. He'd let her go. OMG! She was free. Finally something had gone right. She stood directly next to the exit to wait for Dottie and the 'girls.'

"Why'd you let her go?" she heard O'Reilly ask. "You should have questioned her. She could be smuggling something."

"Yes. She could. And the same could be said for everyone on this cruise ship from Alaska. But her record is clear. It's not against the law to wear a wig and some make up. It's coming up to break time. As soon as I'm done here, I'm going to Tim Horton's and getting a nice cup of coffee and then going back to sit at my desk and spend the rest of the day doing paperwork."

She heard the *thunk* of the stamp. "Now, if you want to question the rest of the ladies that were with her, be my guest. However, think about how long that will take you, how much paperwork that will generate and how much chatter you will have to listen to from those ladies and ask yourself if it's worth it to you."

There was a long pause. Dani held her breath. She heard O'Reilly's voice. "You know, Tim Horton's sounds good."

Just then Dottie walked through the back of the tent with a big grin on her face. "Yes!"

Dani reached out and hugged her. It was so spontaneous she didn't even have time to think about what she was doing. Dottie hugged her back. Dani needed to get herself back under control but she would savor this small moment of joy.

The rest of the ladies trickled out of the tent.

Dani turned her back to the ship and the water. In front of her was a long white multi-story building shaped like a ship. It had a series of what looked like garage doors about thirty feet apart, and they were all open. The inside appeared to be some sort of museum. "Where is the bus to the airport?"

Dottie pointed toward the street.

Dani nodded. "Okay, that's where I'm going. What about you?"

"I'm taking a tour of the city with the girls. Our flight isn't until tonight." She turned around and waved toward the girls. They hurried along the pier and caught up to Dani and Dottie.

Ann burst out, "That was fun!" There were murmurs of agreement from the others as well.

Dani smiled. "I don't know how to thank you ladies."

"It was our pleasure," Ann said. Then she turned. "Do you mind if we go to the bathroom before we find our bus, girls?" She pointed inside the building. "I want to make sure I don't have to hop off the bus in search of a bathroom later."

"Sounds like a smart idea," Dottie agreed. "Off we go." The ladies headed across the pier and inside the building."

"Wait," Dani said, "What about your wig and your muumuu?"

Elenore looked torn.

"I gave you my address last night. Mail them to me," Dottie yelled and waved. Elenore nodded, and the two of them picked up speed, catching up with the others.

Dani looked around. A wave of loneliness crashed over her unexpectedly. She used to prefer to be alone. Well, except for Carly. Her mind flicked to a picture of Gage, and she swallowed hard again. She'd just have to get used to being alone again. He'd made his choice, and so had she.

CHAPTER TWENTY-SIX

Keeping her head turned toward the building, Dani walked in the direction Dottie had pointed. There was a turn in the dock ahead blocking her view of the street. She took a quick peek back over her shoulder and saw two men lounging on this side of the customs tents across from the gangplank. They had to be Gage's brothers. They were just as he described them earlier.

A kaleidoscope of butterflies took flight in her stomach as she adjusted her sunglasses. She was glad she was still disguised. She had no interest in meeting up and explaining herself to Gage's brothers, but guilt cramped her belly. She wanted them to know he was inside with ship security so they could help him.

She wandered over and stood next to one of the open doorways of the building, right by the turn in the pier. *Forget him. Get on the bus.* He had been clear where he stood. It didn't matter how she felt about him. She knew exactly how he felt about her. He'd called her a harlot. That hurt like she'd been stung by a thousand wasps at once. She'd been called all kinds of things, but nothing had left her ever feeling so stunned and in pain. She owed him nothing.

She should just keep walking. Round the turn and forget everything. She watched Gage's brothers. They were worried. Logan was on the phone and Mitch was looking up and down the pier. Logan put his phone in his pocket and shook his head.

Dani's lip stung when she bit down, undecided. She should email them or call them or something to let them know Gage was stopped by security. Indecision gripped her insides. She shouldn't care, but she did. Gage's brothers weren't the only ones who were worried. He should have been out by now.

She grabbed the phone Gage had given her out of the pocket of the muumuu and sent off a text to Janet.

Tell Logan and Mitch that Gage was taken by ship's security. They need to track him down onboard.

She didn't want direct contact with the guys because then they would have her number and she didn't want to ditch this phone without another one to replace it.

She leaned on the doorway with her back. People moved in every direction in front of her. Many going in and out of the building, but the majority of the crowd was heading toward the street. She saw Dottie and the "girls" in line for the restroom.

Her phone dinged, signaling she'd gotten a text.

Where are you? Are you still on the ship? I thought you all were leaving together.

Dani's fingers flew across the small screen. *No. Change of plans. Tell Logan and Mitch they need to look for their brother. He's still on the ship.* She bit her lip while she waited for a response. Finally her screen lit up.

Where are you? How do you know what's going on with Gage if you're not with him?

Dani let out a groan of frustration.

On the pier. Just tell them!

Dani waited. Logan looked down at his phone. Thank God. Janet had sent the text.

She searched for the tattooed men. The three of them were still at the "bow" end of the pier. One of them seemed to be talking on a cell phone. Then they started to move. They were walking back down the pier toward the gang-plank. Toward Gage's brothers.

"No," she mumbled. Logan and Mitch didn't seem to be paying attention. They were looking at the ship.

"Turn around," she begged under her breath. Her heart hammered in her chest. Why weren't they turning around? Mitch and Logan had to know they were in trouble. The Asian men were walking directly toward them.

Dani ripped off her sunglasses and fired off another text to Janet, asking her to warn the brothers. She watched and waited, hoping to see Logan get another text, but nothing. She bit her lip. She couldn't let this happen. She didn't want anyone to get hurt because of her.

Dani was still standing in the doorway. She was at least a ship's length from the guys. She could yell, but they wouldn't hear her. Even if they did, who was she to them? She wasn't sure Gage gave them her picture or anything, and she was still in the disguise.

She made up her mind. She went into the building and started walking along the inside aisle that ran parallel to the pier, keeping her eye on Gage's brothers through every doorway.

She glanced back and caught Dottie's eye. Dottie waved but must have seen something in the way Dani was moving because she dropped her hand and then brought out her phone.

Dani got a text.

Everything okay, doll?

No. The Asian men are back, and I think they are going to hurt Gage's brothers.

Dani stopped texting and started to jog up the aisle. She came to the last doorway where she was directly across from Logan and Mitch.

She stumbled sideways, tripping on the muumuu again. She slapped her hand on the doorjamb to catch herself but caught a bunch of hair from the wig as well. It went sideways on her head. Swearing up a storm, she righted it as quickly as she could.

One of the Asian men was looking in her direction and nudged the others. They all shifted slightly so they were heading directly for her instead of Logan and Mitch. They were maybe thirty yards away from her. They'd definitely recognized her. They'd seen the wig debacle for sure.

She looked around. There were a lot less people at this end. Everyone was heading toward the bathrooms or the street. No one was close enough to offer assistance even if she asked for it.

The situation she'd been trying to avoid was playing out in slow motion before her. She wanted to be done with Gage and his brothers, but she'd wanted to warn them. Now she needed *their* help. She started waving her arms frantically.

The tattooed men started to run toward her.

The taller one of Gage's brothers, Logan from Gage's earlier description, looked up at Dani. His brows went down, and he frowned. The blondish one, Mitch, turned to see what was going on. His expression immediately changed. He must have put two and two together because he hit Logan and started racing in her direction.

He and Logan were only steps away when one of the tattooed men yelled and tried to grab her. Mitch punched the tattooed guy in the kidney, dropping him to one knee.

Mitch then positioned himself in front of her, and Logan followed suit. Dani was left facing the ship with a wall of Callahan men directly between her and the bad guys.

The other two tattooed men came to an abrupt halt a few feet away. "Give us the software."

"Not a chance in hell," a voice said over Dani's left shoulder. She turned to look. Gage strode up the aisle, brushed by her, and came to stand, shoulder to shoulder with his brothers in front of her. Dani's knees went weak. Gage was fine. The air rushed out of her lungs. It was like she'd been holding her breath for hours.

Then a wave of nausea washed over her as she saw the water off to the right. She backed up into the building. There was a yell from down the aisle but it was just a kid. Dani was tempted to run, but who knew how many more bad guys were around the bend in the pier?

She couldn't see what was going on and she didn't want to be next to the water, but there was no way she was getting by. The Callahan men were doing their job and protecting her. They weren't going to let her be exposed.

She moved slightly to the side to get a better view. Sweat immediately broke out on her palms. Two of the men had guns out, pointing the wicked looking barrels at Gage. The tallest of the men, who was wearing a black T-shirt and jeans, demanded, "Give us the software and the programmer." The "or we'll shoot," part was very clear. He seemed to be the leader. He was flanked by the two gunmen.

One of the gunmen kept his gun low but waved it around a bit. He was wearing jeans with work boots and a tight-fitting white T-shirt. His long black hair was pulled back in a ponytail. He was the one Mitch hit. A mixture of pain and rage warred on his face.

Dani would have thought of the gunman as good looking in any normal circumstance, but this was so far beyond normal—even her normal which was borderline crazy for anyone else.

Did he think they didn't notice his gun? Dani wiped her palms on her muumuu and tried very hard not to hyperventilate. She needed to go with the men. She didn't want anyone to get hurt.

She must have made a small sound because Logan, who was standing in the middle with Gage on his right and Mitch on his left, turned slightly and shook his head once.

"You gentlemen need better manners," Mitch said. "We're visitors to this country, and you aren't being very friendly."

Oh my God. What was he doing? How could he antagonize them? He'd already punched the one with the ponytail. Dani wanted desperately to tell him to shut the hell up, but her voice locked in her throat. Her hands shook as she held on to her backpack through the muumuu. She didn't want to give the men her laptop. Carly needed it, but she wouldn't get anyone killed over it either.

"Excuse me. We're lost. Do you think you can help us find the bus for the city tour?" Dottie's voice floated over the men. She'd come up the outside of the building and was now standing directly behind the men.

Dani had forgotten she'd texted Dottie, and she'd been so engrossed in the men with the guns she hadn't noticed the gaggle of ladies approaching.

"No," she whispered. She'd wanted to shout it, but her voice was not working. She swallowed and tried again. "Dottie, no," but it was too late. The ponytailed gunman turned around to face the ladies.

"Oh, my God! He's got a gun!" Ann exclaimed. Her eyes were the size of golf balls. Elenore, who was standing immediately to Ann's left, shrieked and stumbled back a few steps.

Dottie swore a blue streak and then hit Ponytail in the

arm with her carryon bag. He staggered back under the assault and came within arm's reach of Gage. It was all Gage needed. He reached out and grabbed the guy, wrapping his left arm around the gunman's neck. He grabbed the arm with the gun and slammed it against the doorframe.

It made a horrible thunk, but the man dropped the gun. It went under a display case.

"Yay!" Dottie whooped but her joy was short-lived as the second thug grabbed her and put the gun up to her head.

Gage immediately stopped struggling with the first gunman.

"Let him go," the tall guy demanded.

Gage released Ponytail with a shove. Ponytail stumbled but righted himself and turned back around.

The leader said, "Now give us the software and the programmer, or we'll kill the old lady."

Dottie's eyes were big, and for the first time, there was fear in them. Dani whirled around, frantic to call for help but their end of the building was empty and there was no security in sight.

"Like I said, no way in hell. Let the lady go." Gage wasn't giving an inch.

Logan spoke up, "Ladies, please step away from these men." He gestured toward Ann and Elenore and pointed them to the next doorway over. "We wouldn't want any of you to get hurt."

Dani wasn't going to let Dottie get hurt either. Not instead of her. This was her mess. No one else was going to be put in the crosshairs.

"Move," she demanded, but the Callahan brothers ignored her.

Dani saw out of the corner of her eye a phalanx of security officers coming down the aisle toward them. She turned back. "Security is coming," she said quietly so that only the brothers could hear her.

The tattooed men must have amazing hearing because they glanced at each other. The leader shrugged slightly. "An exchange. The old lady for the software and the programmer. We'll be in touch." They started backing up away from the doorway.

Gage threw them a cell phone. "Don't wait too long."

"Otherwise we'll miss you!" Mitch piped up.

The gunmen each took one of Dottie's arms and held her tightly as they walked down the pier while their leader strolled along behind them. They disappeared around the bend in the wharf.

Dani watched them go. "Can't you go after them? They're taking Dottie!"

"If we chase them, there's a chance that when they get close to their vehicle, they'll shoot Dottie or someone else. We don't want to take that risk." It was Mitch who spoke.

Dani protested. "But—"

"Is there a problem here?"

Dani turned to see the security officers standing behind her. "Ummm—"

Logan came to stand at Dani's elbow. "No, sir. We're just collecting our friends and leaving." He put his arm around Dani and walked her out the doorway onto the pier. Gage and Mitch fell in beside them.

Dani's knees were wobbly. She stumbled, but Logan caught her. He moved his arm from her shoulders to her waist and kept it there. Gratitude swept through her. She couldn't have handled being near Gage at the moment, but she couldn't walk on her own.

"What about the girls?" She gestured toward Ann and Elenore who looked so pale they might pass out.

"Don't worry, Mitch will get them."

As Logan spoke, Mitch moved over and put an arm around each woman. He brought them in close and started chatting with them. She couldn't hear what he was saying, but Ann leaned into Mitch.

She closed her eyes. What a mess Dani had made. All she'd wanted to do was help Carly, but now she'd put the people who'd helped her in danger.

CHAPTER TWENTY-SEVEN

They pulled up in front of a hotel, and the doorman rushed out to the SUV. He opened the door for Dani and the other women, then reached in and tried to help Dani out of the truck. She paused, blinking. *What was this guy's deal?* Then she remembered the disguise. She even had her sunglasses on. She hadn't wanted the other ladies to see her cry on the ride over. She just kept seeing Dottie's big eyes full of fear. She sniffed as she got out of the SUV.

"Sorry for not being able to get closer to the sidewalk. The construction makes it difficult." The doorman smiled apologetically.

Scaffolding were covering the front of the hotel and construction machinery created an obstacle course of sorts. "Not a problem," she said quietly as she moved toward the sidewalk.

The doorman waved over a couple of bellmen. One came up beside her.

"That's okay. I—"

"No arguing. We don't want you to have an incident in the middle of the street." He took her arm and started guiding her toward the sidewalk, but a skateboarder zoomed by just in front of them.

"Ahhh," Dani yelled and jumped. She'd had her head down so she hadn't seen him coming.

"Damn kids," the bellman said. "Such a menace."

The kid went up the ramp just to their left and made a jump. The ramp was part of the construction to help workers get wheelbarrows over a load of gravel in the street to load it onto the scaffolding. The kid arced over the gravel and landed down the street. It was a good jump. The kid had skills.

"Here you are." The bellman deposited her on the sidewalk and then went back to get the luggage out of the truck. She saw her bag. Gage must have sorted stuff out with the cruise line. She looked down at the muumuu she wore and grimaced. It would be nice to have her own clothes again.

Another doorman held open the door and ushered her, Elenore, and Ann inside. She walked into the lobby and stopped dead.

The lobby was done in a white marble with cream and brown furniture. A long fireplace dominated one wall, a few people sitting in front of it. The shops were all upscale boutique places that carried high-end clothing and jewelry.

The woman at the reception desk smiled at her and, automatically, Dani smiled back. The hotel was part of the five-star hotel chain called the Jasmine Door, which was owned by Jameson Drake. The initials JD were everywhere. It screamed opulence.

Logan approached the desk and spoke with a female receptionist. A moment later, she handed him two keys. He nodded and came over to Dani.

"Right this way, ladies." He gestured toward the elevators. Ann and Elenore, who were standing beside Dani, started moving. Neither woman had said much since the scene at the pier. Dani couldn't blame them. What was there to say? She'd gotten one their best friends into a life and death situation. It wasn't exactly time for small talk.

Mitch came in between the two elderly ladies and offered each an elbow. That elicited a small smile from Elenore and a slight nod from Ann. He walked them into the elevator.

Logan had the ladies' luggage, including Dottie's, and he followed them. He hit the button and the doors closed.

"We'll take this one," Gage said and gestured at the empty car next door.

Dani nodded and walked in. Gage followed with their luggage. The doors closed. Gage reached over and hit the button for the twenty-fifth floor.

Dani took a deep breath. Her heart slammed against her ribcage as she stood staring straight ahead. She didn't need a lecture from Gage on how her irresponsible behavior and poor career choice had put Dottie in danger. She already knew that. He could say "I told you so" all he wanted and she wouldn't argue with him.

Gage cleared his throat.

While she might not have deserved his vicious attack before, she certainly deserved it now. She braced herself for the onslaught.

"It's not your fault." Gage's voice was low and gravelly.

"Wha-what?" Dani blinked and turned toward him.

"I said it's not your fault. You didn't get Dottie kidnapped."

Tears welled up, and Dani did her best to blink them back, but one slipped free and slowly ran down her cheek. "Yes, I did," she mumbled.

"No. You didn't. Ponytail and the others were never going to shoot us on the pier. They couldn't get away, no matter how fast they were. They were always going to take someone. They just wanted it to be you. We weren't going to let that happen. They would've taken one of us if Dottie hadn't stepped in."

"But it was my fault she was there. I texted her there was trouble, and she came to help. If I hadn't texted her, none of this would be happening."

The elevator dinged. Dani quickly took off the sunglasses and patted her face with the sleeve of her muumuu. She didn't want to smear all the makeup Ann had spent so much time applying to her face. *Not that it mattered now.* She saw Gage's frowning reflection on the elevator doors just before they opened.

They disembarked and turned left down the hallway. Logan, Mitch, and the ladies were only a few steps ahead.

"Ladies, this is your room." Mitch opened the door with a flourish.

Ann and Elenore entered, murmuring appreciatively. Mitch followed them with their luggage.

"This is your room," Gage said as he opened the door directly across from Ann and Elenore.

Dani slid by him into the room. The "girls" were right. It was gorgeous. There were floor to ceiling windows that had a beautiful city view on the opposite wall from the door. A king-size bed was located in the middle of the right wall with a doorway to what must be a bathroom.

There was a blue suede sofa on the remaining wall to her left. It was filled with fluffy cushions, and it had a coffee table directly in front of it with a small chair angled next to it. The carpet was a deep cream-colored shag, the same shade as the duvet on the bed. A blue throw across one corner of the bed matched blue lamps on the bedside tables positioned on either side of the bed.

Gage closed the door and then smiled slightly. "Nice view."

Dani nodded. Finally, a view that didn't include water.

She walked over by the sofa and dropped her sunglasses on the coffee table. There was a knock on the door.

Gage turned around and looked through the peephole. He opened the door to admit his brothers.

"Hey," Logan said as he entered, followed by Mitch who was close on his heels. The brothers walked around Dani. Logan sat on the far end of the sofa and Mitch plunked down on the chair. Gage moved over to stand next to the coffee table, closer to Mitch's end.

"I gotta say, your disguise is amazing," Mitch said. "No wonder you got off the ship with no one noticing."

Logan nodded. "It's very well done. Come and sit." He gestured to Dani.

"Ann is a former theatrical makeup artist. She did a great job. I really do look like an old lady. Except for my hands." Dani moved around the coffee table and was about to sit but then thought better of it. She reached up and pulled off the wig then tugged the muumuu over her head.

"Jesus," Mitch mumbled. "Did you wear this all day?"

Dani just nodded and bit her lip as she slipped her backpack off. Her back was killing her. She collapsed on the sofa.

"Do you want water?" Logan asked.

Dani nodded. Gage walked over and grabbed a couple of bottles off the nightstand. He came back and gave her a bottle and then offered one to Mitch, who declined.

"So," Gage said. "What are we going to do to get Dottie back?"

CHAPTER TWENTY-EIGHT

Gage winced as he sat on the floor of the hotel room. He'd pulled something in his back when he'd grabbed Ponytail guy earlier.

"What do you know about the Triads?" Logan asked Gage and Dani.

Mitch was across the room on the hotel phone.

Dani blinked as she took another sip of water. "Um, they're organized crime from Hong Kong and Macao. They've branched out all over the world. Why?"

Mitch hung up and announced, "Food's on the way." He came back over and sat in the chair. "I spoke with Ann and ordered some things for the ladies as well."

Dani nodded to him. Under normal circumstances, Dani would be starving, but if Gage had to guess, he'd bet she was anything but hungry.

He knew he was staring, but he couldn't take his eyes off her. He'd been scared out of his mind when he'd seen the tattooed guys facing off with his brothers on the pier. He figured that the little old lady behind them had to be Dani but it had taken him a minute. Mitch was right, the disguise was a work of art. Thank God his brothers had been close. He wouldn't ever have been able to forgive himself if something had happened to Dani.

She looked pale to him, but it was hard to tell under all the makeup. He'd wanted so badly to wrap his arms around her in the elevator. She was taking all of this on as her fault. It wasn't. It was his for overreacting last night. For being an asshat. He'd find a way to make it all up to her. Everything. After they got Dottie back.

Logan turned back to Dani. "Have you ever had any dealings with them?"

Dani hesitated. "That's sort of a hard question to answer."

"Try," Logan growled.

When Dani shot him a frown, Gage caught Logan's gaze and shook his head slightly. Dani wouldn't respond well to being yelled at. *He oughta know.*

"It's not that simple." Dani licked her lips. "In the past, I did collaborate with some other hackers. I didn't ask who the clients were. I got paid by crypto currency. So I can't say for sure one way or the other. In the last couple of years, no, I have had no contact with the Triads."

Mitch blew out a breath. "We discovered they are the ones who are after you. Not the Chinese government. The Triads have Dottie."

"The Triads? Why are they involved? How did they find out about the project?"

"The pictures you sent of the guys from the cruise ship, they are Triad members," Logan said. "I called some FBI friends and asked them to run the pictures through NCIC. Turns out they're wanted in California and over in Hong Kong. If we can figure out how they found out about the software, we might be able to figure out the bigger picture."

"Bigger picture?" Dani asked.

Mitch nodded. "Someone has been after Drake for

months, first trying to buy the software and then trying to steal it. But other things have been happening, too. Some of his business deals are falling through, and some of his sites have been sabotaged. We think it's all connected. The sabotage started before the push for the software."

Mitch ran a hand through his hair and winced. He took his hand down and looked at his knuckles.

"Did you hurt your hand when you punched Ponytail?" Dani asked

"Not much. Just scraped my knuckles a bit." He winked then asked, "So was it just by chance the software came into it, or was that the target all along? Did they even know about the software in the beginning?"

Logan piped up, "Our people back in New York are working on sorting it, and they are making some progress, but not enough."

"The mole," Gage stated. "My guess is the mole told the Triads about the software."

Logan raised his eyebrow. "What makes you think so?"

Gage shrugged. "Word wasn't on the street about the software a few months ago. In fact, there's still only a handful of people who know about it."

Dani nodded. "That's right. When Drake first came to me with the idea for the software, he hadn't told anyone else. There was no paperwork. Nothing. He'd put the word out that he needed a hacker to build some software, but he didn't offer any details. A go-between I use sometimes mentioned the job to me. Said he thought it would be challenging and I could make a lot of money but even he didn't have details. Just a vague mention of it having something to do with facial recognition. I didn't get more until I spoke directly to Drake. So there is no way the Triads knew about the project at that point unless Drake told them."

Logan nodded slowly. "I see where you're going with this."

"Right. Once I agreed and managed to get the base code for it, I contacted Drake and told him what I would need. That's when others were brought in to help gather the necessities. We're talking early spring here. Maybe four months ago. When did the sabotage start?"

Mitch took a swig of water and swallowed. "Beginning of the year. It was already well underway by the time we were brought on."

There was a knock at the door. All three men jumped up and moved toward the door. Mitch grabbed a vase from a side table and nodded at Gage. "Who is it?"

"Room Service."

Gage looked through the peephole and nodded at Mitch. Logan stood to one side. Gage stepped back and opened the door. Mitch moved out from behind the door but leaned on the wall gripping the vase down by his side. The room service attendant rolled the cart into the room.

"Where would you like it?" he asked.

Logan stepped forward. "You can just leave it like that. We'll take care of it." He signed and handed the guy a tip.

The waiter smiled "Are you sure you don't want help setting up?"

"Yes. We're good. Thanks."

The waiter gave a little bow and left. Gage closed the door after him and came back and sat down.

Mitch dropped the vase softly on the carpet and then moved over to the food-laden cart. "What about the food? I'm starving."

"You're always hungry. It will keep for another few minutes." Logan gestured toward the chair Mitch had vacated. "Have a seat."

Mitch grabbed a roll and grumbled on his way over to

the chair. Gage smiled at his brother and sat back down on the floor.

"You were saying?" Logan looked at Gage.

Dani cut in. "What's with the vase?"

Mitch grinned. "Since we can't bring guns into the country we have to make do with whatever's on hand."

"Right," Dani said and shook her head.

Gage piped up. "As I was saying, it has to be the mole. The mole found out about the software and told the Triads. They went from sabotage to trying to get the software. It would make sense for them to want a copy, for sure."

No one said anything as he took a sip of water. He continued, "If I had to guess, I would say they were trying to sabotage Drake's stuff because they want a way in. Think about it. Drake has hotels all over the world just like this one. Some are even bigger, huge thousand-room places but he also has small boutique inns. If the Triads could get access, they could launder money, drugs, and human trafficking all through one system. It's a gold mine for them really."

Mitch looked at Logan. "He's got a point. It makes a lot of sense. We've been wondering about the sabotage for months. This theory makes all the pieces fit in place."

Logan agreed. "It does." He stood up. "I'll call the office and give them an update. It may give them another angle to check."

"Why don't you give me a shot at it?" Dani asked.

"A shot at what?" Mitch raised an eyebrow. "You mean figuring out who the mole is?"

Dani nodded. "I'm rather handy with a computer." She smiled slightly.

"I bet." Mitch grinned back. "Well, if you're half as good on the computer as you are at disguises, we might be in business."

When Dani reached for her laptop, Gage hopped up and

went around the coffee table. He took her hand and refused to let go when she tried to pull it back. "But first, we eat. Don't know if we'll be getting another chance anytime soon."

She frowned at him, but the loud rumble of her stomach told him he was right.

He pulled her off the couch. "You need to keep your strength up. Dottie needs us to be on point."

Dani glared at him but then nodded.

Thank you, God. He'd been so afraid she would deny herself food with the excuse she needed to work. She'd done it on the ship. Dani didn't function well without food. He smiled at the memory of her calling him an "asshat" when she'd been hungry. The smile died. He *was* an asshat. She'd never forgive him for what he'd said, and he didn't blame her. But he could make sure she ate and took care of herself.

Her hips swayed as she walked to the room service cart. She stood in front of it and stared. She didn't pick up a plate.

"Are you alright?" Logan asked. He'd just gotten off the phone and came to stand beside her.

"Um, yeah. Just tired and hungry, I guess."

Logan frowned. "Dottie's still alive."

She bit her lip and nodded quickly. Unshed tears glistened in the corners of her eyes.

Gage's gut knotted. Pain tore up his insides as if he'd been shot. She was going to cry again, and it was his fault. If he'd followed her…if he'd just kept his cool, the whole scene outside the cruise ship wouldn't have happened.

Logan squeezed Dani's arm and then rubbed his hand up and down. "We'll get her back."

Gage ground his teeth and fisted his hands. It had damn near killed him when Logan had put his arm around Dani at the pier. Now he was touching her again. Logan already had a woman in his life. He should not be touching Dani.

Mitch glanced at Logan and Dani as he finished loading his plate. When he turned and saw Gage, he grinned.

Gage opened and closed his hands again. He really wanted to wipe the smirk off his brother's face. Mitch chuckled as he went by and winked at his brother. Gage turned and glared at Mitch.

"What?" Mitch asked while trying to look innocent, but he couldn't hold it in and burst out laughing.

"What's so funny?" Logan asked as he led Dani back over to the coffee table.

Gage glared at Mitch. If he said one word, Gage was going to take him out.

Mitch put his hands up in defeat. "Not a thing." He winked again at Gage.

Gage shook his head and went over to put some food on a plate. He wasn't hungry, but he knew he should eat. Plus, he needed some breathing room. Being so closed to Dani and not being able to touch her was like dying slowly. He didn't need Mitch's knowing looks to aggravate him anymore than he already was.

"Logan's right, Dani. Dottie will be fine. From what we saw at the pier, she knows a thing or two about handling herself." Mitch smiled.

Dani picked up a piece of buttered croissant. "Yes, but she's an…older woman and she's been kidnapped by a group of thugs." She put the croissant back down. "What is taking them so long? Why haven't they contacted us?"

Mitch took a sip of his drink. "It takes a while to organize an exchange. They have to pick their place and, if they're smart, they'll want someone on hand who can test the software. Gage mentioned earlier they grabbed a USB before and thought they had it."

Gage nodded. "They won't make that mistake this time.

I'm guessing they are waiting for their tech guy to arrive. So he can make sure it's the real thing."

Dani took a deep breath and blew it out slowly. She nodded and then looked at Gage. "We need a plan."

"Way ahead of you," Mitch said through a mouthful of food. "Finish your lunch and then have a shower. We need a bit more time to work out some details. We'll lay it out for you later this afternoon. Have a nap if you want."

Dani nodded. Exhaustion hung like a shawl off her shoulders.

Gage stood up and signaled his brothers. Logan immediately understood, but Mitch sat in his chair chomping away. "Mitch," he growled.

Mitch took a bite of his bacon and egg sandwich and then looked up. "What?"

Gage shook his head and then pointed to the door.

"Why don't we go and give you some time to yourself," Logan said as he crossed the room to the door. After pulling it open, he turned to Mitch and pointed to the hallway.

"Alright. Alright, I'm going." Mitch popped the last bite of sandwich in his mouth and then stood up and walked over to the trolley. He put his plate down and started wheeling it out.

"What the hell are you doing?" Gage asked as he grabbed his brother's arm.

"What?" Mitch asked. "I'm still hungry. She's finished her food. I want more. There's plenty left. I'm taking it with me."

"Seriously?" Logan shook his head.

Gage wanted to smack some sense into this brother. "Leave it," he said through clenched teeth.

"No. It's fine. Please take it. Mitch is right. I'm finished, and it will just go to waste."

Mitch turned and shot her a smile over his shoulder and

then pushed the trolley out the door. "Thanks. We're just down the hall, room twenty-five thirty, if you need us."

Gage turned. "Uh, lock the door after us. Make sure you check to see who is there before you open it, and don't open it to anyone but one of us or the ladies across the way." He leaned on the doorjamb. "Dani…I…"

She peered at him over the top of her water bottle. Fatigue mixed with sadness marred her features.

He wanted to apologize, to make her understand how sorry he was for what he'd said. He wanted to make her see that it was his fault Dottie was taken. Dani was his responsibility, but he'd screwed up, which led to their current situation. This was the exact reason sleeping with the client was a bad idea.

"Get some rest. It's all going to be okay. Promise." He stood up straight and walked out into the hallway, closing the door after him. He was determined to keep that promise. Even if it killed him, or more likely, someone else.

CHAPTER TWENTY-NINE

Dani rose from the sofa and went to the bathroom. There was no nap in her future, but a shower definitely sounded good. She looked in the mirror and studied her face. The makeup was streaky. There were rivulets on her cheeks from her tears like a reminder of the nightmare she was living. So was this what she would look like when she was old? Would she live long enough to find out?

Carly's face flitted through her mind. She closed her eyes. She'd missed the call with Carly last night. As soon as she was out of the shower, she needed to speak to her sister. Carly was always a ray of sunshine and, right now, Dani needed all the sunshine she could get.

Her thoughts ran to Dottie, who was older but still full of life. If anything bad happened to her, Dani would never be able to forgive herself. Who was she kidding? Something bad had already happened to Dottie.

Now Dani had to fix it somehow.

Gage had promised everything would work out. He meant rescuing Dottie. She wanted to believe him. She trusted he would do his absolute best to save Dottie. It remained to be seen if he would actually succeed.

Dani leaned over the sink and turned on the tap. She scrubbed at the make-up wishing she could wash away her fears as easily. She peeled off her clothes and stepped into the shower. The spray pounded on her back, massaging away the ache, but leaving fatigue in its wake. Finally she gathered enough strength to turn off the spray. She wrapped her hair in a towel and her body in a big fluffy robe.

After grabbing the laptop from her bag, she climbed on the bed and booted up the computer. She initiated a call to Carly. There was no answer. She glanced at the clock. Maybe she was having some sort of test? Or maybe she was in the bathroom? She waited another few minutes and tried again. No response.

The low-grade fear bloomed into a state of high panic. Where was Carly? Was she okay? They would have called her if something had happened. Dani's stomach dropped. They didn't have her number. She'd gotten rid of her other cell when she left Juneau, and she'd forgotten to call the hospital and give them the new one.

What if they'd been trying to reach her? What if something had happened to Carly? What if she…? Dani's throat closed over with unshed tears. No. She wouldn't think it. She grabbed her cell and dialed the number she knew by heart. Her hand shook as she held the phone. She connected with the switchboard and hit all of the appropriate buttons to get to Carly's floor, praying the whole time that Carly was just gone for testing or something.

The phone rang and rang, but no one picked up. Not totally unusual. Sometimes, it just happened no one was at the desk. She stared unseeing, willing herself to remain calm. Where was everyone? It was probably a busy day on the ward and the hospital staff was occupied.

She tried running lines of code in her head, but she couldn't calm her thoughts. The weight of missing the calls with Carly sat heavy on her shoulders. She swallowed the huge lump in her throat. First she'd let Carly down and now Dottie. She was a hot mess.

Rubbing her face with her hands, Dani realized she owed an apology to Ann and Elenore. She'd put them in danger. She owed them a lot more than an apology, but it was a place to start.

Dani closed her laptop, deciding to get dressed and go across the hall before trying again. It was lunchtime so maybe there were fewer people on the floor at the hospital. That was probably why they couldn't answer the phone. She rubbed her belly, where the few morsels she'd eaten sat heavy, making her queasy.

She took a deep breath and then went and got her suitcase. She pulled out a pair of skinny jeans and a black cashmere sweater. She normally didn't bother with nice things, but she loved the softness of cashmere. It was like wearing a hug, and she needed a hug right now. She needed all the warmth she could get.

Dani dressed quickly and then brushed her teeth. She finished in the bathroom and sat down on the bed. She wanted to call Carly, but if they didn't answer again, she would panic. She couldn't seem to get herself under control. It was like once the damn broke when she was with Gage, she couldn't stop the overflow of emotion.

There was a knock at the door. Dani pulled herself off the bed and went over and looked through the peephole. Gage. She just didn't need this right now.

She blocked the tiny viewer with her hand and called out, "What do you want, Gage?"

"Dani, can you open the door please?"

She sighed and rested her forehead against the door. She

was too much of a hot mess to deal with Gage at this moment. It had been difficult to just sit in the same room with him earlier. She'd been so damn happy to see him when he'd appeared out of nowhere. She wanted to scream at him for saying those horrible things to her, but she also wanted to jump into his arms, overjoyed that he was safe.

She took a breath. She was terrified about Carly, terrified for Dottie, and she was angry. Angry she let Dottie get involved in her mess. She was on the knife's edge of keeping control, and there was no way in hell she was going to cry or show any other emotion in front of him. He'd called her a harlot. She knew where he stood. He knew where she stood. She was a hacker and he was an asshole.

"I'm busy. What do you need?"

"Dani, this is not something we should discuss through a door. Not sure who's listening. Let me in."

"Fuck. Fuckity, fuck, fuck." Dani squared her shoulders. "Fine." She opened the door.

Gage strode in.

"What do you want?" Damn if he didn't look fine in his black collared shirt and blue jeans with his damp hair flopping over his forehead. She cursed silently as she slammed the door. It wasn't fair.

Gage turned to face her. "How far along are you on your software? Does it work?"

She blinked. She wasn't sure what she thought he was going to ask, but it wasn't that. "Yes, it works…to a point." She was loath to admit it, but it eventually broke down and froze. Worse, she had no idea how to fix it. She crossed her arms over her chest. "Why?"

Gage hesitated. "We're probably going to have to give it to the kidnappers."

"There's no way—"

Gage put up his hands. "I know you don't want to, but

they are definitely going to want to test it before they let us have Dottie."

Dani's eyes narrowed. "How do you know? Did they call?"

Gage's mouth compressed into a flat line as he nodded.

"They did? They called? When?" Dani snarled.

"A little while ago." Gage ran his hand through his hair and then turned and walked farther into the room.

Dani put her hands on her hips and followed on Gage's heels. "Why didn't you tell me?"

Gage dropped into the chair. "We wanted to have some sort of a plan before we said anything." He gestured to the sofa. "Please sit."

"No. I'm not sitting," she said through clenched teeth. "What is going on? When is the exchange? What exactly did they say? I. Want. Details."

Gage remained silent for a second and eyed Dani. "Okay. They called about thirty minutes ago. They demanded the software in exchange for Dottie. They said they'd call back at 6:00 p.m. tonight and tell us where and when."

Dani took up pacing.

After an eternity, Gage asked, "What are you thinking?"

Dani stayed silent and continued to pace. She needed to think, and Gage talking to her wasn't helping.

"Dani."

She whirled around to face him. "What?"

Gage took a deep breath and rested his palms on top of his thighs. "Dani. Just calm down—"

"Don't you dare patronize me! I want to know exactly what's going on. It's my fault she's in this mess."

Gage shook his head. "It's not your fault. It's mine."

She advanced to stand directly in front of him and pointed at his chest. "You're right. It is your fault!" The air crackled with her accusation. "You were supposed to protect me! You were supposed to keep me safe! Dottie never should've been there. You should've had a way to get me off the ship and to your brothers safely."

She pointed to her own chest. "I should've been working on the software the whole trip, not hacking the ships systems. I could've had the software totally functional by now." She pointed at him again. "It's all your fault!"

Gage shot out of the chair to stand inches from her. "If you'd told me where you were so I didn't waste time running around Europe looking for you, you would be safely back in New York!" He glared down at her.

Anger, anxiety and frustration coursed through her. The heat from his body hit her chest. His scent swirled around her. She couldn't hold it together any longer. She was either going to burst into tears or... She pushed him backwards. Hard. He let out a curse as his ass hit the cushion. She didn't give him a chance to recover. She crawled into his lap and planted her lips on his.

She drove her tongue into his mouth, invading him, tasting everywhere at once. He responded in kind. Their tongues rolled with each other, matching move for move. Hot, wet kisses and tiny bites kept their mouths occupied while she jammed her hands into his hair, locking him in place. His hands cupped her ass and pulled her close but it wasn't enough.

She shifted so her knees went deeper into the cushions, getting closer to him. He was so hard she couldn't stop herself from grinding against him. He scooped her up and stood, breaking their kiss. She wrapped both her legs around his waist. He looked toward the bed but her laptop was on it. He took her to the sofa and laid her down. He lowered himself on top of her. He was hard as rock, and it felt so, so good.

Wanting to feel his skin, she started pulling at his shirt.

She needed to feel it, drown herself in him, and forget about Carly and how she was letting the little girl down. Forget that it was her fault Dottie was in trouble. She just wanted to forget period.

"Gage," she moaned. She desperately tore at his shirt, consumed by the desire to run her tongue over his muscles and feel them flex and ripple under her touch. With a growl low in her throat, she finally pulled hard enough to get the shirt off over his head.

He trailed kisses and small nips from her ear to the hollow of her neck. He stopped for a brief second as he pulled her sweater over her head. When he saw she was wearing a black lace bra, his grin turned greedy. Groaning, he pushed the lace aside and dropped his lips to her nipple.

Heat uncoiled from her core. She fisted her hands in his hair and threw her head back, pushing her breasts forward as he took the other bud in his mouth. A shot of desire ripped through her when he tugged on her nipple with his teeth.

She pulled his head away to reclaim his mouth, her tongue rolling with his in a deep kiss. He reached back and undid her bra and then lifted her slightly so he could pull it off. He let it hit the floor. He pulled away from her mouth and dropped his gaze to her breasts. With a groan, she lifted her hips and ground against him again.

Catching his eye, she slowly rolled him over so she was on top. She ran her hands up his bare chest before leaning forward and taking his nipple into her mouth.

"Dani, you are driving me crazy," he growled.

She swirled her tongue, then nipped him harder in response to his groan of pleasure. She undid the button of his jeans, and while still kissing his chest, she started to push them and his black boxer briefs down. He lifted his hips to help her. She ran her fingers over his hips and then wrapped her hand around his length.

He grabbed her head and brought her mouth to his; his scorching kiss made heat coil in her belly. She needed him. This. Now.

She grasped his shoulders, and shifted her weight so she could get her jeans off. He helped her slide her clothing over her hips, and then off all together. They dropped in a pile on the floor. She wanted to be closer. Needed to feel him. She shifted again, and rubbed against him.

THE SIGHT OF HER NAKED STOLE HIS BREATH. SHE WAS magnificent. Her lips all plump from their kisses, black eyes roaming over him. She was a goddess.

Her breasts were high, round, and full, as perfect as her rounded hips. He pulled her down on top of his length. He couldn't help it. And she was ready, hot, wet, and very willing. When he cupped her ass, she arched her back and he plunged into her. He captured her gaze. Her eyes turned coal-black and her mouth opened on a small moan.

He claimed her mouth at the same time he went deeper into her core. A growl escaped him as he tried to take her slowly. She wouldn't let him. She rolled her hips faster, meeting each stroke. Swearing, he cupped her ass.

When he pressed into her, she rocked back. "Faster," she demanded, and then she growled. It was the sexiest sound he had ever heard. He drove into her faster and faster until he felt her tighten around him. A cry of raw pleasure ripped from her throat, and with a roar, he fell over the edge with her.

She flopped across his chest and lay there, straining to take in enough oxygen. She was amazing. They fit together so well; it was like she was created just for him. He started to wrap his arms around her but she pushed away from his chest and stood up.

"Dani?"

"Leave, Gage."

She didn't even pause in her step or look back at him. She walked across the room and disappeared into the bathroom. Her words cut the joy from his body. Pain filled the crevasses where happiness had just flowed. Here he'd thought they had made up somehow. That the sex had signaled she'd forgiven him. It was clear now he'd been dead wrong.

She just used him in the moment. It meant nothing to her. Maybe she really was a… *No!* He refused to believe she didn't care at all. She was just overwhelmed. When this was all over, when sanity returned, they would talk. He would apologize and… and what? She was never going to change. She was a hacker with a loose moral code, and he just couldn't stomach that. It went against everything he believed. He rubbed his chest as if he were in physical pain.

He stood up and got dressed. He gathered her clothes and left them in a pile on the chair. He was done. He didn't need this, any of this. When this job was over, he was done with Dani. He walked across the room and opened the door. He walked through it, closing it quietly but firmly behind him.

DANI HEARD THE DOOR CLOSE AND PROMPTLY BURST into tears. She'd needed Gage in that moment, but having sex with him again had been a major mistake. She'd given in to her weakness. She should've just kicked him out. Now she'd just made it so much harder on herself. She needed to quit Gage like he was a drug—cold turkey. It was the only way she'd survive.

She took a deep breath, but his scent filled her nose. She quickly turned on the shower and stepped in. She gasped as the cold spray hit her like an ice storm. She gritted her teeth and stood under the water until it gradually warmed up. She took the soap and lathered her whole body. Once. Twice. She needed to wash off all remnants of Gage Callahan.

When she was finished in the shower, she wrapped herself in the robe again and went out to lay on the king-size bed. She needed a second to regroup and then she would call about Carly and make a plan for the exchange so she could get Dottie back in one piece. She closed her eyes. What if she made a few modifications to the software? It was her last thought as she drifted off to sleep.

CHAPTER THIRTY

"Gage!" Janet yelped, sounding startled. "Where are you?" There was a muffled sound and then, "I thought you'd be in the air by now. Wait, are you in the air?"

"Um, no. It's a bit of a long story, but we haven't left Vancouver yet."

"Oh. Okay. How can I help?" Janet asked, sounding more like her usual efficient self.

"Ah, well…we need some guns. Our resources are very limited in Vancouver. Time is running out. It will take longer to get them than we have. Can you help?"

"Guns." There was silence. "Should I ask what's going on? I'm sure Mr. Drake will be interested."

"Best if you don't know. Not a good time to explain things. I'll explain everything to Drake later." There was more silence. "Janet?"

"Well, that's not what I had anticipated."

Gage frowned and glanced at his brothers. Logan was tapping his fingers on the arm of the chair and Mitch was lying on the sofa.

"We ran into an issue up here. It's a long story and I'll tell you later, but we kind of need the guns in a hurry."

"I'll check with Mr. Drake, and if he okays it, then I will have someone drop some weapons to you in an hour or a little more. Does that work?"

He gave his brothers a thumbs up. Logan leaned back in his chair and Mitch grinned. "That's perfect. You're amazing, Janet! Thanks."

"I'll call you when they're ready." Janet hung up.

Gage put the cell down on the coffee table. "We're in business."

"Thank you, Janet," Mitch said.

Logan smiled slightly. "Now we just have to figure out a game plan for the exchange."

Mitch leaned back in his chair. "I'm glad we didn't have to use the backup plan. I haven't seen Stinky in a long time, and I'm not sure he's still in town."

"Why am I not surprised you know someone named Stinky?" Logan shook his head.

"There's a great story behind the nickname," Mitch said. "You see—"

"You two start on it. I'm gonna grab a shower," Gage said as he walked toward the bathroom. He had no interest in knowing a damn thing about Stinky. His brothers' eyes bored into his back, but neither one of them said a word. They were both smart enough to keep their mouths shut.

Gage grabbed a shower. The scalding water was just what he needed. His muscles were tight, and he was running on fumes. It seemed like it had been weeks since he'd felt one hundred percent physically. He finished under the spray and dried himself off. After grabbing clean clothes, he got dressed.

Mitch and Logan were hovering over a piece of paper,

presumably they were talking about various scenarios for the exchange.

Gage grabbed the cell phone and looked at the screen. Janet had texted. "She has the guns." His brothers looked up. "I'm texting her now to have her person meet me in the lobby of the hotel."

"Sounds good," Mitch said. Then he went back to looking at the paper.

Another text came in. "She says to be in the lobby in ten minutes."

Logan looked up. "Do you want backup?"

"Nah. It'll be fine. I'll head out now. When I get back, I want to hear your plans for getting us out alive."

Both of his brothers grunted.

Gage went out of the room door, hopped on an elevator to the lobby. The doors slid open and he scanned the area, locating an empty chair by the fireplace. While he waited his mind turned to Dani. She was such a conundrum to him. He shouldn't be thinking about her at all. She was everything he fought against. Her attitude toward what she did was entirely backward. Did she really not care about the long-term effects of her hacking?

He ground his teeth. He needed to stop thinking about her all together. The phone vibrated in his hand. The person with the guns was out front but couldn't find a place to park because of all the construction. Gage hoped the courier brought more than just handguns but beggars couldn't be choosers.

Gage texted that he would meet the courier. He moved through the lobby and out the door of the hotel. He saw the black sedan idling just beyond the hotel entryway, past the construction equipment. He picked his way through the loose debris over to the car.

Gage tensed as he approached the car. He wasn't loving the blacked-out windows.

The window rolled down, and Janet's face appeared. She was in the driver's seat and leaning over toward the passenger side. "Gage. Get in."

"Janet? What are you doing here?" he asked. "Why didn't you tell me you were in town?" He opened the door and got into the passenger seat.

"I didn't really have time, and I wasn't sure if I was going to be able to come myself or not." Janet pressed the window button, and it rolled up again.

Gage smiled. "Well, I'm glad to see you. We can really use your help."

She hit the lock button and then pulled away from the curb. "I'm glad to see you, too. I admit you made me nervous there for a minute, but it's all good now."

"What are you talking about? Where are we going?" Gage asked. When Janet glanced at him, his gut knotted. Her eyes were cold, and her voice had taken on a weird tone.

She laughed. "Your request for guns surprised me, I have to say. I expected you to have your own resources up here, but this whole business has been full of surprises."

"Since the start, many things have gone sideways because of you and your brothers, not the least of which is the Triads grabbing some old woman instead of Dani." She smiled coldly. "But then you called and, well, everything is back on track. Now I'm certain your brothers will give us the hacker."

Gage tried to hit the unlock button, but he heard a distinct click. "Keep your hands on the dash where I can see them." He glanced over his shoulder and saw Ponytail from the pier. He was holding a gun.

Gage was silent for a second. He couldn't believe what was happening. He'd been ambushed. It had never occurred to him that Janet was involved. Adrenaline rampaged through his veins.

"What do you want?" he demanded.

Janet laughed. "I have what I need for now, and soon I'll have the software, too."

Ice stabbed through his heart. She knew where his brothers were. Worse, she knew where Dani was. *Fuck*. She knew all about the resources they had in this city as well, or the lack there of. He'd told her himself during the call. He curled his fingers into fists. He needed to distract her. Find out her plan.

"I know what you're thinking and, yes, we are aware of your skills, if not your plans exactly, and we are well prepared to handle your brothers at the exchange."

The cold smile was back. Gage had to figure something out, or Dani and his brothers would be like lambs led to the slaughter.

CHAPTER THIRTY-ONE

Dani's eyes popped open as she bolted into a sitting position. She whirled around and looked at the clock. 5:45 p.m. "Shit!" She'd fallen asleep. She hopped off the bed and ran to her clothing piled on the chair. She pulled it on as quickly as possible and started out of the room. She ran back, grabbed her room key, and headed out again. She'd forgotten her shoes, but she wasn't stopping to go back for them.

She dashed out the door and down the hall. She banged loudly on Gage's door. It swung open, and she barreled into the room, brushing by Logan. She saw Mitch out of the corner of her eye.

"I know who the mole is! We've been so stupid! I should have realized earlier—"

"It's Janet. We know," Logan said as he went back over and sat down in the chair.

"Uh, what? How did you figure it out?" Dani asked as she walked over and plopped down on the sofa.

Logan looked at Mitch, who sat down on the sofa next to Dani.

"Well," Logan began and then cleared his throat.

"We fucked up. That's how we found out." Mitch spat the words like they tasted bad in his mouth.

Dani frowned. "I don't understand. What happened?" She looked around the room. "Wait. Where's Gage?" When she glanced at Logan, her skin went cold. Her heart hammered in her chest. Her palms got slick. Nausea rose from her belly, and her lunch tried to claw its way up her throat. She swallowed hard. "Where is he?" she whispered.

Logan leaned forward in his chair. "We asked Janet for some guns. We don't have any resources in Vancouver."

Mitch ran his hands over his face. "We let him go by himself to pick up the guns. It was only down to the lobby, but we should've gone with him. It just never occurred to us he would get kidnapped as well. They already have one hostage. Why would they need two?"

"They have Gage?" Dani's voice was still a whisper. Her mouth was Sahara dry. She couldn't seem to swallow.

Logan frowned and ran a hand through his hair. "Yes. When he didn't come back after twenty minutes, we got concerned. We went in search of him, but he was gone. Mitch got the security tapes from the hotel. Gage got into a dark sedan with blacked-out windows, and it drove away. We already traced the plates. It was stolen."

"Then how do you know it's Janet?"

Mitch sighed. "We watched the video for about ten minutes before the meet. Thankfully, she had to go around the block because of the construction so we caught her on camera through the windshield. No doubt, it was Janet."

"How did you know it was Janet?" Logan asked as he leaned back again in the chair.

"What?" She blinked. This couldn't be happening. Gage was now in trouble, and all because of her. She rubbed her hands over her face, then sank back into the sofa cushions.

"I fell asleep, and I guess my subconscious put it

together. If I hadn't been such an idiot, I would have put it together earlier this morning." Was it really only this morning that all this had happened? "When I saw you waiting for Gage outside of the ship, but he didn't show up, I got worried. I texted Janet and asked her to text you two so you would know Gage was still on the ship."

"Why didn't you just text us directly? Didn't you have our number?" asked Logan.

Dani's stomach rolled. "I…um, didn't want you to have my number. I needed a new phone first. I wanted to go it on my own. I'm used to being by myself. Having Gage around just…complicated things." She kept her eyes on her hands.

"Understood," Mitch said, "but how did that tell you the mole was Janet?"

"Because the minute after I texted Janet, Ponytail and his crew started heading your direction. That's why I started running toward you. I wanted to warn you. Then they saw me, and I…needed your help. Those guys walked right by you two like they had no clue who you were. It wasn't 'til after I texted Janet that things changed." She swallowed the tears that clawed at her throat. "This is all my fault."

"No," Mitch said and shook his head. "This is our fault. We should have picked this up ages ago. Drake was having problems long before you entered the picture. We should have figured out it was Janet a long time ago."

"Well, playing the blame game isn't going to help anyone and, for the record, the only person at fault is Janet. So, let's figure out what the hell we're going to do to rectify the situation." Logan got to his feet and went over to yet another room service trolley and poured himself some coffee. He held up the pot, but both Mitch and Dani shook their head.

Coffee in hand, he walked back to the chair. "I still don't understand why she would do it. Why jeopardize your entire life for this? Was she always a mole for the Triads? I'm not following the logic. Drake pays well, and I know he takes care of his people. When I told him earlier, he was distraught. He didn't believe me at first. He thought of Janet and her son as family. Why destroy that? He's so angry I wouldn't be surprised if he put a hit out on her, assuming she survives today."

"Her son. It's about Micah," Mitch said. "She was crazy about her kid. I'm willing to bet she blames Drake for his death somehow."

"So she wanted revenge?" Logan asked. "I guess that makes sense."

"Does it really matter why?" Dani asked. "Who gives a rat's ass why she did it? We need to fix this. I just care about getting our people back. So what are we going to do? Are they still calling at six?" she demanded, leaning forward again.

"As far as we know," Logan responded.

Mitch nodded. "The deal is Dottie and Gage for the software. At least, we think it is. I have no idea if that's changed. The only bit of good news is Stinky came through and we have more guns. We're going to need them."

Dani leaned forward again. She hadn't brought her laptop with her. She'd been in such a hurry to come, she'd forgotten it. Ann and Elenore. She'd forgotten them, too.

"Ann and Elenore?" she asked.

"They are in their room watching a movie. They ordered in dinner. The other ladies in the group caught their flight home. Ann told them Dottie wasn't feeling well, so they were going to stay a day or two longer."

"I'd still like to know why they want the software in the first place," Logan said and then took a sip of his coffee.

Dani laughed without humor. "That's easy. I'm sure it's because it would give the Triads the ultimate weapon against law enforcement. All they'd need is access to personnel databases, and then they would know if anyone is a mole in their organization.

"Not to mention they could find anyone they wanted as long as they can tap into a video camera system like the traffic cameras in a city where they think that person is hiding. It would be very difficult to get away from the Triads if they have the software. No one would ever be safe testifying against them again."

"And they want you because it's not quite finished." Logan took another sip of coffee. "Makes sense. I have to say, your software is as impressive as it is scary."

Dani frowned. "Thanks. I think."

CHAPTER THIRTY-TWO

Gage winced as he shifted his weight once more. His shoulder was aching. Apparently, Ponytail wanted revenge for this morning because he'd zip-tied Gage's hands behind his back and then slammed him to the ground. His left shoulder had taken the brunt of the impact. Ponytail tried to kick him in the ribs, but the tall guy, whose name was Phil, pulled him off.

Gage was worried he was going to have permanent damage with his hands tied so tightly behind his back. It made the pain radiate down his left arm. At least his ass wasn't numb.

He was thirsty, though. Janet had refused to give him anything to drink. He shivered slightly in the cold, dank air of the deserted factory. The building had that abandoned look when they'd walked through it earlier. Broken windows, garbage on the floors and it smelled of mold and dead things. They'd taken him and Dottie to an office in the far corner.

The springs of the old couch he was sitting on poked him in the back. His feet were unbound out in front of him. Not that it mattered since Phil was standing just outside the office with a gun pointed in his direction. The gag was making his jaws hurt, and he was so damned parched his tongue was like sandpaper. He coughed. The deep, gurgling sound concerned him, but he had more trouble on his plate than not feeling one-hundred percent.

He glanced at Dottie at the other end of the sofa. She appeared to be dozing, her color pale, but other than that, she seemed okay. Her breathing was even and didn't appear to be labored.

Gage looked at Janet and shook his head again. He still couldn't believe he and his brothers had missed it. All of his guys at Callahan Security had missed it, too. How could she betray Drake? She'd been with him for years and years.

He'd watched her for the last couple of hours as she typed and answered calls. She was the picture of efficiency in her navy suit with a white blouse. Red nails matched her red high-heeled shoes. Her silver hair was pulled into a tight, low bun. Her makeup was understated. She was exactly what Gage pictured when he thought of the perfect high-powered assistant. It was just so bizarre. He coughed again.

"Would you still like a drink of water?" she asked as she finished typing something on the screen and then looked up. Gage nodded. She looked at Phil, who was leaning in the doorway, and said, "Give him water. Not too much. Just enough to keep him going. He's no use to us if he passes out or he can't stand up."

Phil's eyes narrowed. "I don't work for you, lady," he said, but he moved over and put his gun on the desk. He grabbed a bottle of water from the crate on the floor and opened it. He flipped his Seattle Mariners ballcap around, then tilted his head back and drank half the bottle. Then he walked over to Gage. He took out the gag and poured the rest down Gage's throat. Gage choked but managed to swallow some.

"That's all you're getting so don't ask for more," Phil

snarled. He threw the bottle in the garbage can and made to put the gag back in Gage's mouth, but Gage turned his head. Phil drew a hand back and punched Gage in the jaw.

Gage's head snapped back. Phil packed a hell of a punch, but Gage could deal. When Phil reached for the gag again, Gage said, "What about Dottie?"

"She's fine," Janet said. "I had to give her a sedative. She talked non-stop even with the gag in her mouth. Truly aggravating."

"Can I have more water?" Gage asked, grasping at straws. He wanted to engage Janet, maybe find out what the plan was.

"No." Phil grabbed Gage's jaw and tried to hold his head in place while he replaced the gag. His cell went off, so he stepped back as he pulled it out and glanced at the screen. He answered it and moved out into the hallway, speaking what Gage assumed was Cantonese.

He asked Janet, "What I don't understand is how you hooked up with the Triads? I figure that's who these guys are. With all the tattoos and the English names and speaking Cantonese. Screams Triads." He wanted to verify the information from his brothers.

A lightbulb went off in his head. "Devon. You did it through Devon. This whole time we've been thinking Devon relapsed, but he didn't, did he?"

The cold smile was back. "Darling Devon. Such a stupid man. He actually thought he could hide his gambling from Jameson Drake. Not possible."

"Not for him," Gage mused, "but for you, everything is possible."

"Yes. I'm Janet, his assistant, his right hand, his lady dragon, keeping the world at bay. And his mother when he needs one. For me, it's all just there for the taking."

A flush crawled up her neck and a smile lit her face. She

was so proud of what she'd done. There was another emotion. Malice. Her eyes glowed with it. She wanted to hurt Drake.

Gage's skin crawled. This woman was truly evil. It suddenly dawned on Gage. "Your son. It's about your son, isn't it?"

The flush was back. Rage and loathing both fought to be the expression on her face. "Yes, my son," she spat. "You've figured it out, Mr. Callahan. Are you proud? Do you feel better? My son is the reason for all of this. Jameson Drake killed my son."

Gage's eyebrows went up.

"You're surprised. Well, you shouldn't be. He did. He killed my son as sure as if he'd shot him. I brought Micah to a party on Drake's yacht one night when I had to work. That's when he tried drugs for the first time. He was instantly hooked. Jameson paid for rehab because he felt guilty. He knew he was responsible.

"It didn't matter. Micah couldn't kick the habit. He overdosed. Drake was kind. He gave me a few weeks of vacation to grieve, and then it was back to business as usual. Well, not for me.

"That was it, you see." She snapped her fingers. "The moment when it all clicked. Jameson Drake droning on about business all those years, I couldn't help but learn a thing or two." The malice was back in her smile. "I went on to apply everything I learned from Drake to bring about his own downfall. The irony was delicious. It was all so *fun*." Janet's eyes filled with an eerie light.

Gage shivered again. This woman was out of control. He shifted on the couch again. Thoughts swirled in his head. They'd been right about the Triads wanting to use Drake's hotel chains. They'd just been wrong about who was behind it all.

"Money laundering, human trafficking…you helped the Triads set that up in Drake's businesses." It was unthinkable what this woman had done.

"The money laundering came first, using the hotel's cleaning services, and we branched out from there. We moved to selling drugs using the concierge and certain clients, and then, well, the sky's the limit."

Gage couldn't believe his ears. She was part of money laundering. That was bad, but helping the people that had indirectly caused her son's death to sell the very thing that killed him? She was…beyond words. The coldness in Janet's soul was indescribable.

"You're shocked. It's written all over your face." She smirked. "Don't you see? That's the glory of it. No one would ever suspect me of being behind everything. That would be ludicrous." She laughed. It was a weird and haunting laugh that set Gage's teeth on edge. Where the hell was Phil?

"The Triads are so entrenched in Drake's hotels now, he'll never get them out. And the best part is there's an article written all about it. It will be released when I give the word. It's just waiting on one more little thing."

"The software," Gage croaked. His voice was shot. He needed more water badly.

"Yes, Mr. Callahan. The software. It's my golden para-chute. Once the Triads have that and I get paid an enormous amount of money, I'm finished. I will be retiring to some sunny spot where I can live out my days enjoying the sun, sand, and downfall of Jameson Drake."

"How do you know the Triads won't double-cross you? It's not like they are known for being upstanding." Gage shifted again. He leaned on his right arm to try to take the pressure off the left.

"Please do give me some credit. I've been dealing with these people for some time now. I have things set up appropriately. They will follow through because there will be consequences if they don't." She glanced at her wristwatch and rose. She smoothed out her skirt. The cold, creepy smile slid back into place. "And now, Mr. Callahan, it is time for you and your brothers to die."

CHAPTER THIRTY-THREE

Dani looked out the car window as they drove into Stanley Park. Almost a thousand acres of West Coast rainforest on the water's edge in Vancouver. It was ginormous. How could it even exist in a city? And how were they supposed to find the specific part of some small path to meet for the exchange? Mitch said they had given him exact coordinates and also explained the location in great detail, so she didn't ask questions.

"Why pick here?" Dani asked from the back seat.

Logan shrugged. "I have no idea."

Mitch piped up, "I think it's because they have a boat nearby. They are either holding Gage and Dottie on a boat or it's their getaway vehicle. Or maybe they just like the restaurant here. Who the hell knows?"

"It just seems weird. I mean it's a very public place." Dani sighed.

Logan tapped the window. "Not today. With the major storm coming in, people aren't staying."

He was right. The wind was picking up. No one else seemed to be on the way into the park, but traffic was heavy on the way out. Just as well. They didn't need any more innocent people involved in this mess.

They parked in the lot, hopped out and started walking. They saw one person with their dog coming from the opposite direction, and that was it.

"So, you know the plan, right?" Mitch asked.

"Yes. No need to go over it again. It's not complicated." Dani was finding it hard to focus on what Mitch was saying. She kept her head turned away from the water. Just smelling the salt air turned her stomach.

"Okay. The meeting spot is about a fifteen-minute walk from here. We're going to follow this gravel path." He indicated with his hand. "And then Logan and I are going to enter the woods farther down and make our way over to where you are supposed to meet them. We'll guide you to where you have to turn off the main path. Don't worry. We'll keep an eye on you the whole time. Nothing will happen." Mitch raised his gun.

It didn't make her feel better the way he probably thought it would.

"Here's your earbud. You'll be able to communicate with us the whole time."

She nodded. She liked the look of the wide gravel path. It turned away from the water.

Logan smiled and gave her arm a quick squeeze. "It's going to be fine."

She nodded again. As they walked away from the lot, it amazed her how quickly they lost sight of the parking lot. The path was wide but the trees were densely packed. Who knew there was such a large forest in the middle of the city? If she didn't know better, she could be back in Alaska. A few minutes later, Mitch and Logan disappeared into the woods.

Being suddenly alone, fear sizzled in her belly. Surrounded by trees, the wind howling through the leaves had the hair on her neck standing on end. She just wanted this to be over with. She needed to be done with all of this.

A few minutes later, her earbud crackled and Mitch instructed her to turn left. She turned and stared at the woods. There was a very narrow pathway. She couldn't see anything or anyone, but that was the whole point.

She crept slowly down the path. Where the other one had been small stones. This one was all wooded. It was a trail with roots and pine needles on the ground. She shivered. After she'd gone another hundred yards or so, Mitch told her to stop.

Even though it was still daylight, the forest around her was shrouded in gloom. The lack of light made the forest eerie and threatening. The smell of moisture and dead foliage filled her nose. If she listened hard, she could hear ocean waves hitting the shore. *No need to do that.*

Twenty minutes later, Dani rubbed her sweaty palms on her jeans yet again. She couldn't relax. Her blood was roaring in her ears. Her breathing was getting shallow.

"Take deep breaths. Be calm. You're going to hyperventilate and pass out."

Mitch's voice in her earbud was meant to be reassuring, but it wasn't. She wasn't sure anything would ever be okay again. She'd finally gotten through to the nurse's station at the hospital just as they were getting out of the car here at Stanley Park. The nurse had said to come quick. They'd been trying to reach Dani, but the calls wouldn't go through. Carly was dying. There wasn't much time.

Dani was numb. "What?" Dani asked.

Mitch's voice snapped with irritation. "I said you need to pay attention. We need to be ready."

"Right." She nodded, but Mitch and Logan couldn't see her that closely, so it was wasted on them. She needed to focus. The call had come in at exactly 6:00 p.m., just like they said it would. The meet was set for Stanley Park on some foot path at 7:00 p.m. They'd had very little time to prepare.

At least they knew Gage was on the way this time. They'd insisted on speaking to him, if only for a second. She'd collapsed on the sofa at the sound of his voice. He'd said Dottie was okay as well. Dani managed to find a small bit of solace in that. She'd been so worried that once they had Gage, they would decide they didn't need Dottie.

All these years, she'd always seen herself as strong and capable. Being alone had never been an issue, and yet only a few days with this man, and she was lost without him.

"No." She corrected that thought. Not lost. She'd be fine on her own. He just…mattered to her. She would be lost without Carly, though. Carly. Tears stung her eyelids.

"What did you say?" Logan asked.

"What? Who? Me?" She hadn't realized she'd spoken aloud. "Nothing. Just talking to myself." She swallowed hard.

Great. They were going to think she'd lost her mind. She shrugged, shifting her backpack. The wind blew hard, and she stumbled a step. *Stupid tree roots.*

The storm hadn't broken yet, but it wasn't far off. The locals said gray skies were typical in Vancouver, but these clouds were dark purple and pregnant with rain. Lightning looked like it could be a distinct possibility. She needed to be out of here before that happened. She needed to be out of here as quickly as possible.

"Come on," she mumbled.

Logan's voice cut through the wind. "They're here."

CHAPTER THIRTY-FOUR

G age looked up and saw Dani whirl in his direction. His gut knotted. He didn't want her here, not that he had a choice, but he knew the hell she must be going through. She would be blaming herself for all of this.

The world spun a bit, and he stumbled over the roots on the path. Dottie tried to help him, but her hands were tied. Her eyes narrowed as she looked at him. He knew he didn't look so good.

All that time on the ship without eating and drinking much, plus his time in captivity, had made him very dehydrated. He knew the signs. The dizziness, the dry mouth, the orange-colored urine. He was in trouble. At least they'd switched to having his hands tied in front of him. Less strain on his back and shoulder this way. He needed to save every bit of strength he had.

He tried to focus. *Work the problem.* The rain came harder now, not that he was feeling many drops. The foliage was blocking most of the water. He licked his lips, hoping to pull in whatever moisture he could. He needed to figure out what plan his brothers had made so he could help them.

He had to be ready for anything because, knowing them, anything was possible. He glanced over at Dottie. He needed her to be ready, too, but he had no way to convey that to her. Janet had never let them speak to one another. Dottie caught his gaze and winked. He would have laughed if he could've. This old gal was up for anything, and he loved her for it.

Ponytail and the other gunman, whose name Gage had learned was Andy, came to a stop quite a distance from Dani. Gage stumbled again and shivered. His phlegmy, hacking cough shook his body. He was pretty sure he had a fever.

He licked his lips again and ran his eyes over Dani. She didn't look good either. She was scared, but beyond that, there was something else. The spark was gone from her eyes. There was fear there instead and…sadness. She looked incredibly sad. Worry consumed him. *Focus*. He could worry about Dani's feelings later.

He looked around. Where were his brothers? They had to be in the trees, but the forest was too dense to see them. That was a good thing, but they had to know that Andy and Ponytail knew they were there as well.

What would he do in their situation? He studied the setup and Dani. She must be wearing an ear bud. If it were him, he would be in the woods with guns. He and Mitch thought along the same lines; they'd had similar training.

If Gage could help line up the shot, then Mitch and Logan could take out Andy and Ponytail before they even started the negotiations about the software.

He glanced at the woods again. Were they in the right position? Probably not since Andy and Ponytail were still standing. There was a group of trees with branches overhanging the path. He would be to the left of that, if it were him, because there was a boulder to hide behind. If they were there, they didn't have a clear shot. The branches were too thick and would block the view. Gage needed to get Andy and Ponytail to move ahead a couple feet.

He took a tentative step and tried to make it look like he was stumbling forward, but instead of moving with him, Ponytail and Andy just yanked him back.

Dottie looked at him. Gage tried to gesture with his head, but she wasn't getting it. Then her eyes lit up. She moved a few steps forward before one of the thugs could grab her. Gage tried to move with her, but Andy grabbed his arm and held him back.

It suddenly hit Gage there was another problem. Phil. He was pretty sure Phil was lurking somewhere. That might put a crimp in the plan.

"Where is the software?" Andy yelled.

Negotiations had begun. And still no gunfire. His brothers didn't have a clear shot.

Gage mumbled, "Fuck."

CHAPTER THIRTY-FIVE

Her knees almost gave out. Gage was stumbling between the two men. Dottie looked like she was being half dragged along as well. The two gunmen from the pier. They had Gage's hands zip-tied in front of him. Dottie was tied up the same way. Gage looked cold. His shirt was ripped, and his jeans were stained. His face was flushed, almost as if he had a fever. Dottie looked tired but otherwise okay.

She heard them ask about the software, but she couldn't seem to get her lips to move. "I—" Her voice was a whisper. Her mouth was dry. She swallowed hard and tried again. "I have it." She turned slightly so they could see the backpack.

"Give us the software," the short, skinny guy yelled.

Dani shook her head. "You need to let them go first."

Mitch said, "I can't get a clear shot from where I am. Logan, what about you?"

"No. They need to move up closer to Dani. Otherwise, I'll have to move to get a shot."

There was some sound through the ear bud and then a

loud whistle. Dani winced and rubbed her ear. She dropped her hand immediately, but it was too late.

"You can take out the earpiece. It doesn't matter now anyway." Ponytail gestured to her left with his chin. Logan and Mitch were being marched down from the tree line with their hands laced behind their heads. There were two more tattooed guys behind them, one with a Seattle Mariners baseball hat on. They had guns pointed at Mitch and Logan.

Fear made Dani's stomach heave. Puking would not help, she reminded herself. The guy with the hat walked Mitch and Logan up close to the path and then made them stop. She could see them in her peripheral vision when she looked back at Gage.

Gage. He didn't look good. She was pretty sure he was sick and most likely in pain.

"The software. Now," Ponytail demanded.

Dani turned to look at Mitch and Logan. Mitch nodded. She shrugged off the backpack and let it slide to the ground. She squatted down and started unzipping her sack.

"Hey. Do that slowly."

She looked up at Ponytail and nodded. She slowly unzipped the bag. She reached in and brought out her laptop while holding her other hand in the air. The last thing she wanted was to get shot. She stood up, holding the laptop.

Ponytail gestured to her to come. "Okay. Now walk over here and give it to me."

"What about Gage and Dottie? You need to let them go first," Dani yelled over the wind. They'd stayed about twenty yards apart on the path, and with the rising wind and rain, it was getting harder to hear them.

"Nah uh. That's not how this is going to work. We're going to test out the software, and if it works, then they can go." He shoved Gage, who stumbled. The other gunman had to grab Gage's arm to stop him from falling.

Dani looked at Mitch again, who nodded. She started over slowly. Her feet felt mired in fast drying cement. Her knees wanted to give out. She wiped the palm of her empty hand on her jeans.

Big, fat raindrops started to fall faster. Her gaze locked with Gage's. She could do this. For him, she would do this. His eyes were overly bright, but she could see encouragement in them, and something else.

"Stop right there." Ponytail pointed to the ground. "Put the laptop down and step back."

Dani did as she was instructed. She was only a few feet from Gage now. He was sick. He had a fever. She could see it clearly in his face as he blinked slowly several times.

Dottie looked exhausted and a little pale. She also had a bruise on her cheek, but other than that, she seemed fine. She was in better shape than Gage. The woman was amazing.

Ponytail pointed again. "Back up more."

Dani did as instructed. This time when she glanced at Mitch and Logan, she realized that Ballcap had moved them in closer. They were slightly behind and to her left. Gage and his captors were directly in front of her. Trees surrounded the group. There was nowhere for her to run.

Her eyes locked with Logan's for the briefest second. The plan had been for Mitch and Logan to shoot the guys before negotiations started. Plan B called for her to run like hell when the brothers distracted the men with the guns, but Gage was obviously sick, and Dottie didn't look like she could run far. Plus, there was nowhere for her to go.

Dani took a deep breath as the rain started in earnest. Her hands shook. She took another breath, deep and slow like Gage had taught her. She could do Plan C. The one no one else knew about.

Ponytail stepped forward and grabbed her laptop. He put his gun away and balanced the laptop in his left hand and opened it with his right. The other gunman saw Dani looking and gestured with his gun. She couldn't do anything because he would shoot. Not to mention the two men with guns behind her.

Ponytail tried to keep his body between the sky and the keyboard while he started typing away. He was surprisingly fast.

He whipped out his phone and hit a number while angling the lid a bit to keep water from the keyboard. He spoke briefly. He waited and watched the screen. He spoke on the phone again. He put the phone in his pocket and typed some more. He brought the phone back out and said something else.

"There's no signal. We have to get out of the woods." He gestured to the guy in the hat. "Phil, you lead and have those two between you and Andy. Then you." He pointed at Dani.

She hesitated.

"Go!"

She turned and followed Andy. She glanced over her shoulder, hoping to see Gage or Dottie, but it was Ponytail.

The walk was short. Only a few minutes. The sound of the waves grew louder. They emerged from the trees and went down a slight hill to the car lane that lined the perimeter of the park. Dani looked in either direction, but it was empty.

Ponytail pushed her between the shoulder blades, encouraging her to move faster. They crossed the lane and ended up on the seawall. Dani was sure she was going to pass out. She immediately turned away from the water to face the trees.

They were in almost the exact position they had been in the forest. Gage and Dottie were in front of her flanked by Ponytail and Andy. Mitch and Logan were behind her off to her left with the other two gunmen slightly behind them.

There was nowhere to run. And they were getting wetter by the minute.

Ponytail opened the laptop and put it on the seawall this time. He clicked away on the keys and brought the phone out of his pocket once more. No more than twenty seconds later, he raised a fist in the air. The software had worked. Ponytail hung up the phone and closed the laptop.

Dani felt no relief. She'd known it would work. That wasn't the hard part. The hard part had been making the software disappear after they verified that it worked. Or at least appear to vanish.

She said, "You got what you wanted. Now let them go."

Ponytail laughed. "Fat chance. Now we kill you all." He raised his gun in her direction.

"You might want to open the laptop again," Dani said in a voice that sounded so much calmer to her ears than she felt.

Ponytail frowned and hesitated, gun still raised. "Why? What did you do?"

Dani shrugged. "You'll have to open the laptop to see."

Ponytail turned and put the laptop back down on the wall. He opened it up and hit a few buttons. Then a few more. "Where is it?" he yelled.

"Not until you let them go. All of them." Dani pointed first to Gage and Dottie and then to Gage's two brothers. She needed to make sure they were all okay. Not just Gage, but all of them. They all had people to go back to, unlike her. After Carly, there was nobody.

Ponytail waved his gun at her, but she didn't flinch. It was funny how having nothing left to lose made her stronger than she'd ever been. Gage was already lost to her, and Carly was soon to be gone forever. What did it matter now if she made it out or not?

CHAPTER THIRTY-SIX

D ani shook her head. "I can bring it back, but only after you let them all go." The wind picked up and the rain was almost coming in sideways.

What the hell was she doing? Gage glanced at his brothers. Logan looked alarmed, and Mitch shrugged slightly. This wasn't part of the plan. Gage needed to think of something quick, but the fever was getting to him. His brain was foggy, and he couldn't stop shivering. He needed to create a distraction, something his brothers would recognize and know to act on.

When Ponytail waved his gun around, Gage knew he was trying to decide what to do. Finally Ponytail reached into his pocket and pulled out his cell. He hit the call button.

Lightning lit up the sky, followed immediately by a clap of thunder so loud the whole seawall shook. Ponytail jumped and knocked the screen of Dani's laptop. Almost as if the whole thing was happening in slow motion, Gage watched the laptop tilt and start to slide off the wall into the ocean.

Dani acted instinctively and dove for it. She closed her hands around it, but her momentum carried her too far forward. She was off balance. She was trying to regain solid footing, but she tripped over Ponytail's foot.

Dani began to go headfirst over the wall into the water. He ran to catch her as a shot rang out. When Ponytail dropped to the ground in front of him, Gage jumped over him to reach Dani as she plunged toward the rocks and the water below.

Two more shots rang out as Gage's hands closed around Dani's right ankle. Her weight and momentum pulled him tight against the wall, but he dug his feet in and bent his knees to stop them both from going over.

There was crunch in his wrists and pain radiated down his left arm. He yelled in agony as he leaned over the wall. He could see Dani's face. It was getting hit with spray from the waves.

She was paralyzed with fear. She wasn't breathing, and he knew the blood was rushing to her head. She was going to pass out. She closed her eyes.

"Breathe!" he yelled. "Dammit, Dani! You have to take a fucking breath! Don't you dare pass out!"

DANI TOOK A DEEP BREATH AND THEN ANOTHER. SHE opened her eyes, and her field of vision expanded. She was still hanging upside down above the waves, but she was awake and alert. She was holding the laptop with both hands.

She tilted her head and saw Gage holding one foot with both of his hands still zip tied together. She saw his mouth moving and realized he was speaking to her. "You need to try, honey."

"Try what?" she asked. It was so hard to hear him over

the storm. The lightning continued to flash, and the thunder made everything shake.

His eyes were wide, and his mouth was in a grimace. Panic. Panic and pain. That's what was on his face. "You need to reach for me, hon. Curl up and reach for my hands. I can't pull you up like this. I need you to grab on to me so I can haul you to safety."

"Okay," she said, but he couldn't hear her, so she just nodded. Then she let go of the laptop with one hand and tried to swing up and grab his arm, but it was impossible. She needed two hands.

Gage understood the problem. "Just let go of the laptop."

Dani blinked. The laptop had been her life for the last few months. It was like another limb for her. It was where she wrote her code. It offered her peace and solace. It was her lifeline to Carly. Carly, who had decorated it with Frozen stickers as a joke. Carly, whose smiling face lit up the screen. Carly, who was dying.

Dani's throat closed over. She could feel Gage's fingers slipping on her ankle. She looked up at him again, and their gazes locked. His eyes pleaded with her to drop the laptop. What did it matter now? She took a deep breath and let the laptop go. It fell into the angry, churning water and disappeared under the black waves.

CHAPTER THIRTY-SEVEN

Gage gritted his teeth. His arm was being pulled out of the socket. He was losing his grip on Dani's ankle. "Dani, please, honey. Please swing up and grab my arm. I can't hold you like this much longer."

Dani looked up at him, her expression bleak. She said something he couldn't hear and then nodded. She gave a violent swing and latched on to his right arm just as he lost his grip on her foot.

He started to move backward to pull her up since he couldn't grab hold of her. But it was a losing battle. Panic gnawed his arm and twisted his gut. He was going to lose her, and she was going to die on the rocks below. He swore and pulled with everything he had. He managed to get Dani up another couple of inches, but not enough.

Firm hands grasped his shoulders. His brothers had appeared, one on either side of him. Mitch leaned over and grabbed Dani by the arms. Logan pushed Gage out of the way and helped Mitch pull Dani over the wall to safety.

Gage collapsed, sliding down the wall to sit on the walkway. His left arm was on fire, the pain shooting down it like lightning strikes. It was as if everything was happening in slow motion.

He blinked, but it was hard to see clearly through the rain that was coming down in sheets. He looked around and saw Ponytail and Andy dead on the ground. Phil was talking into a radio, and police were filling the area like ants at a picnic. Dotti was beside him, wrapping something around him. She felt his forehead with the back of her hand.

He blinked again. Dani was sitting not too far away, and his brothers were crouched in front of her. Relief flooded his veins. Dani was here on this side of the wall and not down on the rocks. He was glad his brothers were okay as well, but Dani had scared him. Losing her scared him far more than anything else ever had.

Lids heavy, his eyes slid shut. Someone shook his shoulder. He opened his eyes to find Logan leaning over him with Dottie standing just behind. He could see Logan's mouth moving, but there was no sound.

"What?"

Concern flickered across Logan's face. When he touched Gage's left shoulder, Gage groaned. Then he touched Gage's forehead. There was fear in his brother's eyes.

He wanted to tell Logan it was nothing. Just a bit of a cold. But he couldn't seem to get his mouth to work.

Logan gestured and Mitch joined them. Their mouths formed words he didn't hear and then both of them stared down at him. He tried to smile. He wanted them to know he was okay but, more importantly, he wanted to know for sure Dani was good. She hated being by the water. They needed to get her out of here so she could relax.

When Phil appeared in front of him, Gage started to try to get up. He wanted to help Dani. He tried to speak again, but the words wouldn't come out.

Mitch put a hand on Gage's good shoulder and shook his

head. He leaned down and said directly into Gage's ear. "Dani is okay. She hurt her ankle, but she's going to be just fine."

Gage nodded his thanks and breathed a sigh of relief. He attempted to get up again, but his limbs just didn't want to obey him.

Dottie leaned over. "Dani is fine. You are not, however. You're sick, and you need to stop trying to move until the ambulance gets here."

Gage nodded. It was all he could manage.

Then he leaned his head back and closed his eyes.

CHAPTER THIRTY-EIGHT

Dani limped along the seawall on her way back to the parking lot. No one had noticed her slip away. They were all too concerned about the dead bodies and getting Gage the help he needed.

She was glad Dottie was okay as well, and she knew Dottie would make sure Gage was looked after until the ambulance came. That lady was something else. Dani smiled slightly.

She was also happy that Gage's brothers were there to take care of him. She owed him her life. She would have smashed onto the rocks, and the waves would have pulled her out to sea. She would always be grateful. She just couldn't stay. If there was a chance she could see Carly once more before she was gone forever, then she had to try.

She limped along as quickly as she could. The storm had moved off some minutes ago, and the rain had slowed down to a fine mist. She rounded the last corner and came to the parking lot. It was full of cop cars but no one was paying attention to her. Not really surprising. They had just bagged a few Triad members. It was a great day for them.

She pulled the keys from her pocket as she limped over to the car. She'd felt badly when she'd picked Logan's pocket but desperate times…She unlocked the door, threw her now empty backpack on the passenger seat, and got in. Saying a silent apology to Mitch and Logan, she started the car, put it in gear, and pulled out of the parking lot.

She'd paid attention when they'd driven to the park so she had a fair idea of how to get back to the hotel. It was a pretty straight shot. Of course, if she had a phone or her laptop, she'd have a map.

Her laptop. Her chest squeezed. Carly. It was their connection. Dani was suddenly aware of how quiet everything was. She could hear the sound of the tires on the pavement. The occasional swipe of the wipers.

But her brain was quiet. For the first time in months, she wasn't working on the software. She always had ideas running through her brain. Things to try. Lines of code. It was always there like white noise. But now her mind was silent. Was this what it would be like without Carly?

She quickly turned on the radio and cranked the volume, drowning out the silence. The emptiness. She gasped for air. She hadn't even noticed she'd been holding her breath. Her hands shook on the steering wheel. What was going on? She needed to focus. She tried to dig up some snippet of code to think about, some random lines of symbols that would challenge her mind, but she drew a blank. It was as if her brain had switched off.

The sound of horns blaring made her jump. The light had turned green. She accelerated quickly and shot down the street, only to come to a complete stop a few feet later. Traffic.

The construction at the hotel seemed to be causing quite a mess. She sat staring out the window at the line of taillights ahead of her. It was going to be a long wait by the looks of things. She watched the traffic lights at the end of the block. They changed from red to green and back to red again with no one moving. She tapped her fingers on the steering wheel.

A car pulled away from the curb about three car lengths ahead on her right. It took a right turn and disappeared around the corner. An open parking space. She was only a few blocks from the hotel. If the traffic moved just a bit, she could park and walk the rest of the way. She willed the traffic to move, and five minutes later pulled into the space.

She limped as fast as she could, but her ankle hurt like a bitch. She had her backpack slung over one shoulder. She had the room key and her wallet in it, but not much else. She missed the weight of her laptop.

The sun had come out, and she was sweating in her damp sweater. Her hair was hot on her neck.

The anger and frustration were building with every step. Everything she and Carly had gone through. All for nothing. Her hands curled into fists. She walked faster, pushing herself. She half fell off the curb at the light and almost landed on the hood of a car.

Stepping back, she uncurled her fists and hauled in a calming breath. Then another, and another. Being angry wasn't going to help. She needed to occupy her brain. Again, she tried to call up some line of code, but nothing was coming.

She looked up and saw she was standing at the lights across the street from her hotel. Traffic was flowing freely again.

The light changed, and Dani stepped off the curb into the crosswalk.

There was a squeal of tires on the now dry pavement. Someone screamed. Dani looked up and saw Janet behind the wheel of a black Town Car bearing down on her. Janet's face was a mask of hatred. She must have tromped harder on the accelerator because the car leapt forward. It was mere feet from Dani, who was in the middle of the crosswalk with nowhere to hide.

The woman in Alaska flashed through Dani's mind as she made a mad leap and flew toward the sidewalk. Dani felt the rush of air as the car sped by her before she landed hard on the sidewalk in front of the hotel.

Dani looked up in time to see Janet hit the ramp that was part of the construction site and launch into the sky.

The front passenger side of the car caught the scaffolding and tore it from the front of the hotel. The car flipped over onto its roof as it hit the pavement and skidded.

Dani covered her head as the scaffolding smashed down on top of the car and the sidewalk. The deafening sound was followed by an eerie silence. Dani lifted her head again. Janet's car was crushed by scaffolding and concrete.

Dani got up slowly and dusted herself off. A woman asked if she needed help, but she refused. She looked over at what remained of the twisted wreck that held Janet. There was no way she was alive. Probably for the best. Dani could hear sirens in the distance. She turned and limped into the hotel. She had somewhere to be.

CHAPTER THIRTY-NINE

Gage opened his eyes and squinted against the sunlight. Wait…sunlight. How long had he been out? He opened his eyes again and tried to sit up.

"Slow down there, brother. You need to rest."

He looked over at Mitch, reclining in a chair with his feet up on the end of Gage's bed. Pain shot through his left shoulder. He winced and looked down. His arm was in a sling. "What happened? What day is it? Where's Dani?"

Logan was standing by the window, talking on his cell. He hung up and moved to stand beside Gage. "It's still the same day around nine at night. The sun is just setting. What happened is a tough one to answer, and as to where Dani went, the police are trying to figure that out as well."

Gage laid back on the bed, and Logan used the remote to move him into a sitting position.

"Dani's disappeared? When did that happen? Why am I hooked up to IVs?" Gage asked.

Logan put a butt cheek on the bed. "What do you remember?"

Gage thought for a minute. It was all a blank and then,

click, the images raced before his eyes. He blinked. "She was okay after you guys helped me pull her up. Her ankle was injured, but nothing else, right?"

Logan nodded. "The scene got a bit crazy with all the cops and everything. We had a lot of explaining to do, and I had to do some smoothing over of ruffled feathers. By the time we looked around, she was gone."

"In our rental car," Mitch added. "The cops were kind enough to give us a lift here so we could see about you. I gotta say though, brother, as happy as I am to see you're alright, nothing would make me happier right now than a shower and a hot meal. These clothes smell." Mitch fingered his black T-shirt and dirty jeans.

Logan snorted. "News flash…you stink as much as the clothes."

"You're no bunch of roses either with your navy button-down and jeans. Who goes to a hostage exchange in a button-down shirt? Seriously!" Mitch scoffed.

Gage rubbed his head. His brothers were giving him a headache. "Dottie. How's Dottie?"

Mitch laughed. "She's fine. She's telling the nurses how it was in the old days. Apparently, she was a trauma nurse back in the day. They are going to keep her overnight just in case, but she'll be on a plane home with Ann and Elenore tomorrow."

Gage nodded. "Good. What's with the IVs? For dehydration and a cold?" he asked.

"Try dehydration and walking pneumonia. Apparently, adults don't normally get it unless their immune system is weak. They want to run some tests." Logan looked concerned.

Mitch laughed. "I explained to the doc that you've been running around Europe for a couple of weeks without taking care of yourself, and then you were running from killers and held hostage. He seemed to think that would do it."

Logan smiled. "I can see his point. Still tests wouldn't be a bad idea."

Gage snorted. "I don't need tests. I'll be fine." He gestured to the two IVs. "I'm assuming they're pumping me full of saline and antibiotics."

Mitch nodded. "And some pain meds for the shoulder. Looks like you strained it badly but at least you didn't do serious damage to your rotator cuff. They want you to stay for a couple of days while they monitor you. The police also want to interview you."

"Detective Lau sends his apologies and his well wishes for a speedy recovery," Logan added.

Gage frowned. "Who the hell is Detective Lau?"

It was Logan's turn to laugh. "I believe you know him as Phil. He apologizes for hitting you, but he said he had to make it look good in front of that 'nutcase.' His words."

"Jesus. He could have pulled it a bit." Gage rubbed his jaw. "I can't believe he's a cop. He was very convincing. What about Janet?" Gage asked. "That woman is seriously scary. She really needs help."

Mitch nodded. "Lau filled us in. I've been dealing with Janet for months, and I had no clue."

Gage grimaced as he moved his arm. "I know what you mean. I think losing her son set something off in her. Revenge became her sole reason for living."

"That was pretty much Lau's take on the situation as well." Mitch frowned. "I've never been so off base about someone before, though. It's damn scary that I never picked up on her being the mole."

Gage nodded, but his mind was on Dani. Where the hell did she go? She wouldn't have wanted to be around cops, to be sure, but he didn't expect her to cut and run like that.

Maybe he should have, though. She was a hacker. He frowned.

"Is your arm hurting you?" Mitch asked.

"More likely his heart," Logan retorted.

Gage scowled at his brother.

Mitch grinned. "Trouble in paradise?"

"I believe our dear brother is missing someone, and it might be causing him some pain," Logan said with a smile.

"No." Gage shook his head. "She's a hacker," he said with finality, as if that explained everything.

"What's that got to do with it? Do you care about her or not?" Mitch demanded.

Gage shook his head. "It's not that simple."

Mitch rolled his eyes. "Uh, yes, it is."

"For once I agree with Mitch, Gage. It really is that simple. Do you care about her?"

Gage frowned at Logan. Did he care about her? If he was honest, then the answer would be a resounding "yes!" But she was part of something he hated. "I…I do care about her." He thought about the insane amount of fear and agony he'd felt when he saw her go headfirst over the wall. "A lot." He shook his head. "But she's a hacker. Someone who causes damage. Someone who works for the wrong side. The dark side."

Mitch burst out laughing. "Sorry, dude, but seriously? You worked for Navy Intelligence. It doesn't get much darker than that." He held up his hand. "I know you're going to tell me you did it to protect your country and for the right reasons. I agree. I was a SEAL for the same reasons, but we still caused damage. The dark side, as you call it, is all a matter of perspective. She saved your asses on the ship with her hacking abilities. And she was working on the software to help Drake find his sister, not to sell to the highest bidder."

Gage didn't bother to explain about Dani's true motivation, helping Carly. He got his brother's point. Still…

Logan shook his head. "I can't believe I am saying this, but Mitch is right."

"Yes!" Mitch crowed.

"Look at Mitch's girlfriend. A thief—"

"That's former thief!"

"Are you telling us she doesn't steal anymore?" Logan asked.

"Er, well, sort of?" Mitch grinned.

"That's what I thought." Logan turned back to Gage. "The point is Alex is a good person, and her extracurricular activities have come in handy for Callahan Security on more than one occasion. You didn't seem to have a problem with that. There's a lot of gray area in what we do, and you've never seemed to mind using it before."

"But..." he started then stopped.

"It's personal," Logan finished for him. "I know." Logan let out a big sigh and sat back farther onto the bed. "I had a hard time with Lacy. She's not only the daughter of one of the biggest arms dealers in the world, but she used to organize the logistics behind the deliveries to clients. Trust me, that's a hard nut to swallow. But I love her, and even though she's getting out of the business, that life will always be a part of her. Hell, we've used her contacts while working on this Drake mess. It is what it is. You have to decide if living with Dani being a hacker is worse than living without her."

Gage swallowed. His brothers were right. He did have a choice to make. "It just feels like a betrayal."

"To Cutter?" Mitch asked.

Gage nodded. "He was a good man. He was my best friend. We went into the service together. Do you remember when you stole his girlfriend, Mitch?"

"I didn't steal her," Mitch said while trying to look innocent. "I can't help it if she preferred me to him. She had good taste."

Logan laughed. "I seem to remember you drove Dad's Porsche to school. I think she just had good taste in cars."

Mitch grinned. "Dad damn near strangled me over that one. But Cutter forgave me, if you recall. And you're right Gage, Cutter was a great guy," Mitch said. "I liked him a lot. But Dani is not the hacker that sold out Cutter. And if anyone would give Dani a second chance, it would be Cutter. That's what he believed in, second chances."

Gage closed his eyes and swallowed the tears crawling up his throat. Mitch was so right. If anyone would look beyond Dani being a hacker, it would be Cutter. Gage could hear Cutter's voice in his head. *What the hell are you waitin' for? She's awesome. You're a dope for even stopping to think about it.*

Gage smiled. "I guess you're right. I'm being an ass about this. I need to accept her for who she is. She said as much." Gage's face fell. He'd called her a harlot. She'd been clear at the hotel that she wanted nothing more to do with him. How was he going to fix that?

Mitch said, "Oh, I know that look. You said stupid stuff to her. Been there. Still end up there occasionally, but the make-up sex is great!" Mitch's grin was infectious. Logan joined him, and the two started to laugh. Gage had to hold up his hand to make them stop.

"Please don't shake the bed. My arm is killing me."

Logan's phone rang. He got up off the bed to answer it.

"So…now what, brother?" Mitch asked.

"Now I have to find Dani and ask her to forgive me."

"Sounds like a plan."

Logan hung up. His face had lost a bit of color.

Gage's stomach knotted. "What is it?"

"That was Lau. They were looking for Janet. They found her in a car in front of our hotel under a pile of scaffolding and concrete. She's dead."

"There's more, isn't there?" Gage demanded.

"Yes. She was after Dani. She tried to mow her down. She wanted to do a hit and run but she hit the construction site and brought it down on top of her. Hotel security video caught the whole thing. Lau said Janet aimed right at Dani and hit the gas."

"Dani?" Gage could barely get the word out. Icy fingers gripped his heart.

Logan shook his head. "She's gone. Disappeared. Cops are still looking for her."

CHAPTER FORTY

D ani squeezed Carly's hand. She'd arrived a few hours ago, but the little girl hadn't woken up yet. She looked so small under the hospital blankets with all the big machines hooked up to her. She'd lost weight since Dani had seen her last. Dani willed her to open her beautiful blue eyes one last time.

"She knows you're here," Carol said.

"What?" Dani turned to the nurse.

"Carly knows you're here. She hasn't rested this peacefully before."

Dani just nodded. Tears rolled down her cheeks. She didn't try to hide them or stop them. They were going to be the first of many. This little girl was the only family Dani ever really had. She thought momentarily of Gage, but shook her head. That was done. She knew the score. People like her were meant to be alone. Except for Carly. Carly had kept her going. Kept her sane when even her computer hacking hadn't. This little girl was her world, and she was losing her.

She sobbed.

Carly's eyelashes fluttered. Once. Twice. They stayed

open the third time. Dani got up off the chair she'd been sitting on beside Carly's bed and leaned over the little girl.

A smile lit Carly's face. "I knew you'd come before I had to go." Her words were soft, and Dani had a hard time hearing them. She moved closer.

"I wouldn't miss seeing you, Squiggles. How's it going? The nurses tell me you're being a pain in the butt again. Something about too much chocolate."

"There can never be too much chocolate." Her lips barely moved with the words.

"Agreed," Dani said, and she wiped her face on the sleeve of her black sweater.

Carly closed her eyes and then opened them again. "We need to talk," she said.

"We are talking."

"Serious stuff this time."

Dani nodded, unable to get any words out.

"I'm not going to be around much longer."

Dani bit her lip to contain it, but a small sob slipped out.

Carly squeezed her hand slightly. "It's okay. I'm okay with it, but I'm worried about you. You need to promise me you'll go to school." She paused and took a deep breath. The machines beeped and then settled again. "You like school. Your eyes shine when you talk about making video games. Promise me you'll go and do that."

Dani nodded. "I promise," she whispered.

Carly's lashes were pale and spiky against her white cheeks.

"Please don't go yet," Dani begged. "I haven't found your family. I promised I would."

Carly smiled and opened her eyes. "Silly, you are my family. You always have been. I never cared about finding my real parents 'cause I had you."

Dani blinked in surprise. "I—"

"You need something to do when you're nervous or in pain or scared. You've been terrified the whole time I've been in here. And you hate hospitals." She smiled again. "I hate them, too, but this one has been alright. The nurses are nice. Anyway, I didn't want you to be unhappy so I said it would be good to find my family. I knew it would keep you busy." She gave a small laugh. "Tricked you." Her eyes closed again.

Dani started to cry in earnest. This little girl, this little fragile girl, was only thinking of Dani, wanting Dani to be happy. Guilt washed over her. "I'm so sorry. I should've stayed with you. I should've never left your side."

"You didn't leave me. We spoke every single day. We watched movies and ate popcorn and chocolate. You sent me all the best stuff. It was awesome. You didn't miss a thing. You were here"—she touched her own heart—"always."

Dani gasped for breath. "And you are here"—she put her hand on her own chest—"always." She pulled a small box out of her pocket. "This is for you, Squiggles."

Carly smiled. "What is it?"

Dani pulled the locket out of the box and held it up so Carly could see. "It opens up."

Carly reached for the locket and opened it. She smiled when she saw the pictures of the two of them inside the locket. "I love it. Sisters forever." She took Dani's hand and squeezed one last time.

Then she quietly faded away.

The machines started beeping and the nurses rushed in. They moved some of the equipment around, and Carol felt for a pulse. She flipped a few more switches and silenced the alarms. She spoke to another nurse. "It's time. Call the team. They're already on standby."

"What? What's going on?"

Carol disengaged Dani from Carly's bedside and took her

outside. "Carly wanted me to tell you that, because you will always be in her heart, she wants that heart to live on, so she donated her organs. There's another little girl, three floors up, waiting for a new heart."

The room spun, and Dani started to fall. Carol gripped her under the arms and helped her to a chair. She gestured to a third nurse, who ran and got her water. She handed it to Dani.

Dani gulped it down. "Normally, a child can't make this decision on their own, but no one but you ever came to see Carly. She told us her wishes and that you were traveling but would sign the paperwork when you got here. It's all…irregular, but Carly was such a special kid. We did what she asked." Carol hesitated. "Will you sign the paperwork? We need to have someone's signature on file."

Dani nodded because she was incapable of words. Carol rose and went to the nurse's station and then came back with the papers. Dani didn't even bother to read them. If this was what Carly wanted, then she wanted it too. She signed the papers.

Carol took everything from Dani and handed it to another nurse. She then went on to explain what would happen in a while when things were set up. "Would you like to go back in and sit with Carly until it's time?"

Dani nodded and trudged back into the room. She sat down and looked at Carly. She wouldn't open her eyes again ever. Tears rolled down her face as she processed the loss of her sister.

What would she do now? She promised Carly she would go to school, so there was that. The emptiness hurt her chest. It was as if her own heart was physically breaking in two. This little girl was the only person on Earth who had ever made her really smile.

Well, that wasn't strictly true, but Gage didn't count. At least not anymore. Sitting there next to Carly's bed, she could finally admit to herself she loved Gage, even if he did call her awful names. She'd been hard on him, and he'd lashed out. God knew she understood how that worked. Yes, she truly loved him, and she was sad without him. Heartbroken. About Carly. About Gage.

Dani would leave the hospital that day without either of the people who meant the world to her in her life. What would she do? It was tempting to be angry. It danced around the edges of her world. But she'd been angry long enough. Carly wouldn't want her to be angry. Carly would want her to be happy. Find a new project to work on. Write new code. Start a new chapter.

She heard a rustle of fabric that meant Carol was back. "It's time." Carol smiled encouragingly.

Dani stood up. They positioned everything they needed with Carly and started wheeling her out of the room. Dani followed behind. When she entered the hallway, tears fell like the sheets of rain had in Vancouver. The entire hallway was lined with doctors and nurses that had treated Carly during her time at the hospital. They all came to send her off and say their thanks. Dani's tears streamed down her face.

It was too much. The joy and laughter and love this little girl had given her was gone, and yet she was still able to give a last gift. The most precious gift of all.

They turned the corner, and Dani followed suit. She couldn't believe all the people who had come for Carly. Dani looked down at the little warrior one more time. The bed stopped rolling, and Dani knew this was her cue to say her final good-bye. She leaned down and whispered. "I love you, Squiggles."

When she stood up, she came face-to-face with Gage. He

was leaning against the wall. He had a bruise on his left cheek and his left arm was in a sling. He straightened up and opened up his right arm. She moved forward into his embrace. As his arm closed around her, she sobbed uncontrollably.

CHAPTER FORTY-ONE

A week later, Dani sat on a bench on the shore of Lake Champlain. As she looked out over the water, she marveled that it ever had any power over her. Losing Carly and everything else she'd gone through had put so many things in perspective for her. It was all different now. She was more settled. More grown up. She took a sip of her tea and glanced at Gage over the top of her cup.

He leaned against a split rail fence, finishing up a call. He hadn't left her side since Carly died. She couldn't believe he'd flown to Vermont to be with her. He'd not said a word about anything other than to ask her what she needed or if there was anything he could do. His quiet support and his strong embrace had gotten her through the worst of it.

She wasn't fooling herself. There would be gray days ahead. There always were when someone disappeared from her life and, this time, she'd lost two people. Carly was gone, and soon Gage would be. He'd been her rock during the day and her solace at night. He'd never asked a thing from her, but she knew it was time to rip off the bandage.

Gage hung up and turned to face her. "You good?" he asked.

She nodded. "You?"

He nodded. She knew he was feeling better. His color was back to normal. He'd been positively gray when she'd seen him at the hospital, not that she'd realized it at the time.

In the days after Carly, Gage had filled in the details she'd missed, including his illness. His brothers checked on him daily, multiple times. It annoyed him, but she understood it completely. He was family.

She smiled at him, even though she was dying inside. He needed to go back to his life, and she needed to find one. He deserved better than hanging around, taking care of her.

"Gage, come have a seat."

There was a wariness in his eyes as he sat down next to her. He knew something was coming. She could see it. She studied his face, committing every detail to memory. She wanted to be able to call it up whenever she needed comfort.

"Relax. I'm letting you off the hook."

He frowned.

"I really appreciate you being here for me. Taking care of me. Helping me through losing Carly. It's meant the world to me. Really. But it's time to move on. I need to think about my next steps, and you need to get back to your brothers and your work. I've held you here long enough.

"I know you promised me you would protect me even after everything was over, but that was back when we thought the Chinese government was after me. Since it was the Triads, I don't think we have to worry anymore. They will be otherwise occupied with Drake and his law enforcement connections. We've spoken and he's launching an all-out war on them so he can be free of their influence in his companies."

It was harder than she thought. She was going to cry. She

bit her lip and shot off the bench. She turned to face him. Tears clogged her throat, and her heart was being ripped in two all over again, but she was determined to do this. They both had to move on.

"Thanks for everything. If you ever need anything, just let me know. I sent Logan an email address I can be reached at always." She stuck out her hand. She didn't think she would be able to let him go if she hugged him.

Gage blinked. He looked at her hand and then up at her face. "Are you serious right now? A handshake? You're blowing me off with a handshake?"

She frowned. "What? Do you want a hug?"

Gage leapt to his feet and towered over her. "A hug? No, I don't want a fucking hug. I want all the hugs."

Dani shook her head. "What the hell are you talking about? I'm telling you it's okay to move on. You've been here looking after me because you feel guilty and you promised me and you're trying to be a good friend or something. I'm okay now. I appreciate it. It's been great. A real help but, ah, it's time for you to go back home. I'm all good."

"You're all good. Time for me to go back. Guilty. Are you crazy? I'm not here because I feel guilty or because I'm trying to be a friend. I'm here because I love you! I hate seeing you in pain. And I'm not leaving because I'm never leaving without you."

Dani frowned. She opened and closed her mouth. She was having trouble understanding the words Gage was saying. It seemed like… "I'm…what?"

Gage leaned down until they were eye to eye. "I. Love. You. I'm sorry I said all that stupid shit about you being a hacker. I am so incredibly sorry for calling you that name. I can't apologize enough about that. But I love you, and I don't want you to change."

Dani was stunned. Good things didn't happen to her. Life did not work out for her. Ever.

She swallowed. "Huh. That's what I thought you said." What was she supposed to do now? She knew what she wanted to do, but did she have the balls to take the chance? Pain could be just around the corner.

She leaned forward and kissed him hard on the mouth. Then she pulled back. "I love you, too." As the words flew out of her mouth, joy exploded in her chest. Gage blinked, and then a huge grin appeared on his face. He picked her up and spun her around and let out a loud yell. Then plunked her down on the bench and proceeded to kiss her as if her life depended on it. Because after all, it did.

EPILOGUE

"You're sure you're okay with implementing this?" Drake asked for the umpteenth time.

"Yes." Dani nodded. It was taking all of her patience not to be majorly sarcastic to the man, but he was the one paying the bill. She was trying to install her software on Drake's server. All of his interruptions weren't helping any. Not to mention the data center they were in was cold and dry, and she was tired. Too much fun with Gage last night and not enough sleep. She smiled.

Drake continued. "And Gage is okay with this? I heard he wasn't so…keen on the idea."

Dani's eyes narrowed. "I wonder where you heard that?" she asked as she looked around Drake to Jake, one of the guys from Callahan Security standing in the doorway of the security cage.

Jake raised his hands. "Don't look at me." He gestured over his shoulder.

"Dragan?" Dani murmured as she glared at the body-guard who was leaning against the outside wall.

The edges of Dragan's lips turned upward, but he didn't say a word.

Dani went back to the task at hand.

"So is Gage okay with this?" Drake asked.

Dani looked over at him. Jameson Drake was a colossal pain in the ass, but watching him fidget with a paperclip made her take pity on him. He was nervous. He'd waited a long time for this. A chance to find his sister. Dani knew the software would work, but whether or not Drake's sister was still alive was a mystery.

"Let's just say, we've come to an agreement." Dani smiled.

"I just bet you have." Drake's lips twitched. "These Callahan men have such…interesting taste in women."

"Agreed," Dragan murmured.

Dani shot him a look.

Jake burst into laughter. "I'd be careful, Dragan. She's not liking you at the moment. You might suddenly have your identity stolen."

Dani turned back to the keyboard. She glanced at her laptop screen and bit her lip. She wiped her right palm on her jeans. Then after another few keystrokes, she smiled. "Voilà, up and running."

Drake straightened up and immediately looked over her shoulder. On the screen was a picture of his sister from when she was a girl and next to it were images of people flashing so fast one faced blurred into the next in a constant stream. "What's happening?"

"I'm actually running two different servers. One is running my software and comparing your sister's photo to all of the live security feeds from your hotels here in the United States. The other is comparing her picture to all of the previous hours of security video you have on your hard drives. It will continue to do that until it's caught up to your live feeds.

"If your sister enters or has entered any one of your hotels here in the U.S. in the last six months, my software will find her and send a notification to your phone."

Drake blinked and leaned against the cage doorjamb again. "So, you're going to do this for all of my hotels across the world?"

Dani nodded. "Yes. You have all of your servers already stored off site in locations like this one. I think there're twelve in all. I'll go to each location and install my software just like I did here. Then you'll be able to compare your sister's picture to the live feeds from all over the world."

Drake nodded.

"Just remember the software will reboot on a randomized schedule so it doesn't freeze. It's the best I can offer you. As long as you don't try to search for a large group of people at once, the software should function perfectly. If something does stop working I'll be notified immediately."

Drake covered his face with his hands. His shoulders rose and fell.

Dani looked at Jake. He shrugged slightly and shook his head. She bit her lip. "I know how much this means to you. I really hope you find your sister."

Drake dropped his hands by his sides. "Thank you. And thank you for making this possible. This chance…it's more than I could have hoped for."

"It was fun." Dani laughed. "Well, mostly fun."

Drake nodded. "And you think this is secure enough? I know how powerful this is, and I know certain groups would like to have it."

"It's true. It's a very valuable tool and a lot of people would like to get their hands on it," Gage said as he walked by Dragan and Jake. He stood in the doorway just behind Drake. "But these facilities are damn hard to get into. Armed guards, bullet proof glass, retinal scans. It's really state of the art, and at this point there is nothing else that even comes close." Gage stopped next to Dani.

"Is it safe from hacking?" Drake asked.

Jake snorted and Dragan cracked a grin.

Dani glared at the two of them before she answered Drake, "Nothing is unhackable unless it's off grid in a closed, clean room." She shrugged. "Someone somewhere might be able to get in, but then they'd have to be good enough to get by all the security I've enabled, which is as close to ironclad as you can get. And if the hack is that big, if they get that far, we'll know about it."

Drake nodded again. "And Gage, you'll go with her and protect her while she installs this?"

It was Gage's turn to smile. "I don't plan on leaving her side."

Heat crawled up Dani's cheeks. She knew what the wicked gleam in his eye meant, and she had no doubt so did all the other men in the room.

"Drake, since I'll be gone and Mitch is already in Africa, Dragan and Jake will stay with you. They will be your personal security and organize anything else you might need. The Triads know about the software, and even though you managed to get a lot of them jailed both here and in Macau, I think we need to keep security tight around you and your businesses."

"Agreed." Drake glanced at Jake and then Dragan. "I'm sure these gentlemen are up to the task. Callahan Security has not let me down yet."

"Um, I think we're good to go." Dani stood up and closed her new laptop. She ran her hand over the stickers. Frozen and Star Wars. Who knew Gage would be a Sci-Fi fan?

"Okay. Here you go." Drake handed Dani a USB stick.

Gage frowned. "What's that?"

Dani shook her head but Drake didn't see her. "It's the money I owe Dani for all her work. It's in bitcoin and this is the key."

Gage glared at Dani. "Bitcoin?"

"What? You didn't expect me to pay tax on this did you?" she asked with a grin.

Gage shook his head and Drake laughed. "Good luck with her." Drake clapped Gage on the back. "You're going to need it," he said as he walked out of the security cage. Jake and Dragan fell in step with him, and they disappeared around the corner.

"Yes, I am," Gage said and then swooped in for a kiss.

BREAK AND ENTER
CALLAHAN SECURITY BOOK 1

Callahan Security is on the brink of disaster. Mitch Callahan pushed his brothers to expand the family business into private security, and their first major client is a complete pain in the ass. It's no wonder the man has a target on his back, but nothing could prepare Mitch for how seductive his adversary is.

Love hurts. No one knows that better than Alexandra Buchannan, so she uses her talents as a thief to equalize the scales of romantic justice. Your ex still has your favorite painting? Not for long. Alex's latest job is her biggest challenge yet. Her target just hired a new security company, and the team leader is as smart as he is sexy.

Mitch knows he's jeopardizing not only this job but the future of Callahan Security. If only he didn't find Alex so damn irresistible. Soon their game of cat and mouse explodes into a million pieces. Unbeknownst to them, there's another player in the game, and his intentions are far deadlier.

Learn more about the book here: https://lorimatthewsbooks.com/books/

ABOUT THE AUTHOR

I grew up in a house filled with books and readers. Some of my fondest memories are of reading in the same room with my mother and sisters, arguing about whose turn it was to make tea. No one wanted to put their book down!

I was introduced to romance because of my mom's habit of leaving books all over the house. One day I picked one up. I still remember the cover. It was a Harlequin by Janet Daily. Little did I know at the time that it would set the stage for my future. I went on to discover mystery novels. Agatha Christie was my favorite. And then suspense with Wilber Smith and Ian Fleming.

I loved the thought of combining my favorite genres, and during high school, I attempted to write my first romantic suspense novel. I wrote the first four chapters and then exams happened and that was the end of that. I desperately hope that book died a quiet death somewhere in a computer recycling facility.

A few years later, (okay, quite a few) after two degrees, a husband and two kids, I attended a workshop in Tuscany that lit that spark for writing again. I have been pounding the keyboard ever since here in New Jersey, where I live with my children—who are thrilled with my writing as it means they get to eat more pizza—and my very supportive husband.

Please visit my webpage at https://lorimatthewsbooks.com to keep up on my news.

Please stay in touch! You can find me here:
Facebook:
https://www.facebook.com/LoriMatthewsBooks

Instagram:

https://www.instagram.com/lorimatthewsbooks/

Twitter:
https://twitter.com/_LoriMatthews_

Goodreads:
https://www.goodreads.com/author/show/
7733959.Lori_Matthews

Bookbub:
https://www.bookbub.com/profile/lori-matthews

Made in the USA
Columbia, SC
29 January 2022